Alternity

Mari Mancusi

CONTENTS

PROLOGUE

Running.

I am running for my life. That much I know as the heels of my silver boots click a staccato beat against the metallic road below. But where am I? Who's chasing me? And, most importantly, why?

I have no idea.

Run faster. Run harder. Run from the moon.

A strange chant echoes through my head, with urgency I can't comprehend. Endless demands competing with my own frantic thoughts skitter across my brain like a bum needle on a worn record.

Where am I? *Run faster.* Who's chasing me? *Run harder.* And why? *Run from the moon.*

But there is no moon. The corridor is black, skyless, and deep underground. And I'm already running as fast and as hard as I can.

Sucking in a breath I take in my surroundings without slowing down. Trying to think, to process, to find a shred of familiarity in the dark steel beams crisscrossing the tunnel's ceiling, the mammoth fans cut into the walls expelling hot, sour air. It all seems so familiar and yet completely foreign. Like an episode of déjà vu pricking at the dark recesses of your brain, or a name on the tip of your tongue—the one you always remember at 3:00 A.M., when it no longer matters.

Except, this time I think it might still matter. And 3:00 A.M. may be too late.

"Don't let her reach the hatch!"

My heart slams against my chest as I realize my pursuers— whoever they might be—aren't far behind. Sweat pools in the hollow of my throat, then drips down, soaking my breasts. My muscles burn, my lungs refuse to take in air, I can barely swallow, and my vision has gone spotty. Soon I'll have to stop.

But to stop is to die. That much I know. And so I keep running.

I turn a corner and catch sight of a ladder in front of me, embedded firmly into the wall, a potential salvation ascending into the darkness. Where does it go? Could it lead to the hatch my enemies seek to keep me from? To stop and check it out will eat up valuable time—time I don't have. But I have to take a chance. I can't run forever.

I throw myself against the ladder, wrapping my hands around each rung as I climb, step after step. The ground falls away, and with it the dim tunnel lighting. Soon I am engulfed in blackness.

A few seconds later I bang my head against something, almost falling off the ladder from the impact. I steady myself, then reach up with one hand, fingers exploring the ceiling until they come upon a latch. More frantic exploration reveals a handle. There's definitely some kind of trapdoor.

"Up here! Get her!"

I hear feet clanging against the metal rungs as my pursuers start up after me. I don't have much time left. Wrapping my hand around the trapdoor handle, I yank on it with all my might. This is my one chance to escape.

It doesn't budge.

I pound on the door, my heart exploding in my chest as I realize that I likely have precious seconds to live. Surprisingly, my life does not flash before my eyes; in fact, I'm still having difficulty remembering any life at all. Who I am. What I do. How I got into this mess.

Run from the moon, the mysterious voice in my head demands.

"Shut up," I mutter, tired of its nonsensical advice.

The first man reaches me, paws at my feet through the darkness. "We've got her!" he cries. And indeed, it seems he has.

Not willing to give up without a fight, I slam my foot down on his hand, the stiletto heel driving into his palm. A crunch of bone. A yelp of pain. I repeat the blow, then follow up with a wild kick to where I estimate his head to be, all the while clinging to the ladder for dear life. I don't miss. Knocked off balance he loses his grip, falls backward, and hurtles into the blackness below. A sickening thud, followed by silence, tells me he's likely met his maker.

But his death is not enough to save me. The second guy is right behind him and much more prepared for my alley cat tactics. There's a flash of light—a crimson beam cutting through the darkness—then a sharp, icy pain spreading up my ankle, shooting through my veins at a lightning pace, reaching my toes, my fingers, my brain—one after another. My grip loosens, my head swims, my muscles fail. At first I fear he'll just let me fall to my death. But my attacker grabs on instead and starts dragging me down the ladder.

Not good.

At the bottom, the men flip me over so I'm lying on my stomach, spread-eagle. I can't move, my body is Jell-O, my muscles are useless.

But I can see. I can hear. I can feel.

Three men kneel above me, armed with scary-looking tools, including something that resembles a high-tech electric syringe, complete with gauges and lights and a really long needle. I'm not sure what it does, but I know that I don't want it done to me.

One man reaches into his bag and pulls out a small silver box. He presses his thumb against the top. The box beeps and flashes a green light, then pops open, revealing a vial of some sort. He presents the vial to the man with the syringe, who takes it and sticks the long needle inside, sucking up the unidentified contents. The syringe beeps in approval and a few green lights flash in sync.

"Are you ready, my dear?" the man with the gun asks, his lips curled in a sneer. He's big, built like a soldier and sporting a trim gray beard. He's wearing a shiny metallic jumpsuit, pulled tight by a black tool belt.

"Please!" I beg, not thinking for one second that anything I say will make a difference, but at the same time desperate to try. "Just let me go!"

The men laugh, shaking their heads in mirth. "Oh, you'll go all right," replies the second guy. He's smaller than the first, but no less menacing. "Pow!" he quips. "Straight to the moon."

They grab my arm and flip me over. I watch helplessly as they stab me with the syringe, injecting silver liquid into my unwilling veins. I scream and scream and scream, knowing it will do no good. Knowing that there's no escape.

Like it or not, I'm going to the moon.

ONE

"Skye, Skye! Wake up! Wake up!"

I clawed through the blackness, trying desperately to regain consciousness at the sound of my roommate's voice. My eyes flew open, and I struggled to take in a breath. My throat had constricted ... the air cut off to my lungs. I waved my arms frantically in Felicia's direction, praying she would get the message before I asphyxiated in my own bed.

She did. Not surprising, I suppose. It wasn't as if this was the first time I'd woken up to a full-on asthma attack. Especially recently, when I'd been trying to cut back on my medication and use yoga to control my breathing instead. A moment later I felt my inhaler being stuffed into my mouth, sending lifesaving Lunatropium into my airwaves.

My muscles relaxed, and I sunk into the pillow, allowing myself a luxurious sigh of relief. I was back. I was safe. I was me again. I pulled the inhaler from my mouth and scanned my dorm room, enjoying each and every shred of familiarity. My raggedy teddy bear, Melvin, at the foot of my bed. My overstuffed bookcase across the room, crammed with well-worn fantasy epics and textbooks. My prized Alienware laptop, souped up to run the latest and greatest video games, on my desk. And my movie posters above my bed. *Star Wars*, *The Hunger Games*, *Phaze Runner*. I smiled a little as Luke, Katniss, and Deckard all glowered down at me, as if daring me to claim that my nightmare adventure had been more hellish than their everyday realities.

"Are you okay?" Felicia asked, peering down at me with concern, her long blond hair framing her heart-shaped face. "That looked like a bad one."

"It wasn't good," I agreed, sitting up and rubbing my eyes. I realized I was still shaking and wondered if it was from the nightmare itself or my abrupt awakening. "But at least it woke me up. I was having the worst dream ever."

"Another one?" Felicia sat down on the side of the bed, reaching out to squeeze my hand. I squirmed under her gaze, not liking the pity I recognized in her eyes. "What was it about this time?" she asked cautiously, knowing I didn't always like to talk about them.

"I can't remember the details," I said with a shrug. "You know how dreams are. But it's like I'm trapped in this underground world, fleeing for my life. Someone's chasing me and I don't know who—or why for that matter. In fact, in the dream, it's almost as if I'm not even myself, but some other person." I trailed off, not knowing what else to say. It sounded so silly when I explained it out loud. How could I convey how terrifying it had been? How real it felt? It wasn't like a normal dream that fled with the break of dawn. It clung to me, even now, as if it were reality and this was the dream.

"Is the guy chasing you hot?" Felicia asked, a mischievous grin crossing her face. "'Cause if so, I suggest you let him catch you next time. I had this one dream a few nights ago where I was being chased by Clive Owen and ..."

I tried and failed to muster a smile. I knew she was just trying to cheer me up. And normally it probably would have worked. But after three weeks of horrible, unrelenting nightmares and asthma attacks, accompanied by very little actual rest, I was in no mood for jokes.

"Look," I interrupted, just as she was getting to the TMI section of her Clive Owen fantasy. "It's really not funny, okay? I don't even want to go back to sleep at this point—just in case I have another dream. It's *that* bad."

Felicia's face softened. She leaned down to give me a comforting hug. "Have you told your parents?" she asked. "Maybe they could have you see someone. I mean, if you're not sleeping ..."

I scowled. Sure, many of my classmates at NYU saw shrinks. In fact, it had become almost fashionable to talk about what "my therapist said" at parties. But I'd always resisted the idea of seeking answers from a stranger. I liked to be in control of my own destiny, thank you very much.

"Maybe you're right," I said noncommittally, mostly so she wouldn't press me. "I'll think about it, anyway. In the meantime, you can go back to sleep. I know you have that big test tomorrow. I'll be fine. I swear. I'll keep the inhaler nearby, just in case."

Felicia looked at me suspiciously. "And what are *you* going to do?" she asked. She knew me way too well, and I felt my face warm at the accusation in her question. I considered lying, but if she woke up again, I'd be busted, so what was the use?

"I was thinking I'd play some RealLife," I admitted. "Just for a little bit. So I can relax and stuff." I added the last part a little defensively, preempting the attack.

Sure enough, my roommate groaned loudly, grabbing Melvin from the foot of my bed and tossing him in my direction. The bear fell short of the bed and landed on the floor with a soft plop. "No *wonder* you're having nightmares!" she cried, rising to her feet and heading to her side of the room. "Staying up all night, playing your little games. That cannot be healthy."

Blah, blah, blah. It was always the same. Felicia was a good roommate, but she would never understand my attraction to virtual play. She lived in the real world—playing lacrosse, shopping on Fifth Avenue, getting manicures at J Sisters. She would never understand the appeal of losing one's self to another world. Her world was already great.

"Have you ever considered playing some *real* real life once in a while?" Felicia added dryly as she slipped under the covers. "You know, maybe start your 'sleeping quest' tonight so you can be well rested enough to continue your 'college graduation' quest chain tomorrow morning?"

"Yeah, yeah." I waved her off. "Go back to sleep, will you? Tell Clive Owen I said hi."

She giggled, and I knew I had won. As she turned to face the wall, I walked over to my computer, slipping my headphones on. After waking up the monitor, I logged on to the server and selected my game character, ready to get down to business.

And yes, I did mean business. These days I didn't just play games for fun. They were my job, too. At age eighteen, I was the youngest paid beta tester at Chix0r, the world's first all female-run gaming company. I'd been working hard all year, testing their soon-to-be-released multiplayer online game RealLife: Medieval Times. The game was scheduled to launch in under a month and had already been hyped by *PC Gamer* as the biggest thing since World of Warcraft. The company had put their trust in me to help them find all the bugs before it went out to the public, and I wasn't about to let them down, nightmares or no.

The launch screen loaded, revealing a virtual medieval village along with my character Allora. The place was deserted, save for some computer-generated, nonplayer characters (or NPCs as we called them in the game biz) wandering around. It was hard to believe that in just a few weeks this silent world would be buzzing with activity—crammed with avatars from around the world. Players logging in to experience an entirely new virtual life. Creating characters to fight fantastical beasts, competing for epic weapons and gear, and even forming lifelong friends with fellow gamers. In short—a life far more exciting and interesting than their everyday reality.

But for now, this world was still empty—and mine to explore. Allora peered out from the screen, tapping her foot impatiently, awaiting my next move. As an all-female company, Chix0r had gone one step further than the traditional guy-centric games like World of Warcraft, where the characters were flat and static and did exactly what you told them. RealLife's characters had their own personalities, their own artificial intelligence built into their code. Sort of like the Sims in chainmail. So while you could control your character's movements and direct his or her path, you couldn't make them do things they didn't want to do. They wouldn't fight if they were hungry. They'd refuse to accept a new quest if they were tired or sick. They got lonely if you didn't properly socialize them and angry if someone did them wrong. Sometimes they were scarily like real people.

"Okay, fine, Allora, let's go to the pub," I whispered, moving the mouse to direct the character to the local tavern. "We'll get you a tankard of ale." Allora grinned in excitement as I directed her to her favorite establishment. Not that she had many to choose from. Because we were only in beta mode, the programmers had temporarily sectioned off Allora's hometown from the rest of the game. My poor character had no idea there was a whole other world outside her city's walls. To her, the outskirts of Mare Tranquilitatis were the ends of the earth.

As I sat her down at a nearby table, an NPC promptly brought her a beer. She raised her glass and drank it down happily. She looked so content it almost made me wish I could crawl into the computer and join her for a pint. Block out my reality for the night and become part of a better world.

But that, I knew, was just another dream.

TWO

I open my eyes.

I'm underground again. Halfway across a large suspension bridge made of fraying rope and rotten planks, anchored by cracked stone pillars on either side. Looking down I see a chasm of undeterminable depth. Above, inky blackness stretches on forever. The cavernous walls emit a dim glow, as if embedded with some sort of phosphorous material. The air smells acrid. Of sulfur, sweat, or really cheap cologne.

I take a hesitant step, gingerly placing a foot down on one of the creaky wooden planks. A slight wind catches the bridge and it sways in response. I grip the handrails tightly, my heart beating fast and furious.

I look up, seeking out my destination and to my surprise I see Glenda, standing at the bridge's end. Glenda's my personal trainer, the one who's been teaching me yoga breathing techniques, to help lessen my dependence on asthma medication. She waves, offering me one of her trademark brilliant smiles.

I try to smile back, but my mouth refuses to cooperate as my mind buzzes with questions. Why is she here? What does she want from me? And why are her eyes, shining through the darkness, glowing an iridescent green?

Realizing there's only one way to find out, I draw in a breath and dare another step. The bridge groans under my weight; it must be ancient and the rope is beyond brittle. I look behind me, but I'm too far to go back now. I have to keep going. I have to hope it will stay together for at least one more crossing.

"Keep walking," Glenda encourages, her voice sounding almost ethereal as it bounces off the walls of the cave. "You're almost there."

The bridge feels endless, but still I persevere. What choice do I have?

Finally, I'm close to the end. Close to Glenda. Close to the safety of solid ground. But just as I'm about to make that final leap, a loud cracking assaults my ears. I whirl around, in time to see the stone pillars disintegrate before my eyes. The rope suspension splits. The bridge shudders and cracks, the far side swinging down into the cavern. A split second later I'm vertical, hanging on to the handrails for dear life.

"Help!" I scream to Glenda, who is standing above me, arms crossed, a serene smile on her seamless face. She's wearing a long white robe, the costume of a Greek goddess. A white star glows from her forehead. "You've got to help me!"

But she doesn't move. "Pull yourself out, Mariah," she commands in a calm voice. "You have the power to do so. You always have."

Terrified, I try to do as she says—to pull myself up, my feet dangling uselessly, clawing for some kind of purchase. I'm not making much progress. My heart pounds. My arms burn. I can't hold on much longer. "Please!" I beg, tears streaming down my cheeks, blurring my already spotty vision. I can't believe she's just standing there when I'm about to plummet to my death. "Help me. Give me your hand."

"You don't need my help anymore, Mariah," Glenda says with another gentle smile. "Look within yourself. You have the power."

I have no idea what she's talking about, but now is not the time to try to puzzle it out. Summoning all the willpower and adrenaline I can muster, I give one last heave and hoist myself onto the bank. My chest slams into solid rock, knocking the wind from my lungs. Automatically I search my pockets for my inhaler, but Glenda steps lightly on my hand with a soft slippered foot.

"No," she says, shaking her head. "Gazers only enhance the pull of the moon. For successful reentry you must stop inhaling."

I open my mouth to tell her she's crazy. That no breathing exercise is going to help me in a time like this. But then, strangely, I realize she's right. I *can* breathe. Large lungfuls of air without any effort. I gulp them in like a fish out of water.

When I've finally caught my breath, I scramble to my feet. Now that I'm confident I'll live, the anger burns in my gut. "Why didn't you help me?" I demand, crossing my arms over my chest. "I could have died, you know."

At first Glenda doesn't answer. Just stands there, smiling her strange, serene smile. At that moment I'm not sure if I want to punch her or hug her.

"You don't need my help anymore," she says at last, placing a small white hand on my arm. Her skin is so pale, it's almost translucent. As if she's never seen the sun. "You're almost ready," she adds.

"Ready?" I repeat, confused. "Ready for what?"

"For reentry," she replies, matter-of-factly. "The Eclipsers have been hard at work to get you out for some time now. Myself included. Our doctors think you're almost there."

Her words prick at my brain. As if they should mean something but don't. "Reentry?" I repeat helplessly, not knowing what else to say.

"You're starting to remember," she says gently. "These dreams are a good sign of that. Soon you will awaken back home. But you've been gone a long time, Mariah, and your mind has been through a lot. Moongazing can cause serious brain damage. While our doctors believe your brain is still intact—all the vital functions still working—we're not sure how your memory will be affected."

I scrunch my face up, trying to make sense of her words. I know she's speaking English, but I can't make heads or tails of what she means. "Why are you calling me Mariah?" I ask at last, the one thing I can manage to focus on. The men in my dreams—they called me that, too.

Glenda reaches out to brush a strand of hair from my face, gazing at me with tender eyes. "Because that is who you are," she replies. Then she glances at her wristwatch. A strange accessory for her otherwise primitive dress. "I'm sorry, there's no time to explain," she adds, her voice reluctant and apologetic. "You must listen carefully. When you go through reentry, you won't know where you are. Or even who you are. You'll be vulnerable, scared, alone. If Duske finds you, he may try to suck you back in—make you promises, get you back on the Gazers." Her smile fades, her lips dipping into a frown. "Don't trust him. We may not be able to get you out a second time."

I stare at her, feeling as if I've walked into a movie twenty minutes late. I don't even know what questions to ask.

Glenda continues. "When you get home, call Dawn. He'll find you and take you to us." Glenda reaches into a small reticule tied to her belt and pulls out a feather pen. She takes my hand in hers and scribbles something on the back.

Don't trust Duske. Find Dawn.

-...- .-- -.

I stare at my hand, confused as anything. "What does that mean? What are these symbols?" I demand.

But Glenda only shakes her head. "I'm sorry, child. We're out of time. It's pulling you back now." Her voice sounds a million miles away. "Just remember—seek Dawn. Avoid Duske."

"Seek Dawn, avoid Duske," I repeat helplessly. I can feel the darkness creep in around me, yanking at the edges of my sanity. "Anything else?"

"Yes. One other thing," Glenda says, her voice grave. "Whatever happens, whatever you do, promise me you won't look into the moon."

THREE

"Miss Brown? Will you be joining us today? Or are you only here for your midmorning nap?"

Laughter erupted in the classroom as I slowly lifted my head from my desk, my brain still foggy from my dream. My face burned as I realized my professor, Dr. Davenport, along with my entire film studies class was watching me with great amusement. How long had I been out? Had I been screaming? Thank goodness I wasn't gasping for breath this time. That would have pretty much zeroed out any coolness points I had left.

"Oh good. I've managed to unplug you from the matrix," my teacher quipped, giving me a wink to let me know I was forgiven. Luckily I was one of her favorite students due to our shared secret love of sci-fi films. Not that she'd ever admit it to the rest of the wannabe filmmaker crowd. For them, if it wasn't *Citizen Kane*, it was crap.

"Sorry," I muttered, rubbing my eyes and trying to regain my senses. My heart was still beating fast and reality still felt a bit hazy. Not surprising, really—the dream had been so real, and so disconcerting. Even now, all I could focus on were Glenda's words.

You're starting to remember ...

Oh, I remembered something all right. Namely my roommate's suggestion I go see a shrink.

"It's okay, Miss Brown," my teacher assured me. "Now, do you care to tell the class why Rick is so furious with Ilsa when she first shows up in *Casablanca*?"

My shoulders relaxed. Phew. An easy one. "He thinks she betrayed him," I replied automatically. "When she disappeared in Paris on that final day."

We'd watched the film two days, but I'd already seen it a billion times at home and at the IFC theater in the Village. Sci-fi flicks aside, it was one of my favorites. The love affair between Rick and Ilsa in the shadow of the Nazi invasion was just so tragic and romantic. And the ending! I mean, not to be all spoiler alert, but the sacrifice Rick makes to save the world? It's so swoon-worthy.

Dr. Davenport smiled at me and opened her mouth, presumably to ask a followup question, but at that moment, the clock struck ten, signaling the end of class.

The room erupted in activity, students bouncing from their seats, grabbing their books and laptops, and heading for the exit, barely acknowledging their teacher's reminder about the night's assignment. As I walked down the row of desks, I felt a determined poke at my back. I whirled around to find my boyfriend, Craig, grinning at me from ear to ear.

"Good save," he teased as we exited the classroom. "I thought you were a goner for sure."

"Please." I snorted. "It'd take more than *Casablanca* trivia to bring *me* down."

He slapped me playfully on the back. "That's my girl!" he praised. Then he leaned over and kissed me on the cheek. I endured it for a second, then brushed him away. He was always trying to PDA me in the hallway, which was more than a little embarrassing. After all, we were in school. Teachers were watching. Not to mention fellow students.

As we walked out of class I couldn't help but release a large yawn. I needed to hit the union for a soda or something before my next class or I'd never make it. While I could hold my own on a quarter night's sleep in film class, calculus was another story altogether.

"Did you get *any* sleep last night?" Craig asked, walking beside me. "I mean, no offense, but you look like total hell."

"Thanks." I muttered, avoiding his eyes.

"I'm serious!" he insisted. "Like, if they threw a zombie contest competition, I bet you'd win. Without any makeup!"

"Hardy-har-har." I turned the corner, finding myself wishing he'd walk away. I knew he was just being his normal silly old self, but his remarks were hitting uncomfortably close to home.

"Oh. come on, Skye!" he cried, grabbing me by the arms and dancing me around the hall. "Everyone knows zombies are *so* hot right now. Why, I bet if you met me at Luna tonight, you'd be the talk of the town."

I sighed. I should have predicted this was where the conversation was headed. Luna was a nightclub on Manhattan's Lower East Side. Back when it was just a decrepit hole in the wall, Craig had scored a prized Friday night DJ gig from eleven to twelve. We used to have fun dressing up, skipping the line, and dancing till dawn. And I had to admit, I'd taken great pleasure in telling the other girls that yes, that was my cute boyfriend up there in the DJ booth spinning the sweet tunes.

That all changed two months ago, when Luna had gotten a write-up in *Guest of a Guest*, which turned it into the trendiest spot in town. The club kids fled as the socialites and Wall Streeters moved in, demanding banquettes and bottle service over dance floor space. The club owners loved it: finally they were making some bank. They tightened the velvet ropes and gave the 1 percent what they wanted. If we weren't already regulars, there was no way the bouncers would have accepted our obviously oh-so-fake IDs.

With that in mind, even if I wasn't exhausted beyond recognition, Luna was the last place I wanted to spend my Friday night. Not that I could explain that to Craig, who'd embraced the new clientele once he realized they came with a pay raise. "Sorry," I said, searching for an acceptable excuse. Saying I was just going to go to bed wouldn't cut it. "I've got work to do on the game. We launch in a couple weeks, and I don't want to miss any bugs."

As I could have predicted, Craig scowled. "It's Friday night!" he protested. "You're not allowed to get your geek on on Friday night. In fact, I'm pretty sure it's against the law. Or it should be, if it isn't."

He was too much. I opened my mouth to retort, but was interrupted by a familiar whirlwind of red hair, red lips, and red fingernails bursting in between us. Oh great. My day was getting better and better.

"What's against the law?" Suzy, my second cousin, demanded, flashing a big smile in Craig's direction and ignoring me completely. You'd think that since we were distantly related, not to mention the fact that she had a boyfriend of her own, she'd consider it bad form to flirt with mine. But evidently she didn't get the Miss Manners memo on that one. And Craig, being Craig, used her adoration to his advantage.

"Skye here refuses to go watch me spin at Luna tonight," my boyfriend informed her, giving me an overexaggerated pout. "Isn't that completely uncool of her?"

Suzy nodded enthusiastically, as she did to pretty much anything Craig said. The girl was a walking, talking cliché. "Completely uncool," she agreed, turning to me. "Especially since you haven't been out in forever. We miss you, you know!"

I sighed. Yeah, they missed me. The old me, that was. The happy-go-lucky club kid who loved to dance and party without a care in the world. Not the new Skye, tormented by nightmares and driven mad by lack of sleep. If only they knew what a downer I'd be, they wouldn't want me there in the first place.

"Sorry, Suze. I'm just not feeling well. I've been having these horrible dreams and—"

"Ooh, that reminds me, I had this crazy dream last night!" Suzy butted in. "Ryan Reynolds and I were all making out at Luna, right? And then Ryan Gosling walks in. And he's all ..."

I groaned as she babbled on in way too much detail about her celebrity threesome. Seriously, was *everyone* hooking up and making out in their dreams while I was busy being chased and tormented in mine?

"I've got to get to class," I announced. At this point I wasn't even going to be able to score that soda. I started to push my way through the two of them. But before I could make my escape Suzy's fingers suddenly locked on to my arm, her fire engine–red nails digging painfully into my flesh.

"Ow!" I cried, turning around, my eyes widening as they fell upon her face. My heart started beating fast as I stared at my cousin.

Gone was the sparkle in her eyes, the laughter on her lips. Gone was the arrogance, the flirtation—all that I knew my cousin to be. Instead there was a strange ... blankness to her expression. Blue eyes but nobody home.

"Uh, are you okay?" I asked, peering at her a little closer. The change was so startling and sudden—it was almost as if someone had flipped a switch. I glanced around to see if anyone else had noticed. But the hallway had become eerily quiet; the other students seemingly vanished into thin air. Even Craig, who was still standing there, seemed so preoccupied, staring down at his phone, it was as if he wasn't actually present.

My heart started beating faster. Something was seriously weird here. Was I having another dream? I reluctantly turned back to Suzy.

"Skye, I *need* you to go to Luna tonight," my cousin was saying in a slow voice that sounded nothing like her normal boisterous tone. She paused, then added, "I think Trent is cheating on me and I need you to find out if I'm right."

I let out a breath, forcing my shoulders to relax. She was just freaked out about her stupid boyfriend, I told myself, that was all. Probably not without good reason.

"You need to go to Luna's VIP room tonight and catch him with this girl," Suzy continued in the same detached-sounding voice. "You need to take a photo of the two of them together and bring it back to me. So I'll have the proof I need."

She paused, waiting for my answer. I stared at her for a second, still puzzled by the weird blankness on her face. Then I sighed. While I could argue with her—I could tell her no a dozen times—in the end, it wasn't worth the energy. Especially when she'd teamed up with Craig. And maybe it'd be good for me to get out for a bit. Maybe it would help me forget the dreams.

"Sure," I relented. "Fine. Whatever."

The words had barely left my lips when the hallway burst back into life. Students once again began streaming past us, chattering happily. Craig looked up from his phone. Suzy's face transformed back to its normal vapid enthusiasm, and she squealed as she leapt into my arms, squeezing me tight and effectively cutting off my air supply.

"Oh, thank you, thank you, thank you!" she cried. "You're the best cousin in the history of cousins."

I couldn't find any words to reply.

"And the best girlfriend, too," Craig agreed. "Trust me, you won't regret this!"

I was pretty sure I already did. But I just stood there, dazed and confused, as he kissed me on the cheek again, then turned and started down the hallway, whistling as he went. Suzy untangled herself from my arms and ran off after him, telling him to wait up.

As I watched the two of them go, my eyes caught a glimpse of something I'd never seen before on the back of my cousin's neck.

A tattoo of the moon.

FOUR

I kept my promise that night, walking past the seemingly endless line, which wrapped all the way around one city block, and wondered once again what had happened to my precious Luna. The once hole-in-the-wall club—with more cockroaches than clients—was now the must-go destination for Manhattan's rich and bored. I was pretty sure the designer bags in this line alone could be sold for a down payment on a Park Avenue penthouse.

I could feel the jealous stares burn at my backside as I shrugged by with a Forever 21 purse on my shoulder and waltzed up to the velvet ropes, giving the bouncer a burly hug. *Why does she get to skip the line? Who does she think she is?* Bruno hugged me back. He looked like total thug life, but was actually a complete teddy bear.

"Hey, dollface," he greeted. "Slumming it tonight?"

I laughed. Bruno had been working the door since the days Luna paid actresses to line up and attract a crowd. He knew as well as I did how ridiculous this place had become. "Just came to check Craig out," I told him. "And see some friends. Do you know if Trent is here?"

Bruno shook his head. "Haven't seen him yet," he replied. "But I'm sure he's on his way. You know he never misses a Friday."

I glanced at my watch. Great. I'd hoped to be in and out of here so I could get back home and get some sleep. Evidently luck was not going to be my lady tonight.

Bruno unclipped the velvet rope, and I did a doubletake when I caught a glimpse of a small moon tattooed between his thumb and forefinger. The exact design of Suzy's neck art. Was this some kind of new trend I hadn't heard about? The symbol of a new band everyone loved? I shivered, feeling unnerved all over again. But Bruno just flashed me a toothy grin. "Have a good time!" was all he said.

Pushing down my growing trepidation, I forced my feet to keep walking down the red carpet, through the main doors, down a black-lit corridor, and onto the main dance floor. It was early, but the club was already pretty packed with hot, blinged-out dancers, gyrating to fast-paced electronica mixed with hip-hop.

At one time I would have jumped right in, dancing up a storm and working up a sweat. But tonight I was just too exhausted. I decided to head up to the VIP room and wait for Suzy's stupid boyfriend to make an appearance. That way I could also say hi to Craig if I caught him between sets. Show him what a good and dedicated girlfriend I was.

I pushed my way through the crowd and soon made it to the VIP gateway. The bouncer, a new guy I didn't know, checked his list then unclipped the rope. I climbed the stairs to the elite, private lounge, where only Manhattan's finest were deemed worthy enough to hang. I felt a bit like an intruder, being far from Manhattan's finest. If only I had some kind of sign around my neck, saying I'M WITH THE DJ, maybe I wouldn't have gotten so many suspicious stares.

Since it was still early, there were only a few other guests. A handful of women, tightly wrapped in form-fitting bandage dresses and hoofed with red-soled Louboutins. A few Armani-clad Japanese businessmen, eyeing them with interest. The lot of them lounged on smooshy couches and velvet chairs, sipping champagne and blatantly ignoring the NYC smoking ban. Trent, as Bruno had predicted, was nowhere to be seen yet. Fashionably late, as per usual.

I sank down into a nearby chair and allowed a cocktail waitress to take my drink order. Diet Red Bull—I was desperate for the caffeine. I caught Craig's eye over in the nearby DJ booth and waved. He grinned, probably thrilled to see I'd really shown up, and blew me a kiss. I returned the kiss laughingly, feeling myself relax as I cuddled into the comfy chair, for the first time in a while feeling kind of good. Even with these newfound cheesy clubgoers, I always felt at home at Luna. It was safe here. Familiar. And best of all, loud enough so I wouldn't fall asleep and dream.

That last dream—the one in class—still hadn't left me. In fact, Glenda's words had been banging around my consciousness all day.

"You're almost ready ..."

I shook my head. Had to give my subconscious credit; it sure was creative. Wait until the real life Glenda heard about her starring role in my mental breakdown. Especially the part of her writing the weird symbols on my—

I stopped short, the laughter suffocating as my eyes fell upon the spidery handwriting scrawled across the back of my hand.

I leapt from my seat, my pulse racing as I stared down at the message, hardly believing what I was seeing with my own eyes. It was impossible. Crazy. How could words from a dream be written on my hand in real life? They weren't there before. Were they? Surely I would have noticed.

You won't know where you are. Or even who you are ...

I shook my head, trying to clear my thoughts. This was stupid. There had to be some logical explanation. I must have written it myself. Sleep scribbling. That was a thing, right?

But if I had done it this morning, why was it only showing up now?

I shoved my hand under my thigh, turning back to the DJ booth, wanting to find Craig again. To focus on something real. But before I could turn my head, a flash of hot white light blinded me, hurling me backward in my chair. My hands flew to the armrests as the floor buckled, as if jarred loose from an earthquake. Panicked, I frantically scanned the room, waiting for the screams, the stampedes, the clubgoers tripping over their stilettos as they fled the premises.

But there was nothing.

The other clubgoers were talking. Laughing. Drinking. Could they not see the streaks of electricity arcing down the center of the room? Could they not feel the aftershocks? Smell the sulfur in the air?

I sat frozen in place, my heart banging against my rib cage as my fight-or-flight mechanism kicked in. Something was really wrong here. Really, really wrong. Was it me? Was I finally losing my mind for good?

"I'd like a Jack-and-Coke, please," a man said. I turned to watch him order his drink, hoping to regain some semblance of normalcy. Focus on something mundane. Something real. Something not ripped from a psycho, delusional brain. A stranger ordering a drink. No big deal.

My heart stopped.

The man across the room was not a stranger at all. In fact, I would have recognized him anywhere. Broad shoulders, trim gray beard. And though he was dressed differently—in a black blazer rather than a silver suit, he was as familiar as the back of my hand.

The man from my dream. The one who'd chased me down. Caught me on the ladder. Sent me to the moon. He looked over, caught my eye, gave me a friendly wave.

My world spun off its axis.

I started to scream.

FIVE

I open my eyes. I'm no longer at Luna, no longer safe and sound in the VIP section of my favorite club. Instead I find myself confined to some kind of box the size of a telephone booth, with all four sides projecting dizzying scenes of swirling color—as if I've somehow crawled inside a kaleidoscope. The ceiling is a mess of wires and tubes and the floor seems to be made out of a metal grate. The air is thick, with a sickly sweet odor that's nearly overwhelming, and I cough.

My hands find my face, and I realize I'm wearing some kind of dark sunglasses. Pulling them off, I blink a few times, my naked eyes struggling to accustom to the brightly lit walls. I feel a tug at my fingers and realize the glasses are attached to some kind of retractable cable. I release them and they're sucked into the ceiling, disappearing from view. I swallow hard, staring up at the mass of wires above, hoping I didn't need them for something.

Where am I? What's going on? I have no idea. All I know for sure is I need to find a way out of this box. Forcing down my rising claustrophobia, I desperately feel around for an escape route. Finally, I find a lever and push down on it, breathing a sigh of relief as the wall in front of me collapses, revealing an exit. But an exit to where?

Stepping outside the box, I enter a long hallway, carpeted with crimson-colored shag. Every few feet there's an identical door to the one I just exited, each with a small gray pad just adjacent, with two tiny red and green lights beside it. All the red lights flash in sync, except for the door closest to me, which glows a solid green. Each door is painted entirely black and emblazoned with a gold crescent moon. My heart stutters. More moons. Glenda's warning comes screeching back to me.

Whatever you do ... don't look into the moon.

I avert my eyes, feeling a bit silly for doing so. I mean, how can a door hurt me? But still ... I draw in a breath.

Half of me wants to shrug this off as just another dream. But at the same time, it feels different than the previous ones. More solid. More real. Not to mention I know I didn't fall asleep in the club. There was no way with all that shaking and bright light. Unless that had been part of the dream.

You won't know where you are. Maybe even who you are.

Glenda's words echo through my mind, making me frown. *But I do know*, I remind myself. I may not know where I am, but I certainly know who I am. Skye Brown. Manhattan teen. Club kid and gamer geek, currently awaiting men in white coats to drag her away to a padded room, forever.

I look down one end of the hallway and then the other. Each seems to stretch off into infinity. Which way to go? I haven't a clue. I force myself to choose a direction and start walking. A moment later I slam into a cleverly angled and mirrored door; the endless hallway was just an illusion.

My hands search the door, wrapping around a hidden handle. Could this be the exit? Or a step into danger? I look back down the hallway. I realize I don't have much of a choice so I turn the handle and push the door open, cautiously stepping out into the next room, a bit terrified to learn what I'll find on the other side. If this is one of the dreams, it could be anything. It could even be my death.

"Ah, you're awake. Did you enjoy the trip?" asks a small, wizened Asian man, bowing low. He stands behind a counter, dressed in an old-fashioned suit, like a character out of a Charlie Chan movie. His name tag simply states PROPRIETOR. I stare at him, not sure how to respond.

"What trip? Where am I?" I ask, completely bewildered.

The man only laughs.

I look around, trying to take stock of my surroundings. The place is gaudy. Red velvet sofas, shiny mirrored coffee tables. Elaborate decorative lamps with golden fringe hanging from their

s. Total Las Vegas brothel chic. I notice a few other teens lounging on couches nearby, chattering and laughing among themselves, their nonchalance making me relax a bit. No one seems to be worried. No one seems to be in danger. That's something, at least.

The girls are dressed in colorful tank tops, flouncy miniskirts, and thigh-high stiletto boots: manga characters come to life. The guys are even stranger, in long belted tunics over tight leather pants—not exactly Jersey Shore couture. I surreptitiously check out my own reflection in a nearby mirror. I'm still wearing my club clothes from Luna. Black corset top, short plaid skirt, platform boots. At least I somewhat fit in.

I look back at the group. One of the girls has pulled out an inhaler that looks exactly like mine. She takes a quick puff, then waves good-bye to her friends as she heads toward the hallway I just exited. I watch her go, puzzled as she disappears behind the door.

I realize the proprietor is still staring at me. I reluctantly turn back to him. He looks me over carefully before speaking.

"A man came looking for you," he informs me. "He left a card." He takes my hand in his own wrinkled grip and presses a piece of paper into it.

I stare down at the card, confused. Someone was looking for me? Here? It's then I notice the name. *Reginald Duske, Senator.*

A chill trips down my spine. The guy Glenda was talking about, the one I'm supposed to avoid, has been here. Looking for me. That seems bad in so many ways. Underneath the name there's another one of those long strings of dashes and dots—like the one written on my hand. "What does this code mean?" I ask the proprietor, my voice trembling.

The man looks at me as if I'm insane. I can't say, at this point, that he's entirely wrong in his assessment. "Phone number," he says in a total "duh" voice. "You need to use the phone?" He picks up a silver, crescent-shaped object that looks like no phone I've ever seen and offers it to me.

"Um, no. I mean, yes?" I decide, having no idea what else to do. I glance down at my hand. Sure enough, Glenda's warning is still inscribed on my palm. Then I shift my focus back to the business card.

Reginald Duske. Who is this guy? Is he really a senator? And what about this other person—Dawn. How does Dawn fit into all of this?

The proprietor frowns and taps his foot impatiently. "Just make the call," he demands, and suddenly the whole situation seems a lot more sinister. After all, why should he care? Unless ... he's in on it somehow.

Whatever "it" might be.

I press my lips together, trying to decide what to do. The man continues to stare me down.

"Can I ... have some privacy?" I ask at last, stalling for time.

I see a hint of annoyance flit over the proprietor's face, but he forces it back and smiles at me. He's got perfectly white and shiny teeth. "But of course," he says, bowing again. He steps back from behind the counter and heads to one of the unoccupied couches. The other teens have all vanished into the mirrored corridor. I wonder what they're doing in there.

I shake my head, forcing my attention back to the situation. I stare down at Duske's card, then at the name on my palm. What should I do? Who should I call? Should I call anyone? I close my eyes, desperately searching for answers. For some reason Dawn's name drifts through my consciousness—a shard of glass washing up on the shore, dulled by the sea. Dawn can help me, I determine. Glenda wouldn't steer me wrong.

I set down the card and use the code written on my hand instead, then bring the phone to my ear. It rings twice before a man answers. "Yes, what is it?" he asks impatiently.

"I'm, um, looking for Dawn?" I stammer, not quite sure what to say now that I've made the call. *I'm having this weird dream and my personal trainer thought Dawn could help me with it?* He'd probably hang up right then and there.

"This is Dawn."

"Oh." I pause, taken aback. "Right. Um ..." Now what do I say?

Silence. Then, "Mariah?" the voice asks with a thread of incredulity. "Is that really you?"

I frown. What is it with this girl Mariah? Why does everyone think I'm her? "Uh, no. This is Skye," I correct him. "And, well, I'm not actually sure why I'm calling. It's just I woke up in this weird place and had your phone number written on my hand." Jeez, he's going to think I'm some drunk chick he met at a bar last night. "I know that sounds really bizarre, but—"

"You've got a hell of a nerve calling here, Mariah," Dawn interrupts.

I frown. "I told you. I'm not Mariah. I'm Skye. I don't know who this Mariah person is, but I can assure you—"

There's a heavy sigh on the other end of the line, followed by more silence. Then: "Where are you?"

Good question. I glance around. "Uh, I don't know. I woke up in some small room with movie screens or something, and walked down a hallway into some weird brothel-looking place and— "

"A Moongazer palace. I should have known," Dawn concludes, not sounding too happy about the fact. "Which one?"

I glance around, looking for some sort of locator. "Um ..." My eyes fall upon a business card, lying on the counter. "Area 52?" I read.

Dawn snorts. "Slumming it, are you?" he says, his voice laced with bitterness. "What, the Senate wouldn't pay for a trip from one of the high-class joints?"

"What? I don't—" I couldn't be more seriously lost in a conversation if I tried.

"Well, at least you're close. There's a rabbit hole on Fifty-third. I'll meet you there in five."

"Uh, I'm not sure ..."

But I realize I'm talking to no one. Dawn, whoever he is, has already hung up and is presumably on his way to collect me. I really hope I didn't make some huge mistake calling him.

I notice the proprietor is staring at me suspiciously from the couch. I pretend to continue my conversation. "Oh yes, Duske. It's great to talk to you, too," I say loudly, forcing a laugh. "I'll see you soon. Good-bye now!"

I click END on the phone and set it down on the counter. "That Duske," I say, shaking my head and smiling as the Asian gentleman rises from the couch and walks back to the counter. Luckily, he seems to be buying my act. "He's coming to pick me up. I'm going to wait outside." I start heading for the front door, wanting to get as far away from this unsettling scene as possible.

"Wait!"

I freeze. Now what? My heart pounds as he shuffles over to me. To my surprise, he reaches out to wrap his fingers around the necklace I'm wearing.

"I need the charm," he says firmly.

"Wait!" I grab for the necklace but he's too quick, yanking it away. The delicate clasp gives way and the chain pools into his hands. "That's mine! My mother gave it to me for my birthday."

He rolls his eyes. "This is my necklace," he says firmly, palming it as he heads back behind the counter, opening a cabinet. I gasp as my eyes fall upon the contents—hundreds of silver necklaces, identical to mine. The Asian man slips my chain beside the others and then proceeds to close the cabinet door. "All right then," he says, turning back to me and giving me a toothy grin. "Goodbye for now. I'm sure I'll see you soon," he adds, a bit too knowingly for my liking.

"Yeah, whatever," I mutter as I push open the door. As if I'd ever return to this creepy old place. I step outside, my eyes widening as they take in my surroundings. I'm not sure what I expected the outside to look like, but it certainly wasn't this.

Like in my dreams, I appear to be underground, with a rock ceiling stretching high above. The neighborhood is lit with dim street lights, casting a sickly orange glow on crumbling cement buildings. Everywhere I look I see barred windows, battered doors, chipped paint. Dawn wasn't kidding when he called this place a slum. At the end of the road, a large fan, embedded into the rock, is blowing hot, stale air down the street and stirring up dirt and debris. But it's the smell that's the worst of it—an overwhelming stench of decay and garbage, inescapable and nauseating.

I turn back to the building I just vacated. Moongazer Palace appears to be the one shining neon gem in this otherwise sepia-palette world. It's big and red and gaudy as hell, with a sign reading MOONGAZE HERE! that buzzes and flickers with age—the Z almost burnt out completely. Its tagline —"Are you ready to look into the moon?" —is more than slightly unnerving, and I force myself to turn away.

Across the palace is a narrow brick alleyway—the kind you'd expect to be tagged with colorful graffiti. But instead of art blooming in the den of darkness, I see only a crimson stain splattered against one wall. Red liquid drips down, soaking into a grimy puddle. Is that blood? Human blood? I glance around nervously, taking an involuntary step backward. Maybe I should have waited inside after all.

A shadow crosses my vision. I whirl around to see a dark

silhouette stepping into the alleyway. Terrified, I back up, only to
hit the brick wall. I'm trapped. And the stranger steps into the light.

It's a guy—around my own age. Tall, lean, and wearing a black
leather trench coat and scuffed brown boots. His eyes are hidden
behind mirrored shades and long layers of translucent platinum
hair fall into his face, almost but not completely obscuring high
cheekbones. I catalog him quickly: he's unearthly-looking, hot as
hell, and both completely strange and so damn familiar all at the
same time. Unnerving déjà vu, once again pricking at the edges of
my brain.

The boy stares at me for a moment, then leaps forward almost
too fast for my eyes to follow. He reaches me in an instant,
grabbing me and squeezing me so tightly he practically cuts off my
air supply. Head buried in my hair, his fingers dig into my back. I'm
his prisoner—flush against him and pinned to the wall.

"Let me go!" I demand, squirming. But it's no use. He's too
strong. And all I can focus on is the smear of blood dripping down
the opposite wall.

He pulls away for a moment, allowing me to suck in a much-
needed breath. I catch my reflection in his mirrored shades, almost
not recognizing my own flushed face. Before I can speak he leans
into me, crushing his mouth against mine. His fingers claw at my
arms, his mouth bruises my lips. Fear pounds at my heart. I realize
I need to do something—fast.

I pull back my knee, then let it go. He falls backward, jerking
away as if he'd been shocked. Head bowed, crouched over, hands
balled into fists. Even with his glasses, the fury is clear on his face.

"Nice to see you again, too, Mariah," he growls, his voice low
and guttural, with an accent I can't place. He starts to straighten.

"Don't come any closer!" I cry out, praying he'll obey. I know
some self-defense—I grew up in NYC and my mom insisted on
it—but I've never practiced on a real enemy. "I've … got a gun and
I'm not afraid to use it." *Yeah, right, Skye. And a bridge to Brooklyn,
too.*

I hold my breath, waiting for his next move. Will he retaliate?
Or let me go?

"I'm sorry," he mutters, surprising me. "That was uncalled for,
I guess, given the circumstance. I was just … I don't know. Happy
to see you. Stupid, I know."

"No kidding that was uncalled for!" I cry, rubbing my sore

back, glaring at him. "You can't just grab some random stranger off the street and start kissing them like that! I mean, who do you think you are?"

He turns to me, ripping off his shades for the first time. I gasp. His eyes are the most brilliant blue I've ever seen. They're so intense they practically glow. I'm mesmerized, and for a moment I can't look away. This is, without a doubt, the hottest guy I've ever laid eyes on.

Also, perhaps, the angriest.

"Are you for real?" he demands. "Who do you think I am? Come on, Mariah. I don't have time for these games."

Mariah. Oh my god. The pieces start falling into place.

"Are you Dawn?" I ask in a hesitant whisper. "The one I called?" This guy is Dawn? The one Glenda said could help me?

He cringes, presumably at the incredulity in my tone. "Yeah," he mutters. "I'm Dawn. Once more with feeling." He rakes a hand through his platinum hair as he stalks the alleyway like a tiger, his steps eating up the concrete. "I can't keep doing this," he mutters, more to himself than me. "I just can't keep doing this."

"Doing what?" I ask, feeling confused and also annoyed at my confusion. "What are you talking about?"

He whirls around. "You think you can just waltz back into my life after what you did?" he demands, his voice cold and furious. "That I'll keep taking you back—time and time again—no big deal?" His beautiful eyes flash fire. "Well, you're wrong, Mariah. This is the last time I rescue you. Then I'm done. I'm truly done. I'm not going to let you screw with my head anymore."

I'm screwing with *his* head? He's the one who attacked me and kissed me for no reason whatsoever. Not to mention calling me some other girl's name, even though I've clearly stated who I really am. And now he has the nerve to accuse me?

"Look," I say, gritting my teeth. "My name is Skye Brown. I only called you because my personal trainer, Glenda, told me you could help me." God, that sounds so stupid when I say it out loud. "But obviously she was wrong. So just forget it. I'm going back inside."

I push past him and head toward Moongazer Palace, as fast as my boots can take me. I'll figure my own way out of here. Or I'll just wait until I wake up. Either way, I don't need Mr. Psycho's attitude. I wrap my fingers around the door handle, ready to pull it open.

"I'm sorry," Dawn says suddenly, causing me to freeze in my tracks. He pauses, then adds, "I know you're not yourself. I didn't mean ... it's just hard, you know." He sighs, then adds, "No, I guess you wouldn't know, would you? You wouldn't know anything at all."

He sounds so sad that I find myself, against my better judgment, abandoning the door handle and turning back around. There I find him standing alone in the middle of the street, looking as if he's lost his best friend.

"Talk to me," I beseech him, seeing my opportunity. "What's going on? Where am I? Why am I here?"

At first, he doesn't speak and I'm afraid I'll get nothing from him. But finally he opens his mouth to reply. "The Eclipsers," he says, his voice tired and drained. "Glenda and her gang. They felt you were still worth saving." He stubs his boot into the dirt. "I told them not to bother. That you'd made your choice. But they couldn't accept that. They never could."

"Then why did Glenda tell me to call you?"

Dawn shrugs. "She probably figured if I saw you again, I'd take pity on you. Forgive you for what you did. Hop back on the Eclipser bandwagon." He looks up at me and I notice his beautiful, angry eyes are shining. Wet. "But I don't forgive you," he says in a choked voice. "To me, you'll always be a traitor."

His icy words send a shiver down my spine. He turns away quickly, but not before I can see his expression crumble. Pain radiates through him as he leans against the wall, stone cold, but ashen-faced. Whatever this Mariah girl did to him, it had to be really bad. I find myself fighting the ridiculous urge to walk over and give him a hug.

"I'm sorry," I say in my gentlest voice, daring to approach. I place a comforting hand on his right shoulder. I don't have a clue as to what I'm apologizing for, but I feel the need to say something to make him feel better.

He turns around slowly, looking down at me with his glorious eyes, and for a moment I think he's going to kiss me again. Instead, he reaches up and strokes my cheek with the back of his hand. His touch is soft, tender. The wisp of a butterfly's wing against my skin.

"Look 'Ri, we can't stay here," he murmurs. "It's too dangerous for a Dark Sider to be so close to Luna Park. We must go under."

My pulse kicks up at his words. "Um, 'under'? What do you mean?"

"I'll bring you to my place. At least you'll be safe there. You can rendezvous with the Eclipsers later." He offers a hand. "Come on. Let's go."

I hesitate. I want to believe him. But ...

"I don't know if that's a good idea," I hedge. "After all, I don't even know you."

"Right." Dawn squeezes his eyes shut with frustration. "Of course you don't." He stares up at the sky. "Oh Glenda, you so owe me for this," he mutters.

He reaches into his pocket and pulls out a small silver blade that gleams under the streetlights.

"I'm afraid you leave me no choice," he says in a terse, but even voice. "If you value your life—or what's left of it, anyway—I must insist you come with me."

SIX

I leap back, surprised, shocked, stunned. Isn't Dawn supposed to be one of the good guys? The one Glenda told me I should seek out? So how come he's got a knife pulled on me? On the Good Guy scale of one to ten, slicing and dicing the heroine hovers a bit below negative two in my book.

That's assuming I *am* the heroine in this story. At the moment, I'm not a hundred percent on that.

Dawn seems to share my confusion. He's white-knuckling the blade, hands trembling. Could a precisely placed kick knock it out of his grasp, or will that impulsive trick only leave me with a bloodied foot? My life may depend on the answer. And right now, my only friend is surprise.

Do it!

A strange confidence wells up inside me. Suddenly, for no logical reason at all, I know—beyond the shadow of a doubt—that I can take this guy in a fight. Steal the blade and turn the tables, draw the power into my own two hands.

And so, as if compelled by ancient training I never had, I hold up my hands in fake surrender and take a step forward, waiting for the moment I see him relaxing his grip, thinking I'll give in sweetly and come along like a good little girl. At that instant, I launch into a roundhouse kick, my heel slamming into his palm. With a shocked grunt, he loses his grasp on the weapon, sending it skittering across the ground. I lunge forward, head-butting him with all my might. Our skulls collide with a sick clunking sound. He flails, stumbling backward. Seeing stars myself, I lose my balance, falling into him, and soon we're both entangled on the floor.

Now I need that knife. I roll off my would-be kidnapper, scrambling to my feet, ready to make a mad dash for it. But Dawn reacts, grabbing my boot heel, and I trip, falling flat on my face, hands and chest, slamming onto hard, cold pavement. For a moment I can't breathe—the wind stolen from my lungs.

Dawn takes advantage with lightning speed, dragging me by my heel, then my ankle. I kick backward, using my free foot to slam my boot into his face. He bellows in rage but can't hold on. I wiggle forward along the ground like a worm, fingers outstretched, reaching, straining only millimeters away from the weapon. Finally I feel its cold metal connect with my hand. Got it! Wrapping my fingers around the knife hilt, I flip over, grasping it in both hands, waving it unsteadily in his direction. Advantage: me.

"Freeze!" I command. "Don't move a muscle."

He groans, but obeys. "Well, well," he says, reaching up to touch his face. I've managed to do quite a number on him. Left eye swollen, a split lip, and his nose is practically gushing. "I guess at least you haven't lost your ability to fight like an alley cat." He makes a move to crawl toward me.

"Don't come any closer," I warn. "I'll gut you."

He sighs wearily and sits back down. "Look, we both know you're not going to do that," he says simply. "So how about we stop this charade and head down the rabbit hole before we end up having a patrol on our asses?"

I hesitate. My fingers caress the knife's hilt, my pulse beating a mile a minute, knowing he's called my bluff. There's no way I can bring myself to drive a blade through an actual person, extinguish their spark of life with my own two hands. Dawn, somehow, seems to know this. And he's using this knowledge to turn the tables once again, effortlessly taking back control.

I reluctantly lower the knife.

"Thought so," he says with a knowing nod, rising to his feet and holding out a hand. I ignore it and scramble up by myself.

"I can always change my mind," I remind him, shoving the knife into my boot. Just in case.

He snorts. "Yeah. Don't I know it."

We stare at each other for a moment, me angry, him still cocky, though with a trace of sadness fluttering beneath the surface.

Neither one of us seems willing to look away first. To submit to the other. That is, until a siren's mournful wail shatters the silence of the city block. Dawn's arrogance fades, and concern takes its place.

"And there would be the Park Patrol," he announces. "Underground. Now." He beckons me to follow as he turns and hurries down the street. He gets a few yards, then pauses, turning back to me, his face beseeching.

"Seriously, 'Ri. You have to trust me. You don't want to be caught out here alone."

I want to tell him to go to hell, but something in his voice gives me pause: serious concern, laced with fear. Could we really be in danger? I remember Glenda's words. *Trust Dawn.* At the end of the day, it's all I have to go on in this crazy world.

"Okay," I agree, not knowing what else to do. I still have the knife, I remind myself. I can always escape later. "Lead the way."

We make a left, walking briskly past Moongazer Palace, and then a right at a boarded-up warehouse. Dawn stops at a small manhole cover in the center of the street, silhouetted in sickly orange by one halfheartedly flickering streetlight above. He gets down on his knees and starts twisting the cover with both hands.

The siren wails again. This time louder. Closer.

Dawn looks up. "Give me a hand with this," he orders. "We don't have much time."

I drop to my knees, still sore from our fight, and help him wrench the cover off. We toss it to one side, revealing a metal ladder leading down into the blackness. Just like in my dream. I shiver.

"Go ahead, I'll be right behind you," Dawn instructs.

I stare down into the hole, trying to work up my nerve. I've always been a bit claustrophobic, even when I'm not running around in some kind of weird postapocalyptic underground dream world. Climbing down into a black pit with no idea of what awaits me below? That's a bit much to swallow.

The siren wails again. Piercing. Right around the corner now from the sound of it.

"They're at Moongazer Palace," Dawn says in a hoarse whisper. "They'll be here any second. Please, Mariah. Just go down the rabbit hole."

The panic in his voice compels me to obey. I suck in a breath, wipe my sweaty palms on my skirt, then stick my legs down the hole. Carefully I find each foothold, securing my step before lowering myself to the next rung. The blackness soon swallows me with only a dim circle of light from the opening above to guide my way. Down, down, down. How deep is this "rabbit hole" anyway? And what if there are multisized doors and cupcakes reading EAT ME at the bottom?

I glance up to see Dawn's silhouette far above as he starts his own descent. He's still way up high. If I wanted, I imagine I could jump off the ladder now and make a run for it. But where would I go? I'm completely at his mercy. Better to bide my time, figure out what's going on first.

And who knows? If I'm lucky, maybe I'll just wake up. Realize this is all just another one of my psychotic dreams. That's still a possibility, right? But something inside me, some niggling know-it-all voice, tells me that this isn't like the other times. Those dreams were ethereal, mystical, ungrounded in any kind of reality. This seems different. Solid. Like I'm actually here.

Dawn drags the cover over the manhole and the dim light above me fades until it is gone altogether. The metal clanks into place, leaving us smothered in blackness. I hold out my hand; it's so dark I can't even see it. Cave darkness. Panic bubbles to my throat, but I swallow it down and force myself to begin my breathing exercises as I keep descending. No time to freak out. I need to keep my wits about me now more than ever.

The ladder ends and my boots struggle to find purchase on a surprisingly slick metal surface. Thankfully, it's a bit lighter down here, with a dull, crimson ribbon of light running alongside what appears to be an underground metal road.

I take advantage of the light to take stock of my surroundings. It appears I'm in some kind of large aqueduct, a smooth stone tube, like a sewer (and it certainly smells like one), but with a metal highway running its length. Every few feet, mammoth fans, cut into the stone, blast hot, stale air through the tunnel, whirring loudly, drowning out most other sounds.

I gasp, recognizing the scene. The tunnel from my dream. It has to be.

What if the dream was a premonition of some sort? What if there are uniformed men just around the corner, ready to chase me, to pin me down, to "send me to the moon"? Should I be ready to run?

My panicked thoughts are interrupted as Dawn jumps off the ladder, landing with a thud by my side. He pulls an industrial-strength flashlight from a utility belt and switches it on. I relax a bit. In my dream I was alone. Here, at the very least, I have my reluctant hero by my side. Can I trust him? I have no idea. But what choice do I have?

"Ready?" Dawn asks, turning to me. "My bike's stashed in a side tunnel nearby. I don't think they saw us, and I did lock the hole, but I don't want to take any chances."

"Where are you taking me?"

"I told you. To my house. I'll contact Glenda and the Eclipsers and let them know you're here." He grunts. "Don't worry, once they come get you, you won't have to deal with me anymore."

"Uh, okay," I say, not liking his sarcasm. But then again, how can I blame the guy? I just beat the crap out of him. I'm probably lucky he didn't decide to turn me into the patrol himself.

I follow Dawn down the corridor, his flashlight casting sharp silhouettes against the smooth cave walls. I resist the urge to grab his arm like a girly girl frightened by her own shadow. Instead I square my shoulders and force myself to keep a brave face. Can't let him know how freaked out I am; he already holds enough of an advantage, thank you very much.

The tunnel breaks ahead, forking into an unlit side passage. Dawn motions for me to wait and then disappears into the darkness, returning a moment later leading a small motorcycle. He straddles it and then instructs me to hop on the back, after handing me a helmet. I hesitate, weigh my options, then reluctantly pull the helmet over my head and climb on.

"No handholds," I remark, looking from side to side on the bike.

"Sorry, princess," Dawn says mildly, "you're just going to have to hold on to me."

Seeing no alternative, I tentatively guide my arms around him, clasping my hands together in front. His chest is solid, toned. Not an ounce of fat encasing his well-defined ribs. I can feel his heartbeat through his jacket, thudding too fast. Matching the beats of my own. He's still nervous about me. Or at least this Mariah he thinks I am.

He starts the engine and the bike roars to life. It's then that I realize this is not a regular motorcycle. Namely because regular motorcycles do not hover six inches off the ground.

Holy crap! I start to exclaim, but my words are drowned out as Dawn releases the brake and we begin to fly down the corridor. Yes, literally *fly*. The wind whips through my hair as we soar down the road.

The ride is fast but smooth; by hovering we avoid any potholes or rocks. Dawn steers the bike effortlessly, tipping to one side and then the other as he maneuvers down the sharp tunnel turns. I tighten my grip around him—we have to be going at least a hundred miles an hour—and I wonder what would happen if someone comes around the corner in the other direction. A high-speed flying collision? No thank you.

About ten minutes later Dawn slows the bike. I tilt my head to get a better glimpse as to where we are. We've come to a large, rusty gate that extends from the ground to the cave ceiling. Two identical spotlights cast shards of illumination against its closed metal mouth.

"Welcome to the Dark Side," Dawn says grimly. He presses a button and the bike sinks back to the earth. I let out a sigh of relief. He dismounts and walks over to the gate.

"The dark side?" I repeat skeptically. "As in, 'Use the force, Luke'?"

"Hardy-har-har," Dawn mutters, not sounding the least bit amused. But he does seem to recognize the *Star Wars* reference. Does George Lucas's presence really stretch this far? "Dark Side. Like, the place where the Dark Siders live," he clarifies bitterly. "Those of us deemed unworthy of mingling with the Indys of Luna Park."

That doesn't exactly clear things up. "Indys?"

He sighs. "You really have forgotten everything, haven't you? Indys—short for Independents. The free citizens of Terra. They live on Level One of the underground strata in their luxurious condos with sparkling swimming pools, tennis courts, and expensive restaurants. While we, the working class, the ones who keep Terra running, are trapped down here in Stratum Two. Doomed to live in the dirt and squalor and work like slaves our entire lives."

"You live underground?" I feel a sudden pang of sympathy for the guy. "That must be horrible!" I mean, I can't even imagine what it must be like to live underground. Never see the sun.

Never see the moon …

Dawn chokes out a laugh. "Funny you should say that." He presses his thumb against a small gray pad embedded in the gate. The device beeps twice, and the gate creaks open. "I mean, seeing how you betrayed the revolution and all."

Before I can reply, he joins me back on the bike and turns over the engine, drowning out my billion questions as we rise off the ground again. We head through the gates and into the tunnel beyond. The Dark Side, I realize quickly, is very unlike the town I arrived in, one stratum above, where buildings, while decrepit, still seemed semi-normal and recognizable. This place feels more like an ant farm, with intricate, twisty-tunnels leading off in all directions. The ceilings are beyond low and dull, dirty metal doors are embedded into the rocks every few feet. The claustrophobia kicks back in—hardcore.

As Dawn bike banks a sharp left, we glide down a corridor, and the narrow passage thankfully opens up into what appears to be some kind of town square. I look around, quickly assessing. Junk stores advertise odds and ends. Tiny grocers are busy parceling out moldy vegetables and crusts of bread. Broken-down trailers with tattered canopies and multicolored Christmas lights squat wherever there's room. And scantily clad women hang out of crumbling buildings advertising their particular services.

Steam rises from the grated floor, and condensation drips from the high ceiling, giving the impression of a drizzly rain. The place is packed, too many people for such a small area, all milling about, waiting in ridiculously long lines for groceries and junk. Most are dressed in gray rags and appear scrawny, impoverished, and blindingly pale.

Dawn parks his bike and we disembark. He gestures to the scene. "Spark any memories?" he asks, a hopeful note in his voice.

I shake my head. Just the opposite—I've never seen anything so foreign in my whole life. I try to imagine what living down here would be like. Trapped in a subterranean world with no hope of ever going back up to the surface …

We pass an old man hobbling down the street on a bent metal cane. I can't help but stare as I realize he's got an extra eye growing out of his forehead. He looks up, his trifold gaze meeting mine. Then, suddenly, his forlorn face lights up like a child's on

Christmas morning.

"Mariah?" he cries, his voice full of wonder. "Is that really you?"

"Oh, great. I was afraid of this," Dawn mutters. "Look, Brother—we're trying to keep a low profile—"

"Hey, everyone, it's Mariah Quinn!" the man calls out loudly before Dawn can silence him. A moment later I find myself rushed by what appears to be the entire town. Encircled, entrapped, and completely engulfed by eager Dark Siders, their eyes shining, their voices animated as they demand to know where I've been. I'm smothered in hugs and questions and requests for help. I look around wildly for Dawn, pleading for his assistance.

"Hey, hey!" he yells over the roar of the crowd, shooing them away. He manages to carve out a small space between me and the Dark Siders. "I know you're excited to see her, but Mariah's been through a lot. She needs some time to recover before you bombard her with requests. I'm sure she'll be setting up visiting hours soon. So just hang on until then, okay?"

"Sorry, Mariah," several townspeople say, looking appropriately abashed. "We're just so glad to see you again." They step away slowly, retreating, respectful. Some touch their caps; others bow their heads.

I look over the crowd, realizing that the man with three eyes is not alone in his deformities. A young woman has an extra, useless arm hanging to one side. A small boy has a tooth growing out of his chin. A middle-aged man has an extra set of ears. They're all mutants. Every last one of them. I glance over at Dawn. Is he deformed somehow as well? But no, he seems normal. Flawless, even. A perfect specimen.

Before I can question this, Dawn grabs my hand and leads me through the crowd. It parts like the Red Sea, heads bowing reverently as we pass. Whoever this Mariah is, she certainly has the respect of the people. Did she really betray them all? I glance back at the sad, downtrodden masses and my heart aches at the hope in their eyes. They are going to be sorely disappointed when they find out their supposed fearless leader is nothing more than a college kid from another world.

Dawn leads me out of the town square and down another tunnel. We come to a metal door, embedded in a stone wall. "Home sweet home," he says as he presses his thumb against the sensor. The door slides open, and we step inside.

I look around; the apartment is no more than a small cave—entirely windowless and scooped out of stone. The walls are smooth, as if they've been sanded down and the decor and furnishings are beyond sparse. A small metal futon couch, coffee table, bookcase—a kitchenette with a half fridge and stove top burners at the far end. Two doors lead off to the side. Bedroom? Bathroom? Do they have plumbing down here? That would be something, at least.

The front door slides silently shut behind me. Dawn walks over to the futon and collapses on it, head in his hands. He scrubs his face, staring down at the rock floor, silent.

"Um," I say, still hovering by the door. "So now what?"

Dawn grabs a small silver phone off the coffee table and presses in a code. He puts the receiver to his ear. "Yeah," he says, after a pause. "I got her. Yeah, she's at my place. No. No, she has no idea who she is."

"Is that Glenda?" I ask, reaching for the phone. Dawn dodges my hand and stands up, walking to the other side of the room.

"No, *you* come get her. I told you I wanted nothing to do with this ... Nice trick, telling her to contact me when she reentered ... Yeah, whatever ... As far as I'm concerned she could have rotted at Moongazer Palace." He grips the phone tightly, his knuckles white. "Yes, I really do mean that. Look, you guys have your own agenda and that's fine by me. But I want no part of it. I told you. I'm done. Ready to lie low. I've no interest in fighting the good fight anymore. And you know what? I don't think your fearless leader even knows there *is* a fight." He pauses again. "Whatever. Just come get her so I don't have to look at her pointy little nose anymore."

I cringe, resisting the urge to reach for my nose. He sounds so angry. So bitter. How can I convince him that I'm not who he thinks I am? That he can't blame me for whatever it was that this Mariah chick did?

Dawn presses a button on his phone and looks over at me. "The Eclipsers are on their way," he says. "So you can relax. You'll be rid of me soon enough."

"Look," I say, figuring now that we're relatively safe I should put all my cards on the table. "No matter what you and the people out there think, I'm not Mariah. I'm Skye Brown—a college kid from New York. I don't know what's going on or how I got here or where *here* even is, but I'd really like to go home now." My voice breaks, the strain and stress and horror of everything I've gone through finally overwhelming me. Tears well up in my eyes. Tears of frustration, helplessness, and rage.

There's a pause, then a crash, as Dawn slams his phone against the stone wall, smashing it into a thousand pieces. "Goddamn you, Duske!" he roars, so loud I think I feel the apartment shake. "Goddamn you and your 'Gazers!"

I jump back, afraid of his violent outburst. "What are you talking about?" I ask, trying desperately to keep my voice steady. "Who's this Duske guy? And what's a 'Gazer?" Even as I ask, I'm not sure I want to know.

He turns to me, his face awash in anger. "Listen to me now," he commands. "And listen good. *You* are not who you think you are. This Skye girl from another world? This college kid from New York? She doesn't exist. Your name is Mariah Quinn. You're from here—Terra. In fact, you've lived your whole life on Terra, till a couple of months ago."

"But that's crazy!" I cry. "I know who I am."

"No. You only think you do," Dawn volleys back. "The Moongazing drugs have made you forget who you really are. Everything about your life in fact."

I scowl; this is ridiculous. I don't take drugs. And I certainly haven't forgotten who I am. "You're wrong," I tell him. "I'm Skye. And I have a whole lifetime of memories to prove it."

Dawn rolls his eyes. "Implanted memories don't count."

"What about my family and friends, then?" I challenge. "My classmates? My teachers?"

"Strangers introduced to your new life. My guess is they were similarly wiped and implanted when you started Moongazing."

I squeeze my hands into fists, frustrated beyond belief. "What … is … Moongazing?"

Dawn doesn't answer, and the sudden silence is unnerving. He sinks down onto his futon, his anger seeming to dissipate into sadness. I drop to the couch, looking at him pleadingly. "Tell me," I beg. "Please."

But he just shakes his head. "I look at you now and see nothing but an empty shell. A shadow of a girl I once loved, with false memories to lull her to sleep while her people suffer and die, lost without their leader." He stares at the wall so hard I half wonder if he'll burn a hole in the rock. "You make me sick, Mariah Quinn."

"I'm not Mariah," I protest again, weakly this time, most of the fight in me gone. I wish he could just accept that I'm not who he thinks I am. I'm not a leader. Or a traitor, for that matter. I've never been here before. I've never laid eyes on Dawn. I've never laid eyes on *any* of these people.

Are you so sure about that?

With perfect timing, my throat constricts. Do I have my inhaler? I pat my skirt anxiously, praying it's still in my possession. I feel a lump and reach into my pocket, fingers curling around my salvation. I pull out the device and put it to my mouth.

Dawn knocks the inhaler from my lips milliseconds before I can take a puff. It skitters across the floor, banging against the rock wall and coming to rest a few feet away.

I stare at him. "What the hell did you do that for?" I demand. I dive for my medication. But he's too quick, jumping in front of me and grabbing it before I can.

"Give that back!" I cry, my voice cracking as I struggle to take in air. I double over, wheezing and choking, my hand out, uselessly begging.

"Look at you," Dawn says, his voice cold. "You're so addicted you can't even breathe without the 'Gazer drugs. Pathetic."

"That's not ... 'Gazer drugs." I wheeze. "It's my ... asthma medication."

"You really think I'm stupid, don't you? Or you're so lost it isn't even funny."

My heart pounds. My skin's clammy and cold. If I don't get my breath under control soon, I'm going to die. Here, in this horrible place. Where no one knows where I am. Or even *who* I am.

Dawn drops the inhaler on the floor and crushes it under his boot.

"No!" I scream, my world flying out from under me. I fall back onto the futon, struggling to fill my lungs. My vision's gone spotty and I'm close to passing out.

Breathe in, hold, one, two, three. Breathe out, hold, one, two, three.

Please don't let me die. Not like this.

Suddenly I feel a presence inches from my face. My eyes flutter open to find Dawn, kneeling in front of me, holding a paper bag to my lips. Desperate, I breathe into it, then suck out the air. *Breathe in, suck out, breathe in.*

"Come on," he urges. "Breathe, Mariah. Just breathe."

After what seems like an eternity, I manage to wrestle my lungs back into submission. Dawn removes the bag from my face and rises to his feet.

"Thank you," I murmur weakly, though I should be yelling at him. Sure, he helped me. But if he hadn't broken my inhaler I wouldn't have needed his help to begin with.

"God, you're in worse shape than I thought," Dawn mutters, grabbing a burlap bag off the floor and swinging it over his shoulder.

"You don't understand," I argue weakly. "My medicine—I could die without it."

"That's what they've taught you to believe," he says, looking down at me with sad eyes. "But you didn't die, did you?"

His logic is irritating. "Um, well, no," I admit. "But that doesn't mean ..." I trail off, not knowing what good it will do to explain. He's obviously got his mind made up.

He glances at his watch. "Anyway, I've got to go."

Panic seizes me. "What do you mean?" I cry, hating how desperate my voice sounds. Why should I want him to stay? He very nearly killed me. But at the same time, I don't want to be left alone.

"I've got to stand in line for rations," he explains. "Besides, the Eclipsers are on their way to get you. I really don't want to deal with them today." He pauses for a second and I catch him looking at me longingly with those beautiful glowing eyes of his. Then he shakes his head and turns abruptly away—stalking to the door and slamming it shut without so much as a good-bye. I hear it locking behind him.

I run to the door, grabbing the handle, but it's no use. I bang on the metal, screaming at the top of my lungs for him to come back, but the door remains closed and locked and Dawn does not reemerge. Finally, after my voice gives out, I abandon the door and walk over to investigate what's left of my inhaler. The glossy purple case is shattered, the vial cracked. Not good.

I turn to the rest of the apartment, desperate for some kind of answers. The first thing I discover, discarded on the coffee table, is an ID card of sorts, with Dawn's image grimly smiling up at me. The ID lists him as *Dawn Gray—Surface Medic, nT Alpha.*

Surface medic? Is that like some kind of doctor? I frown. If he's really in the medical profession, he should know better than to withhold someone's medication.

I discard the ID on the coffee table, walking over to the bookcase. There's only one book, lying on a top shelf that I can't reach. Besides that, the bookcase displays a couple of photos, framed with crude glass and metal. The first is a group shot of a bunch of boys, dressed in identical cranberry school uniforms. The caption below reads ACADEMY ALPHA. I set the picture back on the mantel and turn to the other.

My eyes widen. I do a double-take.

No.

It can't be.

I grab the picture and stare hard, my fingers trembling so badly it's hard to get the image to focus. But suddenly it becomes crystal clear. A black and white portrait of a girl wielding a Japanese sword. The caption read: *Mariah Quinn: Champion Swordswoman, Lunar Park Pro Division.*

And she looks exactly like me.

SEVEN

My fingers fumble; I drop the picture, and it crashes to the stone floor. The glass frame shatters into a million pieces, cutting into Mariah's face.

My face.

I sink down onto the sofa, trying to get a grip, not wanting to lose my breath again. My mind whirls with confusion, trying to make sense of it all. I've never posed for a photo with a sword. Hell, I've never held a freaking sword to begin with. And yet, there's no mistaking it. This is a picture of me. My face. My body. It's absolutely identical, down to the heart-shaped birth mark on my left shoulder—the one Craig likes to nibble on when kissing me in the hallway—and the same winding daisy chain I'd regrettably had tattooed around my ankle last spring break, much to my parents' chagrin.

The girl in the photo—she isn't just a lookalike, someone who could easily be mistaken as me; she's an exact replica. She is, in all respects, me.

But how is that possible?

A loud knock on the apartment door causes me to nearly jump out of my skin. I glance over, nervous. Who could it be? Then I remember. The Eclipsers. Glenda and her friends. At last. Maybe now finally I'll get a chance at some real answers. And hopefully a one-way trip back home.

"Glenda?" I venture. "Is that you?"

The door swings open and a tall, broad-shouldered man steps

through, surrounded by an army of six soldiers, all dressed in silver uniforms. I tense, remembering the uniforms from my dream. Are these Eclipsers? Or some other group altogether?

"Hello, darling," the man coos in a deep-throated English accent. I give him a once-over, cataloging him quickly. He's blond. Handsome. Strong Roman nose, piercing green eyes. Well built, too. As if he's clocked in quite a few hours at the local underground gym. He's dressed much differently than Dawn, wearing an old-fashioned black suit, much like the proprietor at Moongazer Palace, though his is tailored to fit and the fabric looks expensive.

"Thank goodness we found you," the man says, stepping across the room and taking my hand in his. Before I realize what's going on, he pulls me from the couch and gallantly kisses the back of my hand.

I yank my hand away with a frown. Something's wrong. I don't know why, exactly. Just … these guys don't seem anything like how I'd imagined Eclipsers. Not that I had a clear picture, mind you, but still.

"I, um—"

The blond man waves a hand. "No, no, dear," he interrupts. "No thanks necessary. It's my pleasure to rescue you. After all, you wouldn't be in this horrid mess if it weren't for me. I tried to take all the precautions, but he stole you away seconds before my men could arrive. I do apologize for the inconvenience. For making you have to spend time in this" —he looks around the room with disdain—"place." He smiles broadly. "Now, come along. We've got primo reservations at Luna Park Terrace and the maitre d' simply deplores tardiness."

He gestures to the open door, and his guards step aside to allow me to exit. I rise from the couch. What am I supposed to do now? Go with them? I don't even know who they are.

"I don't …" I hedge, trailing off, not even sure what questions I should be asking. I look around the apartment, which up until this moment has been my prison cell. The place I've been dying to escape. So why do I have the sudden urge to stay put?

I catch the man's glance at my shattered inhaler, still lying where Dawn left it. He looks up at me. "Your asthma medicine," he says in a concerned voice. "What happened?"

"Uh, it … well, there was an accident," I say, not knowing why

I feel the need to cover for Dawn. After all, he very nearly killed me and it certainly was not an accident.

The man raises an eyebrow. But "I see" is all he says. "Well, no worries, we'll get you set up with a new one as soon as we're home." He pauses, then adds dramatically, "Skye."

My jaw drops. "You know who I am?" I ask incredulously. "You don't think I'm Mariah?"

The man chuckles. "Mariah. What rubbish. Don't tell me you're starting to believe the Dark Siders' wild tales. You're Skye Brow from New York City. An honored guest here in our humble land of Terra. But surely, my dear, you must know that already."

I let out a sigh of relief. Finally, someone who knows who I am. Who recognizes the real me. And here I was starting to believe Dawn's crazy stories. What an idiot. A million questions tangle in my throat, warring to be asked first. "Why am I here? How did I get here? What's Terra? Why does everyone think I'm this Mariah girl? How do I get back home?" The questions come fast and furious.

The man chuckles again. "All in good time, Skye, all in good time. But first, I think you need your medicine. You're looking quite pale. Come with me and we'll arrange for a new inhaler immediately. Before you have another attack. Then we can discuss returning you home."

I pause again, torn. On one hand, I finally have someone who recognizes me as me. Who is promising a sensible explanation for all of this. Not to mention the offer to help me get home.

On the other hand, shouldn't I wait for the Eclipsers? After all, Dawn said they could help.

Why trust Dawn? asks a voice in my head. *He kidnapped you and tried to delude you into thinking you're someone else. He's threatened you with weapons, dragged you underground, and locked you in his house after almost killing you by destroying your medication. Not really a guy who inspires much confidence.*

I can't argue with the logic and I make my decision: I'm going with the stranger who at least seems to know who I am. Who accepts the fact that I'm from Earth, and isn't going to feed me more disturbing lies. Who's going to get me home—which, let's face it, is mission number one.

"Let's go," I say.

I follow him and his men out of Dawn's cave and down the

twisty passageways toward the town square. To my surprise the formerly bustling city center is now startlingly vacant. I look around; where did the throng of mutants go? At the moment I almost expect tumbleweed to float across the abandoned space.

It's then that I catch the eyes peeking from every window. From around every corner. The people are all hiding. Are they afraid of this man and his guards? I suppress a shiver, trying to convince myself it's just from the draft.

My entourage stops in front of a shiny black limo parked just outside the town's main gates. My host presses a button on a remote and the car doors rise like the DeLorean in *Back to the Future*. Still not positive I've made the right choice but not sure what else to do at this point, I reluctantly crawl inside. The interior is luxurious, made of some rich, soft, leatherlike material. Crystal decanters hold sparkling liquid and the lighting is soft purple. The blond man takes a seat across from me and his guards file in, two up front and four at our sides. The driver fires up the engine and the doors swing silently shut. Like Dawn's bike, the limo rises a few inches off the ground and takes off down the tunnel at great speed.

The silence that follows is more than a little unnerving and I decide it's time for some answers. "So who are you?" I ask. "Since you already seem to know everything about me."

He smiles serenely. "They call me Brother Duske. I'm a senator down here in Terra. A member of the Circle of Eight."

Shit. I stare at him, cold seeping through my insides, even though the car is well heated. This is Duske? The man I was warned about by Dawn and Glenda? The one I was told to avoid at all costs? And here I am, in a hover car with him and his soldiers, flying through the tunnels at top speed. *Oh, Skye, what have you gotten yourself into?*

"Judging from your face I gather you've heard terrible rumors about me from the Eclipsers," Duske says, raising an eyebrow "How embarrassing."

I blush. "It's just that ... well ..."

Well, what, Skye? You think he's evil because some random strangers told you he was? The same people who also told you that you're a revolutionary leader for their downtrodden world? Maybe not the most reliable source, just FYI. In fact, maybe they wanted you to avoid Senator Duske because he would tell you the truth—that you're not the precious rebel leader they want you to be. Ever think of that?

"Sorry," I stammer. "It's just—well, I'm feeling a bit like Alice in Wonderland today. You know, I knew who I was this morning, but I've changed several times since then?"

Duske laughs appreciatively. "I promise, Skye," he says. "All will be made clear to you very, very soon."

His words effectively end the conversation and we continue to zoom down the underground highway going this way and that. I soon lose track of all the twists and turns—the place is like a maze. Finally, we stop in front of a tall, vertical glass tube shooting up into the darkness. As I watch, curious despite myself, the driver presses a button on the car's console and a glass door slides open. He backs the car into the tube and then presses another button. I realize that we must be in some kind of glass elevator. Very Willy Wonka. A moment later, the door slides closed, and I feel the sensation of rising fast.

Suddenly, the elevator shudders to a stop and the doors slide open. The driver steps on the gas and we float back out onto the open road. I gasp as I take in the stunning landscape before us. We appear to be in the center of a city, a hustling, bustling metropolis that looks remarkably like Times Square if Times Square were set deep underground.

Tall buildings crowd the streets, disappearing into the darkness above while strategically placed stadium lighting offers the illusion of daylight on street level. Neon signs and billboards advertise fake tanning, cosmetic surgery, and the latest and greatest in hover cars while bustling people go about their days. Girls in short skirts and high boots. Guys in black trench coats. Fashionable, well-fed, happy-looking people of seemingly every race. No mutants in sight, either.

We pass corner boutiques spilling out onto sidewalks. Restaurants serving heaping plates of food to patrons. There's even (get this!) a Starbucks on one corner! As we ride, I look more carefully at the electronic billboards covering almost every possible surface in a garish Tokyo-esque style. "Are you ready to look into the moon?" one asks. "Try it for a day—or a lifetime!" suggests another. And one tongue-in-cheek ad recommends: "One of these days, POW! Straight to the moon!"

"Is this where the Indys live?" I ask.

Duske nods. "We call it Luna Park. Pretty, isn't it?"

It is. The stone walkways are elegant and well-designed. The buildings are sleek and some made entirely of glass. And the centerpiece of the city, a spiky postmodern fountain, glitters as water droplets capture the lights and fragment them into a shower of kaleidoscopic color.

But how can these people enjoy all of this, knowing what's happening one strata down? My mind flashes back to the grubby mutant children of the Dark Side, destined to live in the gutters their entire lives. Do these people know how their neighbors are forced to live?

"Such a difference from down below," I murmur.

"Yes. It's unfortunate," Duske agrees sorrowfully. "But we're working on that. You'll see."

We leave the town, turning left and driving down a long road until we pull up to a mammoth Tudor-style mansion. It's set high on a hill, is at least four stories tall and made of white stone—with a single candle illuminating every window. It's elegant, but at the same time a bit foreboding, the sharp lightning slashing across the landscape, casting menacing shadows. The driver pulls up and around the circular driveway, stopping in front of the house.

"Here we are," Duske announces. "Home sweet home."

We exit the car and end up inside a majestic foyer that matches the majesty of the building's exterior. The walls and floor are made entirely of marble. Cold. Glittering. A crystal chandelier hangs from a cathedral ceiling. In the center of the room a mammoth staircase—like something out of *Gone With the Wind*—sweeps upward.

I turn to Duske. "Can I have my asthma medication now?" I don't mean to sound ungracious and hasty, but before I get completely carried away by the opulence of this stranger's world, I want to make sure he can deliver on his promises. After all, I'm still not sure who to trust.

Duske nods and claps twice. An old, graying butler wearing a tuxedo enters the room, bowing his head as he approaches my host.

"Brother Thom, could you get Sister Skye her medication?" Duske asks. "And," he says, after scratching his chin, "a dress suitable for dinner."

The butler nods and disappears into the house.

"No offense to your current clothing," Duske says, giving me a somewhat disdainful glance. "But the Park Terrace has been picky about dress codes lately. Forgive me."

I nod absently, more concerned that he didn't tell the butler what brand of medication I needed. But before I can speak, the butler returns. Almost as if he had exactly what his master would ask for just waiting in the next room. More than a little creepy.

But I can't help a sigh of relief as he places the inhaler in my palm and I see the familiar Lunatropium label. Just having it in my possession makes it easier to breathe.

"Thank you," I say. "I was really freaking out there for a bit."

Duske nods knowingly. "My pleasure," he says. "Though I suggest you save the medication for a moment you really need it," he adds. "There's not a full bottle's worth left. Asthma medication can be so hard to acquire here in Terra." He turns to Thom. "And the dress?"

Thom hands me a dress on a hanger, covered in plastic. I hold it up in front of me, to get a better look. It's not just a dress, but a full-on floor-length gown. Halter-top, red, with a slit that cuts to midthigh. Even through the plastic I can see the fabric is seeded with multicolored gems. Very adult and very unlike anything I've ever worn before.

Thom bows stiffly. "One flight up," he instructs. "Two doors to the left. A private bathroom where you can bathe and change."

"Dinner's in an hour," Duske adds. "I trust that's enough time to get ready?"

"Um, sure, okay," I stammer, not wanting to appear ungrateful. But still, when do I ask him about going home?

"One more thing," Duske adds, reaching into his pocket. He pulls out a long silver chain with a sparkling charm attached. He drapes it over my head and it falls just between my breasts. "Beautiful," he proclaims. "Just the piece to accentuate the dress."

I grasp the charm between two trembling fingers. The necklace, I realize, is identical to the one the proprietor took from me. Identical to the hundreds of others hanging in the Moongazer Palace cabinet. What does it mean? Suddenly the sinister feeling returns with a vengeance and it's all I can do not to reach for my inhaler again.

"Um, thanks," I murmur, not knowing what else to say. I drop the charm and it settles, warm, against my skin.

"My pleasure," Duske replies. "After all, it's so rare we are fortunate enough to entertain guests from Earth. So few make the trip *this* way, or even learn of our existence in the first place." He bows low. "I'll see you back here in an hour," he pronounces, then turns and heads into the house, leaving me behind, buzzing with a billion questions. Thom remains standing stiffly in the hall, with an expectant look on his face. I glance longingly at the front door, wondering if I should make a break for it. But where would I go? Duske's the only person who seems to know what's really going on in this crazy world. The only one I can convince to help me get home. Better to just get dressed and get this dinner over with, so I can make my request to return to Earth.

And so I head upstairs, trying not to drag the dress on the ground. I find the bathroom and draw in a breath as I step inside. The entire room is constructed of etched glass and marble. A hundred tiny teacup candles flicker from various nooks and crannies. Some are encapsulated in glass, others float in small vases of water. The Jacuzzi is big enough for three and filled to the brim with steaming bubbles. The vanity is covered with brightly colored soaps, glass bottles of flowery perfumes, and earthen jars of creams. There's a video screen embedded in a wall, playing back some sort of soap opera. I watch as it goes into commercial.

"Are you looking for a new adventure?" the voiceover asks, showing film of a large full moon. *"A new world where all your dreams can come true?"* The video switches to a scene of a sunny beach with bathers frolicking and tanning and downing fruity cocktails. *"Imagine a world where you can lie out in the sun and won't get sick."* The picture switches to a swinging nightclub. *"Where you can dance the night away under the waxing moon."* I stare, my eyes widening as I realize the club is Luna. Is that Craig in the DJ booth? *"Well, look no further than Earth—a new world that mirrors the Terra of old in all the best ways. Try it for a day— or take the journey of a lifetime."* The scene closes with two people cuddling up to each other on the hood of a car under a star-filled sky. *"Are you ready to look into the moon?"* the voiceover asks alluringly.

The commercial ends and the TV goes back to its regularly scheduled soap opera. I shake my head. This Moongazing thing, whatever it is, is everywhere. And they make it look so great. Heck, the commercial made *me* excited about Earth and I've lived there my entire life. But what is Moongazing, exactly? Some kind of tourist initiative to send people to Earth on vacation? Seems innocent enough. But if that's all it is, then what was all that stuff

Dawn had been talking about: drugs, implanted memories, fake family and friends? How did that all fit in?

I shrug. *Duske will explain,* I decide. *I'll get the full scoop at dinner.* I hang the dress on a hook and pull off my dirty, bloodied clothes. Then I test the water with my big toe. Perfect. Everything in this part of the world seems to be flawless—the polar opposite of the world beneath. I feel a sudden pang of guilt at the thought. Should I be enjoying this luxury while so many people are suffering below?

I shake my head. I can't think like that right now. And refusing a hot bath will not feed a hungry child. And so, pushing back the guilt, I lower my body into the tub, trying to force my brain to stop whirring at least for a moment.

But still the questions poke and prod, refusing me rest. Where am I? How did I get here? Who are the Eclipsers and what do they want with me? Why does Dawn hate me so?

And most importantly ...

Who is Mariah Quinn and why does she look exactly like me?

EIGHT

"This place is gorgeous. I've never seen anything like it," I exclaim
as the hostess escorts us to a plush booth at the back corner of
Luna Park Terrace restaurant. And I mean it. The entire room is
carved out of a sort of polished smoky blue glass—the tables, the
floors, even the walls—allowing for a tremendous view of a nearby
lava-filled crater. The lava bubbles and boils beside us, but we're
cool and comfortable. This place is beyond breathtaking. A study
in fire and ice.

"You haven't?" Duske asks. "What a shame. But you have so
many other lovely things where you come from. I hardly think you
should complain."

"Oh," I say, taken aback. "I'm not complaining. I'm just
impressed."

Before Duske can respond, a wrinkly man dressed in a tux and
with a name tag that simply reads WAITER approaches our table.
He bows at the waist.

"How do you do this fine evening, Brother Duske?" he asks
with an impeccable English accent. "It is an honor to have you
patronize our humble establishment."

"It is an honor to be here, Brother Claude," Duske answers
with the same modicum of respect.

The waiter turns to me. "And you, Sister. It is an honor to—"

"A bottle of your finest vodka," Duske interrupts.

The waiter nods, seeming a bit taken aback by the interruption.
"Of course," he says, bowing low again. "So sorry, Brother

Duske." He hesitates for a moment, as if daring to speak again. "And would you like your usual entrees?" he asks at last.

Duske glares at him. "I would like my usual," he says. "But this young lady has never dined in your establishment. So I am sure she would like to hear the specials."

"Right. Right," the waiter stammers. I raise an eyebrow. Does he also think I'm Mariah? A nervousness gnaws at my stomach.

The waiter reaches into his pocket and pulls out a handkerchief, patting his brow. "Today we have a lovely butternut squash ravioli, dusted with sage and swaddled in a soy cream sauce. We also have a black bean and tortilla pie, glazed with a faux honey chipotle."

"I'll take the ravioli," I say, relieved the options aren't cow brains or monkey livers. You never know, right? I glance over at Duske, who nods his approval. The waiter bows once again before retreating to presumably fill our orders. Duske watches him go. "Don't mind him," he says. "Brother Claude spent too much time on the surface during the early years. It's a shame to see a mind go to mush like that." He shakes his head. "In any case, what was I saying? Oh yes, how lovely it must be to live on Earth."

I shrug awkwardly, not sure how to respond.

"We on Terra are quite envious of all the opportunities your world affords. There are people here who would give their right arms to live on Earth." He strokes his chin with his forefinger and thumb. "Come to think of it," he adds, "I believe some have."

I start to laugh until I catch his expression. Is he serious?

"But how rude of me. I promised you answers," he says, waving a dismissive hand. "Perhaps I can start with a little history lesson of our humble world of Terra?"

I lean forward eagerly. "I'd like that."

My host clears his throat dramatically before beginning. "Once upon a time," he pronounces with a playful grin. "Isn't that how you Earth people like to begin your stories?" As I give my assent, he continues. "Once upon a time there was a great land that afforded great opportunities to the people who lived on its surface," he said. "It should have lasted forever. Unfortunately, the people did not take proper care of this great land. Nor did they take care of one another. Instead, they fought over petty lands until the world was split in two. There was a great war and a great bomb that poisoned the land and sent everyone underground. At first it was total anarchy. Governments ripped apart, people scrambling just to survive."

I make a face, horrified at his story. It was hard to believe, even with our own close calls on Earth, that something like this could actually happen. That two warring countries could really go that far—pressing the big red buttons and sparking a raging apocalypse.

"How long ago was this?" I ask curiously.

"Nearly a hundred years ago," Duske replies solemnly. "And still the world above is completely uninhabitable. Fortunately now we have our elaborate cities below the surface and there's no one alive who even remembers living under the open sky."

"That's so sad," I muse, trying to imagine a life like this—lived completely underground. No wonder everyone wants to do this Moongazing thing to Earth. The finest shops and restaurants in the world couldn't replace a day at the beach or a walk in the park.

"Indeed. But the alternative was far worse. The total annihilation of the human race."

"Good point," I agree grimly. "So, how did you all end up here underground?"

"It's all thanks to the Circle of Eight," Duske explains, "the forefathers of our current Senate Circle, of which I am fortunate enough to have been born a member. The original group—a secret society back then—was founded a hundred years before the Great War. At the time, our country's government was corrupt and chaotic. A democracy only in name, it was really a totalitarian regime, controlled and manipulated by the rich, powerful, and greedy. This government felt it was perfectly within its rights to invade other countries and force their sham of democracy on them in order to steal their resources. The Circle of Eight knew the end result of this behavior could only lead to apocalypse once the smaller countries upgraded their nuclear technology and decided to fight back."

I suppress a shudder. This all sounds way too real for comfort.

"So, using their foresight, they bought up large quantities of useless desert and constructed secret underground cities like Luna Park, cave by cave. By the time the war inevitably hit, they were ready and able to welcome the refugees below. They took in people from around the world like a Noah's Ark, trying to preserve as many ethnicities as possible."

I think back to the Asian proprietor at Moongazer Palace, and the wide variety of people wandering around Luna Park. They'd definitely done a good job preserving diversity. I liked that.

"So, the Circle of Eight saved the people," Senator Duske continues. "And you'd think the people would be grateful for their salvation. But sadly, this has not proven to be the case. While some of the people acclimated quickly to their new world—finding jobs, buying homes, raising families—others became depressed and angry, refusing to work to better their society They began preaching that it was the Circle's fault that they were poor and helpless. They wanted handouts—and didn't think they should have to work for their bread. They began to convince people that the great and glorious government who'd saved them was actually brutally exploiting and controlling them." Duske shakes his head, a disgusted look on his face. "In reality, nothing could be further from the truth."

I'm so fascinated by his tale I scarcely notice that the waiter has returned with our food. He pulls the silver cover off my plate, revealing multicolored ravioli that smells of cinnamon. He places a similar plate in front of Duske, then passes him a small black handheld machine. Duske presses his thumb against the sensor and the machine beeps and flashes green. Evidently it's some high-tech payment option, just like the locks on the doors. Thumbs sure are useful in Terra. I wonder if I have any credit on mine ...

"My apologies for the dinner," Duske says, picking up a pair of chopsticks. "I know on Earth you dine mostly on meat and fowl. Here in Terra we have very limited access to animals. The war eliminated most species altogether, and the ones that were saved and brought underground proved sterile. We've been working in labs to clone what we have to increase the population, but the clones are not able to reproduce either. So every animal is precious and protected."

I feel a renewed sense of sadness at his words. Never mind the sun—a world without animals seems unlivable. No dogs to greet you with slobbery kisses. No cats to rub up against your leg with a purr.

"Well, don't worry about the meat thing," I assure him. "I'm a vegetarian anyway."

"Of course you are, my dear," Duske says with an odd smile. "And I trust you will enjoy this meal."

I take a bite, savoring the smooth creamy taste and its subtle kick of spice. "It's delicious," I say, surprised and delighted. "In fact, it tastes just like the kind they serve up at ArtePasta in the Village." I laugh. "Like, exactly. So strange." I take another bite.

"Perhaps Earth and Terra aren't so different after all," Duske comments, taking his own bite.

"Well, I definitely agree with you there. In fact, it's actually pretty crazy," I remark, my mouth full of food. "I mean, we speak the same language. Share the same pop culture. You even have a Starbucks, for goodness' sake."

"Indeed," Duske says. He refills his tumbler and downs the shot. "Which is why we felt your Earth is such a good fit for our people."

"A good fit? What do you mean?"

Duske takes another bite, chews, then swallows. "Terra, as much as we've tried to make it a self-sustaining, viable world, is overcrowded. It has huge shortcomings. We can't make enough food. We can't breed animals. We've lost a great deal of aesthetic beauty because of limited access to trees. There are some surface logging companies that risk the radiation to supply us with wood, but there's never enough."

"Okay ..."

"So, a few years ago, the government came up with a plan to export our people to a more inhabitable world—a world that can support them and give them a comfortable and familiar lifestyle. Even better, it's a life aboveground, where they can dance under the moonlight each and every night without worrying about becoming sick."

He sounds like one of the advertisements. "You mean Moongazing," I conclude. So I was right.

Duske nods. "Well, the technical term is interdimensional relocation. We decided to brand it Moongazing. More commercially appealing, we feel. Gives it an almost lyrical feel, don't you agree?"

"Is it—" I remember Dawn's story about Mariah. "Is it ... dangerous?" I hold my breath, hoping my question isn't offensive.

But Duske only chuckles heartily. "Not at all," he says. "It's quite safe. We did a great deal of research and testing before we introduced it to the public." He pauses, then adds, "Why do you ask?"

I shrug. "Dawn seemed to think so. He said all this stuff about me being addicted to some kind of Moongazing drug. And that my memories were implanted and my friends and family weren't real."

This time Duske full-on laughs, long and hard, shaking his head. "He is just too much," he says. "How did you even keep a straight face when he was spouting off such nonsense?"

I frown, not finding it quite so funny. "He was so convinced I was this girl named Mariah. And then I saw a picture of her in his apartment. We look identical."

"Mariah Quinn," Duske says knowingly. "Daughter of Sister Estelle, a retired member of our Senate and Circle of Eight. She was in training to join our ranks and become a member of the Senate until she got ... distracted."

"Distracted?"

Duske rolls his eyes. "She started socializing with the wrong crowd, a group of rebellious and bored Indys who liked to cause trouble. They brainwashed her into thinking that the Circle was somehow the enemy, and so she abandoned her training and moved down to Stratum Two to start up some silly group she called the Eclipsers with her little Indy rebel friends."

I lean forward, fascinated. And here I had assumed Mariah was just another one of the Dark Siders, unhappy with her lot in life. But it turns out she was of royal blood, in a sense. One of the of Illustrious Eight. I wonder what led her to make that choice—to give up everything she'd been born to inherit—trade in her life of luxury—to help the downtrodden down below. Pretty admirable.

"So, what happened to her?"

Duske shrugs. "She played her little revolution thing for a time, but then realized how silly it actually was. She started Moongazing like all her friends and realized that making a new life on Earth was a lot more rewarding than fighting some silly, unnecessary rebellion here on Terra. And so, in the end, she decided to purchase a permanent migration package. Last I heard she's living quite happily on Earth."

"But the Eclipsers couldn't accept her migration," I conclude, my admiration diminishing. Poor Dawn. No wonder he felt so betrayed by her. "They want her back."

"Right," Duske says. "Poor bastards. They've been searching for her on Earth ever since, trying to get her to come home and continue leading their impotent revolution. It was damn lucky I rescued you before they could poison your mind and convince you that you were her."

"Yeah," I agree absently. "Lucky ..."

"I'm not going to lie. You look a hell of a lot like Mariah," Duske adds. "Which is probably why they think you're her. I can actually see similar mannerisms in you, too. But trust me, Skye Brown. You are not Mariah Quinn."

I nod. Right. Of course he's right. It only makes sense. Dawn, Glenda, the Eclipsers. They made a mistake. A simple mistake.

"So now what?" I ask. "How do I get back to Earth?" Under the table I cross my fingers, my mind begging any higher power who might be listening to offer up a simple way for me to return home.

"Easy," Duske says. "You use one of my private 'Gazing booths at the house. A whiff of your asthma medication and the press of a button and poof—you're back on Earth."

I cock my head in confusion. "Why my asthma medication?" I ask, remembering Dawn denouncing the stuff. What was the connection between the two?

But Duske only smiles reassuringly. "Sometimes the journey can be rough. I'd want to make sure you don't have an attack en route."

Something feels odd about his manner, but I'm afraid questioning him too much might cause him to revoke his invitation. *None of the rest matters*, I remind myself. *I just need to get home.* "Okay. Whatever it takes, I suppose," I say, setting down my chopsticks. "Can we go now? I don't mean to be rude, but I'm anxious to get back."

"Understandable. But first, I wonder if I might ask you a favor."

"Uh, sure. I guess," I say, wondering what on earth I could possibly do for him.

Duske clears his throat before speaking. "You think of Terra much the same way Terrans think of Earth. You're here, living, breathing, and experiencing it all, but at the same time, I can tell that you don't quite believe it's all real," he says. "Well, imagine the Terrans. They've never even seen Earth, and many are afraid. Afraid of the unknown. Afraid of what might happen if they Moongaze. Their fear is holding them back, trapping them here on our dead world when they could be living fulfilling, happy lives on Earth."

"O-kay. So what does that have to do with me?"

"In a way, the Eclipsers did me a tremendous favor by bringing you here. You're the first Earth person to ever set foot in Terra. Almost as if you've come as an ambassador for your world." He smiles again. "What I am humbly asking of you is this. That you continue in that role awhile longer. I'm holding a Moongazing seminar this weekend. I'd like you to attend. In the meantime, you can go back to Earth and take some photos for me. Animals, sunshine, grass, trees. Photograph them all and return to Terra to speak to my people at the convention. Tell them what Earth is really like. How wonderful it would be to live there."

"You want me to take photos? And then come back?" I stare at him, incredulous. This was definitely not the favor I had in mind.

"Yes." He nods. "Together you and I can prove to the people of my world that Moongazing is not just some field trip from reality, but a doorway to a new and better existence."

He says the last part so grandly that I assume it's part of his sales pitch. Is he profiting off this, I suddenly wonder. Is he an alternate-reality travel agent, if you will?

"Why can't you just get the photos yourself?" I ask. "I've seen the TV commercials. Obviously you have stock footage of the place. Why do you need me?"

He shrugs dismissively. "I could take pictures, yes, but the people don't see me as an objective source. To have someone who's actually from Earth—well, that's another thing altogether. You can go beyond the tourist brochure. Tell them what it's really like to live there."

"Right." I see what he's saying. But at the same time ... "Look, I'd love to help," I say cautiously. "But I've got a lot on my plate right now. Midterms are coming up and the video game I've been helping test launches in a few weeks. I really don't know if I have time to play travel agent."

I try to make my voice light and apologetic, but Duske's face darkens at my words, his mouth twisting into a sinister frown.

"Listen to me carefully," he says in a slow, tight voice. Gone is the honey-sweet sales pitch. "I need those photos. And I need you to get them for me. There is no one else."

I swallow hard. "But—"

"If you do not get me my photos within two days," he continues in a terse tone, "though I am a very busy man I will make the time to yank you back to Terra myself. And trust me, it will *not* be to take you to dinner."

I stare at him in disbelief, my heart now thudding in my chest. A moment ago he seemed so debonair. So rational and reasonable. I can't believe he's threatening me. And I'm completely helpless— if I don't do what he says, I'll be stuck here forever.

My throat closes up and I wheeze, trying to take a breath. I reach into my pocket for my inhaler. I can feel Duske's eager eyes on me as I put it to my mouth and take a puff. I pull the inhaler away, disturbed by his reaction, remembering Glenda's warning, Dawn's warning.

"Are you ready to go back to Earth?" Duske asks, suddenly back to his pleasant self.

I should be. I should be more than ready. So why am I suddenly so hesitant?

"Um, yes, I guess I am," I say, shaking the doubt away. Do I really want to be here another moment? No, of course not. I want to go home and forget all of this ever happened.

Duske rises from his seat and I follow him out of the restaurant. As we walk down the dimly lit path and to the awaiting car, a man suddenly jumps out from behind a rock sculpture, blocking our path. His eyes are rimmed in black bruises and his mouth's hanging open sideways. He looks utterly insane.

"Don't look into the moon!" he cries, waving a placard on a stick. "It'll destroy your life—your very soul!"

Startled, I take a step back, not sure what he's going to do next. My eyes lift to the placard. MOONGAZING FTL it reads. I know that in geek speak (at least back on Earth) that acronym stands for "For the Loss"—a video game term that stood for something bad, terrible, and shouldn't be touched with a ten-foot pole.

Nervous, I glance over at Duske. He's talking into some kind of communication device strapped to his wrist. Obviously, he's summoning the cavalry.

"I'm not crazy," the man continues, grabbing my hand and staring at me beseechingly. "I'm an Indy, just like you. I had a job, a family, a life. Moongazing stole it all from me. I barely made it out alive. Whatever you do, don't look into the moon!"

Before I can react, three silver-clad soldiers appear, dragging the man backward. He screams in rage, trying to fight, but they quickly overpower him, stunning him with some kind of crimson-beamed taser.

Like the one in your dream, an inner voice reminds me. I shudder.

"Sorry about that," Duske says, putting an arm around my waist and leading me down the path. "As you can see, like any new program, we have our detractors."

I realize I'm still trembling from the encounter. I glance back at the man. He's now spread-eagle on the ground, sobbing hysterically. Could what he said have any truth to it? Was he a victim of Moongazing just like Mariah was?

And if so, was what I was about to do—go Moongazing myself—a good idea?

I shake my head. Dangerous or not, it's my only ticket home. What, do I want to hang out here for the rest of my life? I need to get back to my world as soon as possible and put all this behind me.

We enter the hover car and zoom back to Duske's mansion. He leads me up the stairs, down a hall, and into a long passageway similar to the one at Moongazer Palace. He stops in front of a red door with a crescent moon carved into the metal.

"Here we are," he says. "Are you ready to look into the moon, Skye?" he quips, quoting the promos. What once seemed an innocent slogan now fills me with dread.

I draw in a breath, remember this is the only way home. "I am."

He hands me a small piece of paper with a website URL scribbled on it. "When you have your photos, upload them to this site. That way I'll know you're ready to journey back to Terra, and I will activate the retrieval program."

"Are you sure you really need me to do this?" I ask. "I mean, there's no one else?"

Duske puts his hands on my shoulders and leans forward, kissing me once on each cheek. "You are my chosen one, Skye," he says reverently. "You will be a great symbol of Earth to all the people of Terra. You'll be a symbol of a better life."

I stifle a sigh, trying to push down the worry gnawing at my stomach. But I'm going back home, I remind myself. That's what's important. I'll worry about the photo thing later.

Duske presses his thumb against a sensor. It beeps once, and then the door swings open.

It's time to look into the moon.

*

My phone was ringing. I opened my eyes, blinking the sleep away. I'd never been so happy to be woken up by the phone in all my life. I sat up in bed and looked around, gratefully taking in the cozy familiarity of my bedroom.

It was all a dream. All one crazy, messed-up, freakish, ridiculously long dream.

Though ... how did I get here? Last thing I remember was being in the VIP section of Luna. Had I had some sort of blackout? Who had brought me home?

Still, no unanswered questions could completely eclipse my joy of escaping the crazy, messed-up nightmare world I'd been trapped in. I felt like singing. Shouting. Jumping up and down. My bed. My books. My computer. My teddy bear, Melvin. All here. I was back. I was free.

The answering machine clicked on.

"Skye? It's Craig. Guess you're asleep. I just wanted to check in on you since you left Luna without even coming over to say hi. Where are you?" He paused and I searched for the phone, unable to find the cordless receiver in the dark bedroom. "Please, call me the second you get this. I'm worried about you."

The machine clicked again, indicating the end of the message. I crawled out of bed and fumbled for the light switch. I'd better call him back before he sent out the National Guard. So, I left Luna suddenly? That was odd. And why didn't the phone wake me up before? Was I in that much of a deep sleep? Did I somehow get dosed with something? And where was my roommate? Had she gone out of town for the weekend and forgot to tell me?

I found the switch and flicked it, flooding the room with warm light. Momentarily blinded, I rubbed my eyes. I was going to look great tomorrow at work. All bloodshot and black circles for sure. I glanced in the mirror for confirmation, dreading to see the state of my face.

My heart stopped.

Mirror girl stared back at me, her expression reflecting my horror.

Because instead of the boxer shorts and T-shirt ensemble I usually wore to bed, I was wearing a red silk gown.

A gown that, in real life, shouldn't exist.

NINE

Half a box of NoDoz, a full carafe of coffee, and three Diet Pepsis later, I found myself buzzed and bleary as I dressed for work. It was 8:00 A.M., Saturday morning, and I'd gotten no sleep. I'd thought I'd been exhausted yesterday, but there was no way in hell I was going to risk shutting my eyes and returning to the crazy world of my dreams. The one where I was able to somehow bring dresses back with me.

I jumped into a cold shower hoping it'd wake me up and tried to ignore my shaking hands as I went through the routine of washing my hair. Hopefully work would be a better distraction. We had less than two weeks to find all the bugs in the game. My bosses were counting on me to be careful and alert. That promised to be real fun on no sleep. Besides, how was I supposed to concentrate on reality? All I could think of was my nightmare come to life.

I got out of the shower and towel-dried myself, then headed into the bedroom to change. My eyes fell to the dress, which I'd hung in my closet. There had to be some logical explanation. Maybe I'd bought it on my way home. Or I'd drunkenly switched clothes with someone at the club. Because what other explanation could there be besides the obvious—and unbelievable—one: that I had somehow traveled to an alternate reality and brought the dress back myself?

I was cracking up. Had to be. Maybe instead of heading to work I should check myself into some psych ward. Don a straitjacket, swallow some hardcore antipsychotics. Drool in a padded corner for the next six years. Didn't sound like a terrible plan at the moment.

But instead, I sucked it up and went to work. I was a professional after all.

On my way up from the subway, a block from Chix0r's HQ, I pulled out my cell, realizing I'd gotten three messages while underground. As I walked down the street, I selected the first.

Hey, Skye, it's Suzy! Did you have any luck at Luna last night? I'm still on the island, so, like, call my cell, okay?

Ugh. Erase. Next.

Hey Skye, it's Craig. Where the hell are you? Seriously, I'm starting to freak out here. Call me.

Sigh. I really needed to call him. Though what I was going to say, I had no idea.

Next.

Two days, Skye. Two days.

I nearly dropped the phone. Oh my god. Was that …? My heart pounded as my fingers fumbled, trying to replay the message. Instead I managed to hit the delete button.

"Good-bye," the cheerful computerized female voice chirped before disconnecting.

"No! No good-bye!" I cried, banging a fist against the phone. Damn it! What was that message? Was it from him? It sounded just like him. But he was just a figment of my overactive imagination. A dream character. Wasn't he? If so, how did he find me? How did he get my number?

Had my nightmare really come to life?

I looked up and down the street nervously, as if I'd catch him, in the distance, watching me. But he was nowhere to be seen, everyone going about their business without a care in the world. It was only me, with my heart in my throat and my fingers shaking. I took a deep breath. What was I going to do?

Take the photos.

I froze. The command seemed to be coming from inside my head.

Take the photos.

Again, more insistent.

"Fine. I'll take the stupid photos," I muttered. "I'll do everything I'm supposed to. And in two days, when I don't get magically flown back to Terra, I'll know for sure, once and for all, that this was just one big, bad, crazy old dream."

"What's a dream?"

I looked up, realizing I was standing outside Chix0r's headquarters with little knowledge of how I'd actually gotten here. My boss, Madeline, was standing in front of me, cup of Starbucks in hand. I remembered the Starbucks I'd seen on Terra and shuddered.

"Getting all these bugs worked out before release day," I halfheartedly joked, pushing thoughts of nightmares to the back of my brain. It was time for work mode.

Luckily, Madeline gave me a knowing laugh and together we walked upstairs into the main offices. She gestured for me to come into her own office, the corner one with the great view and windows. Madeline had founded Chix0r five years ago, after becoming disenchanted by all the sex-laced trash talk commonly heard on guy-centric online role-playing games. She'd imagined a virtual world where girls could feel safe strapping on a sword and contributing to the community with no fear of being smacked down by an arrogant metal-mouthed fourteen-year-old boy who, in real life, would never be able to get a real girl to acknowledge his existence.

"Are you okay, Skye?" she asked, peering at me through her black-rimmed glasses. "I don't mean to sound critical, but the last report you sent in had more bugs than an NYC motel room."

I hung my head. Madeline was the coolest boss in the universe and I hated letting her down more than anything. After all, as she'd said so many times, we weren't just coworkers here at Chix0r. We were family.

"I'm sorry," I said. "It's just … I've been having this horrible insomnia lately. And when I do fall asleep I have these crazy dreams. I wake up feeling like I've been run over by a truck."

Madeline nodded sympathetically. "You sound like me. Prerelease jitters," she concluded. "Don't worry, kiddo, your work is great. And we're in the home stretch. Just got to buckle down now and get through the next two weeks. Then we'll be able to relax a bit."

I threw her a halfhearted smile. Prerelease jitters? If only it were that simple.

"Yeah, you're probably right," I said, not wanting to go into it any further. "I'll get through somehow."

"I know you will." Madeline smiled. "Now, I wanted to talk to you about our redesign of the knight class's talent tree that I'd like you to test. Can you pull up a character for a second?"

Intrigued, I logged in to RealLife on her computer and repositioned the monitor so we could both see the screen. Allora was right where I'd left her the last time I played: in the bar. My character turned and looked out from the game, as if she could see us watching her, then broke out into a big smile and waved a greeting.

"She likes you," Madeline commented. "You must treat her well."

I smiled. It was so cool how lifelike the characters were. "I like her, too. She's very kick-ass."

"Okay, now take her outside and have her attack something."

I looked over in surprise. "You've opened up new terrain?"

Madeline nodded. Evidently the designers had been hard at work during my mental collapse.

I obeyed my boss's directive, using the keyboard and mouse to run Allora outside the limits of the city of Mare Tranquilitatis and into the frozen tundra of Serenitatis. The designers had been working hard, adding weather effects, and it looked as if it were really snowing out. Very cool. I led Allora down the hill, off the safe road, and into the wild. A moment later, a bandit troll jumped on her, initiating the game's fight mode. On my command, Allora whipped out her sword and started swinging.

"This is all good," Madeline commented, leaning forward to get a better view of the screen. "But now, show me her finishing move."

I clicked the hot key to have her execute her special move. Each class had one built in: a deadly last strike designed to finish off one's opponent. Allora's move was to fall to the ground and slash off the monster's feet, leaving them incapacitated. It was all very dramatic.

"Hmm."

I glanced at Madeline. She didn't look quite as impressed. She sat back in her chair and rubbed her chin with one hand. I noticed she had a moon tattoo between her thumb and forefinger and winced. Was *everyone* in on this new trend? And why did it have to be a moon? "Yeah, we're going to have to fix that."

I scrunched my eyebrows. "But why? It's so cool-looking!"

"Sure, it's cool-looking. But it doesn't make any sense when it comes to abiding by the traditional rules of chivalry. True knights, according to medieval lore, fight within a strict set of protocols. They have an inborn sense of honor. They would not suddenly turn rogue and slash out with such a cheap move."

"Well, they should consider it," I argued. "If it helps them defeat their opponent."

"But then it would be a battle fought with no honor," Madeline explained. "And while I'd have no problem with the designers giving that move to a rogue character, seeing as they're supposed to be sneaky and underhanded, I won't have knights fighting dishonorably. We need to stick with the world-building. That's what will set us apart from the other games."

I nodded. She was right, of course.

"I'll talk to the designer," Madeline said, rising to her feet. "And we'll have you test out the new moves once they're in place. But for now, why don't you take the day off? Go take a nap or something."

"But there's so much to do ..."

She smiled. "And knowing you, you'll get it done. But not right now. Sometimes even RealLife has to take a backseat to real life," she quipped. "You can get back to things tomorrow."

I thought about arguing further, but knew that when my boss made up her mind, she made up her mind. Besides, I had photos to take.

*

The hot dog man. The Statue of Liberty. The camels at the Bronx Zoo. The maple trees in Central Park. The rollercoaster on Coney Island. I shot them all. Closeup, panoramic, artsy, straight. Duske wanted photos? He'd get his photos. And then maybe he could leave me the hell alone so I could get back to my life.

I arrived back at my apartment around five and headed straight to my computer to start uploading. Maybe I'd get bonus points for turning in the photos a day early. At the very least I could get this assignment off my plate and move on.

My cell phone rang just as I began the upload—the sudden burst of the *Star Wars* ring tone caused me to nearly jump out of my skin, my heart skipping like a broken record. With trembling fingers I reached into my bag and pulled out the phone. Relief washed over me as I recognized the name on the caller ID. Just Craig. Thank God.

"Hey, Craig," I said, selecting the photos out of my My Pictures folder. If only he knew what I was trying to do. He'd be sending the men in white coats over as we spoke.

"There you are!" Craig cried. "I've been calling all day. I thought you were, like, dead or something. Raped and murdered after you disappeared from Luna."

I swallowed a bitter laugh. Disappeared? He was more right than he knew.

"Yeah, sorry about that. I wasn't feeling well and decided to go home about five minutes after I got there. I, um, came home and crashed hardcore."

There was a beat of silence on the other end of the line, and then: "But I came by your place after my shift. I rang the buzzer over and over."

"My roommate went home for the weekend," I told him, though I had no idea if that was actually true. "And like I said, I really crashed. You know, not having had a good night's sleep in ages. I don't think stampeding elephants could have woken me last night."

"You sure you just didn't have another guy over or something?" Craig asked. His voice was only half teasing.

I forced myself to laugh, trying to push a sudden image of Dawn out of my mind. After all, being brutally kissed by dream guys in postapocalyptic alleyways didn't count as cheating, did it?

"No, no. Nothing as exciting as all that," I lied. "Just lots of drooling on my pillow."

Craig's laugh sounded more genuine this time. "Okay, okay," he relented. "So, what are you up to now?"

Oh, not much. Just playing alternate reality travel agent to the postapocalyptic crowd.

"Oh, not much, just doing some work on the old computer."

"Want me to come over?"

"Um …" I glanced at the clock. Did I want him to come over? Not really. I'd have much preferred to curl up in a ball and fall asleep for the next forty-eight hours. But I knew that wasn't really an option. Duske told me that after the photos uploaded he'd be calling me back to Terra. And when/if that happened, I wanted a witness. Someone to let me know exactly what happened after I blacked out and woke up in Terra. Did my body literally disappear with my mind, sucked into some kind of alternate reality wormhole? Or did I fall into a comalike sleep and only travel in my dreams?

"Skye? Are you still there?"

"Yeah," I replied, making my decision. "And sure. Come on over whenever you can."

"Great." I could hear his relief. "I'm not far from your place, actually. I'll be there in, like, ten minutes. Want me to pick up something from Blue Ribbon for dinner?" he asked, naming my favorite Japanese sushi spot.

"Oh, yum. Yes. I'm totally in the mood for their veggie spring rolls," I told him. "And add in an order of edamame as well, okay? See you soon." I hung up the phone and set it down next to my computer in case he called back for clarification of my food order. Poor guy. All things considered, he'd been pretty patient through my continued mental collapse. Cheerful, loyal, supportive—save for a few zombie jokes. Even when I'd been nothing but a pain in the ass.

I forced my brain back on task and pressed upload, launching the final photo into cyberspace, wondering, not for the first time, where these pictures were actually being zapped. Perhaps the URL was linked to a sort of interdimensional Photo-Mart where Duske could pick them up in an hour? It seemed insane, but hell, if they could send *people* to other worlds, I guess photos would be nothing.

The on-screen message confirmed my pictures had been sent. I leaned back in my computer chair, wondering what would happen next. Would Duske e-mail me back? Would he give me a call? Or would I never hear from him again and live out my whole life wondering at the validity of my memory of this adventure? If I had to pick, I'd go for door number three every time.

But life was no game of Deal or No Deal, and I didn't get to choose my destiny. A moment later the whole dorm started to shake, just as Luna had the night before. Flashes of lightning sliced through the air and my stomach rolled as I swam in and out of a blurry, dizzy consciousness.

Finally, just as before, the darkness came and oblivion gripped me with invisible hands.

Oh God, here we go again.

TEN

I open my eyes. At least this time I know what to expect, though that doesn't really make the experience any more comforting. Once again, a tiny room. Video screens on all four walls, a nauseating kaleidoscope of color.

Yup, I'm back. Once more with feeling.

I smack the wall with the palm of my hand, frustrated beyond belief. I can't believe Duske dragged me back here to this hellhole yet again. At least he could have waited till Craig showed up with dinner. Not that I care about the calories; I'm more concerned with the fact that he's going to think I took off on him again. I imagine him showing up at my door, vegetarian goodies in hand, only to have no one answer the intercom. He'll probably end by breaking up with me. I wouldn't blame him if he did, either. I mean, how can I even explain what's happened in a manner that he could possibly begin to believe?

I shake my head, ripping off my glasses. I've got bigger things to worry about than a boyfriend's disappointment, and I need to concentrate on those. Say, for example, the interdimensional travel I just experienced a moment ago. There's no way I can pretend this is all some kind of weird dream anymore. Whatever's happening to me, it's all real, and I need to deal with it and figure out a permanent way back home. I do not want to be stuck here in Terra for any reason, and I don't want to be dragged back and forth at someone else's whim.

I push the button in front of me and the booth's front panel slides open with a high-pitched whine. Stepping out into the hallway, I find Duske standing there, right where I left him. How long have I been gone, Terra time-wise? Is it like Narnia in reverse, where twenty-four hours on Earth pass in just a few minutes here? I glance down at myself. I'm still wearing the same dress I wore when I entered the booth. The necklace is back around my neck. And a surreptitious sniff at my armpits tells me I can't have been inside that sweatbox for twenty-four hours. There's definitely something slippery with the way time's working here.

Duske bows low. "Welcome back, Skye," he says with a flourish of his hand. "It's lovely to see you again, my dear."

I scowl. I'm not buying his pleasantries this time around. "I'd love to say the same," I counter. "But really, I've got to tell you, I'm not very happy about being dragged back. I was just about to have lunch with my boyfriend and I've got a ton of homework to do." I cross my arms under my breasts and throw him an annoyed look. "I mean, I took your photos like you asked. I uploaded them into the system. So, how about you fulfill your end of the bargain and let me go back to my real life?" I can't believe how confident and cool I sound, considering on the inside I'm totally freaking out.

Duske smiles patronizingly. "My dear, dear Skye," he coos. "I'm so sorry if I've upset your lunch plans. But I did warn you. Your services are needed at my Moongazing seminar two nights from now. There will be Indys from all over Terra gathered in the Luna Park auditorium waiting to hear all about Earth. It will be our biggest, best presentation to date, and I need you there."

"But why?" I demand. "Why do you need *me*?"

"Didn't we already go over all of this?" Duske asks. "You are Terra's first ever ambassador from Earth. You're the only Earthling to ever pass through the interdimensional curtain and visit our little world. Who better to explain the wonders of Earth than a girl who has spent her whole life there?"

"I see your point," I say, trying to be reasonable. "But I don't think you see mine. I didn't ask for this gig, and I don't have time to take it. I'm sure there are a billion alien-abducted, *X-Files* freaks on Earth who would simply love an opportunity to travel between worlds and give motivational speeches. But I'm just too busy to be at your beck and call."

"Yes, yes, you and your important job," Duske says. He's wearing a slight sneer. "Don't you play video games for a living or something?"

I can feel my face heat. I can't stand when people make light of the video game industry. Just because we create fun and games full time doesn't mean our responsibilities and deadlines are frivolous, too. In fact, the designers at Chix0r take their work as seriously as a doctor would take his patients' health and while sure, they're not literally saving lives on the operating table, their customers will find relaxation, joy, and stress relief when they log in to any game. Which will cut down on their ulcers and high blood pressure and perhaps save them from that surgeon's knife in the future. But try to tell anyone that and they'll just start laughing. Whatever.

"Look, whether you respect my future career or not is moot," I retort. "We're talking about my life here, not some game played for your amusement."

Duske's lips twist, as if he's trying to suppress a smile. I glower at him. What the hell does he find so funny? Then he shakes his head and clears his throat. "I know, I know," he says, placing a hand on my shoulder. I shrug it away, not wanting him to touch me. "It's a great inconvenience for you to be here. I understand."

"Yes. It is. And I'd like to be sent home now if you don't mind." I look back to the Moongazing booth. "So, tell me how this thing can zap me back to Earth and I'll be on my way."

Duske is silent for a moment. "What if I agreed to compensate you for it? Would that make things better?"

"Compensate?" I look at him skeptically. "What would I do with Terran money?"

"Play Monopoly?" he suggests. Then he laughs. "Just kidding. I'd give you Earth dollars, of course. American currency. We've been farming Earth for quite some time now. Made some investments, started a few corporations. We've even started introducing Terran technology to your world. You lot are so far behind us it's like introducing the abacus to apes. No offense."

I frown. "So what are you saying? You want to pay me to speak at your seminar? How much are we talking about here?"

Duske rubs his chin with his forefinger and thumb. "Hmm," he says thoughtfully. I narrow my eyes. He's going to try to lowball me, isn't he? Probably offer me like a hundred bucks or something. To him, I'm just a kid, after all. "Would one million suffice?"

I stare at him, eyes wide, doubting my ears, working to stop my jaw from dropping to the floor. Did he just say what I thought?

No, that was impossible. And yet ...

"Does that seem too low?" Duske asks, cocking his head. "Hmm. How about a million five, then?"

"One and a half million," I repeat slowly. "In U.S. dollars?" I had to make sure he wasn't confusing our currency with Japanese yen or anything.

"Yes. American money. We could deposit it directly into your account so that when you return to Earth it will be waiting for you."

I give up on the jaw, let it drop. A million dollars? A freaking million dollars? "Are you serious?" I ask. "You'd really give me over a million dollars just for speaking at your convention?" My mind greedily races with the possibilities a million dollars could afford me. I could pay the rest of my tuition. Pay off those horrible student loans. Buy an awesome computer and maybe even a car.

Duske shrugs. "Sure, why not? It's a good investment for me. Spending Earth dollars, of which I have many, to earn real money here on Terra. You convince a few families to purchase Earth-relocation packages and I'll be a rich man here on my own world. You scratch my back, I'll scratch yours."

My mind whirs as I try to make my decision. A million and a half dollars! And all he's asking for is two days of my life. I have to admit, it was a tempting prospect.

Duske takes my silence for a yes and gestures for me to follow him down the hall. "I'll take you to your suite," he says. "I'm sure you'd like to shower and change."

It's then that I realize I have very little choice in the matter. Whether I accept his money or not, it seems there's no way he's going to send me back to Earth until I give my little speech at his seminar. And arguing with him about it may only cause the monetary offer to be rescinded. All in all, it seems best to play along, at least for now. After all, what alternative do I have? It's not like I can just click my heels three times.

I tune back in, resigned to accept my fate. At least temporarily.

"And I do apologize," Duske is saying, "but I must insist you remain in your assigned room until the convention. It's too dangerous for you to be wandering out and about in Luna Park. Those vile Eclipsers may try to kidnap you again to further their pathetic rebellion." He snorts, making it clear what he thinks of them.

The Eclipsers. In all of this craziness I'd nearly forgotten them. Glenda and her gang claim they are the ones who dragged me to this godforsaken world in the first place. What did they think when they arrived at Dawn's house and found it empty? Discovered the framed photo of Mariah lying shattered on the ground? Did they think I'd been kidnapped? Or did they conclude I'd taken off willingly? Do they know I'm with Duske now? Or do they assume I jumped back to my own world, unwilling to play their reindeer games?

My mind flashes to Dawn's scowling face. At least now he can go around telling the Eclipsers that he was right and they were wrong. Especially once they hear that I'll be speaking at an actual pro-Moongazing seminar in two days. He'll believe that his precious Mariah betrayed the revolution a second time.

I frown and hasten my step to match Duske's long strides. Well, there is nothing I can do about that. Had I really been Mariah, I'm sure things would have been different. But they dragged out the wrong girl. Not my fault. I'm not a revolutionary. Not a rebel leader. So really, what good can I do if I stay down below in their cave world and join their rebellion?

Still, my guilty brain lectures, you didn't have to go as far as to start helping the other side. I mean, what if the crazy guy with the placard is right? What if traveling between worlds—Moongazing— is a dangerous, even deadly, pastime that will ultimately destroy those who practice it? What if my promoting Earth travel to the masses ends up the equivalent of leading sheep to the slaughter? Am I selling out the people of Terra for a million dollars?

That's stupid, I tell myself. Why would the government fund and promote a program that would lead to the deaths of their citizens? Totally counterproductive. Besides, I've 'Gazed twice now. I feel completely fine. And the great Mariah herself, the one they're all in love with, is a 'Gazer. They're probably just annoyed that she left them high and dry to go live a better life. Sure, that was pretty crappy of her, but it doesn't make the program itself deadly and dangerous.

Swallowing my doubts, I follow my host down the hall and up another flight of red carpeted stairs, gripping the golden banister. At the top of the stairs, we come to a door. Duske presses the sensor with his thumb and it slides open. I step over the threshold into an elegant, well-lit room. It's done up in gold and mauve, a canopy bed draped with gauzy curtains serving as its centerpiece. There's a flat-panel TV hanging on the far wall of the room, several armchairs and coffee tables, and a sliding glass door leads out to a balcony. The room smells of rose petals, and dozens of flickering candles on every surface give it a sparkly glow.

"I trust this will suit your needs?" Duske asks.

I nod. It's tempting to be swept away by the luxury, but at the same time I can't get the Dark Siders out of my head. Those sick, mutated people. Their stores of moldy bread and tiny cavelike dwellings. Their desperate poverty and helplessness makes this opulence seem obscene. How can people be content to live like this when they know others are suffering one level down?

"Yeah, I guess it'll do," I reply, glancing over at my host. I catch him staring at me, his eyes fixated on my chest. I squirm, suddenly uncomfortable. Is he really checking me out? Gross. I need to get him out of here before he gets the wrong idea or something. "Um, did you need anything else from me?" I ask lamely.

He smiles. "Only if you want it, my dear."

Ew. As if I'd ever touch this guy. I mean, sure, he's good-looking, but he's also way too smarmy for my taste. Not to mention the fact that he's basically trapped me here in this world against my will. Does he really think that will win my affections or turn me on?

"I, um, think I'm all set," I say, bobbing my head enthusiastically, hoping he'll get the hint. "In fact, I think I'll take a nap before dinner. I'm pretty beat." I fake a yawn to make my excuses more realistic. "So I'll, uh, talk to you later, okay?"

I watch as annoyance shadows Duske's face for half a second; then he shakes it away and offers me a large smile. "Very well, Sister Skye," he says, bowing at the waist. "I will leave you then. If you get hungry, just activate the intercom and Brother Thom will bring up some supper." He backs out of the room and the door slides closed behind him, clicking shut with a high-pitched beep. Instinctively, I try to reopen it with no luck.

I wander around the room, examining everything, but find nothing out of the ordinary. It looks just like any other luxury bedroom you might find on Earth. I switch on the television and am surprised to see *Casablanca* pop onto the screen. Bogart's telling Bergman they'll always have Paris. I watch, fascinated. It's kind of creepy how alike Earth and Terra are. Pop culture, movies, coffeehouse chains. Were the two worlds once exactly the same until one day there was a decision to make—a red button to press? Could one fateful action have caused Terra to spin off its projected course and onto a skewed path of apocalyptic destruction? But then how did my Earth manage to avoid it? Or is Terra's underground wasteland something we have to look forward to in our future? And if Terra is a future Earth, why are they still reliving our past culture hundreds of years later?

I wonder what Terrans think of Earth when they arrive after Moongazing. When they first open their eyes and see sunshine, grass, flowers, dogs, cats—everything that makes Earth's present reality superior to their own. When they first see the mighty ocean waves crashing to shore. When they watch their first bald eagle soaring majestically through the sky. When they climb up the Empire State Building and gaze down at their vast new world. When they realize they can now live aboveground without getting sick. It must be thrilling, but at the same time incredibly frightening. Are they forming their own close-knit Terran societies as American immigrants have done for centuries, carving out small neighborhoods to inhabit and keeping with their own traditions? Or are they adapting, blending in with the rest of us, making Earth friends, marrying Earth people?

I find myself laughing. Homeland Security is so worried about closing the Mexican borders. Imagine if they knew there were interdimensional illegal aliens living among us!

In a way, Moongazing makes a lot of sense. Especially if the Terran world really is as overcrowded as Duske claims. If you have the option, why not emigrate to a better world? And if they bring all their superior technology with them, we'll benefit from the relocation as well.

So then, why are the Eclipsers against it? Are they just jealous because they're not on the guest list? Or could there be something more sinister lying beneath the surface of this alternative reality trip?

It's all too much to think of now, so I continue my exploration of my room, opening the wardrobe door and revealing a closet full of clothes. Anxious to get out of my beautiful, but scratchy, evening gown, I select a black cotton tunic and a pair of leggings and change clothes. Much more comfortable. I'm just slipping on a pair of black boots when a knock sounds at the door.

"Come in," I call, wondering who it could be.

Brother Thom steps in, a silver tray of covered dishes in his hands. He sets the tray down on the dresser and pulls off several covers to reveal a meal of a burger and French fries, with a piece of chocolate cake for dessert. At first I'm about to protest the nonvegetarian selection, but then remember there's no meat here on Terra. Must be soy or something. My mouth waters as the rich smell fills the room. I got pulled back to Terra before lunch and now I'm starving.

"Thanks," I say gratefully, walking over to the table and selecting a long fry. I pop it in my mouth. Salty and delicious.

"You are most welcome, Sister," Thom says in an overloud voice. "I hope you enjoy it." Then he throws a furtive glance around the room and lowers his tone to a barely audible whisper. "Don't worry," he hisses. "We've got a plan in place. They'll come for you soon. Get you out."

Uh, what? I squint at him, swallowing my fry, my mouth suddenly dry as cotton. "What? Who?"

"Brother Dawn should never have left you unattended like he did. They must have injected you with some kind of nanotracker to have found you so quickly. Most unfortunate. But do not fret, Sister. We will free you soon."

I stare at him, my mind racing. This does not make any sense. Unless the butler is secretly playing for the other team. "Wait. Are you ... an Eclipser?" I whisper back.

Thom releases a frustrated sigh. "You have not regained your memories, I see," he says, sounding vastly disappointed.

Great. Here we go again. "You think I'm Mariah," I conclude.

"You *are* Mariah," the butler corrects. "Whether you know it or not."

"But Duske said—"

"Don't you get it? Duske is trying to trick you. He's taking advantage of your amnesia to further his agenda."

I close my eyes, wishing I could just somehow zap myself home. Now I'm back at square one. How the hell can I know who to trust—the guy who calls me by my real name and has offered me over a million dollars to speak at his seminar? Or the determined, passionate rebels who swear that I'm someone I'm not and insist that Duske's up to no good?

"You're going to have to try to trust us for a bit," Thom says.

"Your life will depend on it." He heads to the exit. At the door he turns back to me. "It might be better if you cut up your burger before taking a bite," he suggest cryptically. He leaves before I can ask why, the door sliding closed and locking behind him.

Alone again, I stare down at the plate of food, wondering what he meant. The way he said it—so mysterious—as if it were a hint of some kind. Curious, I grab the butter knife on my plate and slice into the patty. The knife strikes something hard and I pull apart the burger, discovering a tiny, plastic, thimblelike device.

As I slip it on my thumb the thimble constricts, wrapping tightly around the digit like a second skin. It's then I notice it has its own fingerprint. I look over at the sensor on the wall, the one I need a magic thumb to operate. Could this thimble be what I think it is?

Hunger forgotten, I walk to the door and press the thumb against the sensor, praying it won't set off an alarm or something. This won't be easy to explain if someone comes to investigate.

Nothing happens.

I try again, rubbing the thimble over the sensor. Still nothing. Just as I'm about to give up, the door suddenly beeps and the LCD indicator by the sensor goes from red to green. My eyes widen.

I'm free.

The door slides open, revealing my exit. I slip outside, peering up and down the corridor to make sure the coast is clear. There's no one in sight.

I tiptoe down the hall, not sure exactly where I'm going or what I'll do when I get there. Maybe I can find the Moongazing rooms and figure out how to make them work so I can go home. Leave this nightmare world forever. Though Duske might try to come after me. He obviously knows where to find me on Earth, and he'd probably be very angry I slipped away before speaking at his seminar. But maybe there'd be a way to hide. Head out to California or someplace even more obscure. Change my name, become someone else. Find a village in Nepal, a shack on a Costa Rican beach. Somewhere, anywhere that he couldn't track me down and drag me back to Terra.

I freeze as I suddenly hear Duske's voice. I flatten my body against the wall and peer into the room next to me. It's some sort of library, stacked floor to ceiling with dusty tomes. Duske's sitting at a large desk, speaking into something that appears to be some kind of videophone. Luckily, he doesn't seem to be aware of my presence.

I prepare to slink away in the other direction, but his words make me pause.

"Yes, she's here," he is saying. "Oh, indeed, it worked brilliantly, Brother. Kudos to you and your crew. The new memories have bonded completely with her psyche. She's utterly convinced she's from Earth ... Yes! Even after those pathetic rebels tried their damnedest to tell her otherwise ... I know! I would have loved to see the look on their faces when their precious Mariah insisted she's some random girl from Earth."

He chuckles, a low guttural sound, and my whole world skids off its axis. My stomach twists and for a moment I'm sure I'll throw up. I can't believe this. The one person who said he believed me—who swore up and down that he knew me as Skye—has just admitted to his crony that he, like everyone else, thinks I'm her. Mariah.

Oh my God.

"She even logged in willingly!" I hear him continue. "Thought she was going home ... I know, I know. It's priceless ... Oh yes, of course I recorded it. I plan to play it at the seminar. Wait till the Indys see a video of the great Mariah Quinn entering a Moongazer booth. They'll be begging us for the opportunity to hand over all their possessions for a chance to play. Your plan was brilliant. Utterly brilliant. I couldn't be more pleased."

He pauses as the other voice on the video screen speaks. I strain to hear. "So, what are you going to do with her after the seminar?" it asks. "Send her back? Let her burn out on her own?"

"No way," Duske says. "It's too dangerous. As we've learned from this experiment, as long as the people believe Mariah Quinn is alive, they'll continue with their silly little revolution. Natural burnout will take too long, and I don't want to have to deal with the possibility of those pesky Eclipsers pulling her out over and over again, convinced they'll eventually get her to join them. It's expensive and irritating."

"So, what are you going to do?"

"Early retirement," Duske says. He makes a throat-slitting gesture, and I suddenly realize this particular package probably doesn't come with a pension plan.

I've got to get the hell out of here.

I sprint back down the hall, fast as my legs can carry me, no idea where I'm going. I bank a left, then a right. I scurry down stairs and around corners. But no matter where I turn, I can't seem to locate an exit. The place is a maze and I have no idea how to get out.

"Psst"

I whirl around at the whisper, praying it's friend and not foe. A lone figure, encased entirely in black and wearing a black mask and hood, stands in the middle of the hallway. I can tell from her curvy silhouette she's a woman, but all that's exposed are radiant green eyes. She puts a finger to her lips, stilling the questions on my tongue. Then she motions for me to follow.

Should I? What if it's just another trap? But what choice do I have? To stay here is to die. At least if I leave now I'll be able to come up with a plan B. Find Moongazer Palace and get back to Earth.

Duske's words flash through my mind.

She's utterly convinced she's from Earth.

Could it be true? Could my whole life be some kind of lie? Implanted memories, he said. Is that even possible? Could everything I know and love be just an illusion? Impossible. And yet . . .

I nod to the figure, realizing I have little choice but to trust her. Maybe she can lead me to Glenda and the rest of the Eclipsers. Maybe they can give me a better idea of what's going on.

The woman bows her head, then turns and starts slinking down the hallway, her steps light and silent like a cat stalking its prey. She pauses at every turn, peering around each corner before motioning me to move forward. She has a Japanese-style sword—a katana of some sort—slung from a utility belt low on her waist.

We scramble up a flight of stairs, then another and another. Are we running to the roof? Finally the figure stops climbing, pulls off a glove, and studies her hand. I realize she's got some kind of map scribbled onto her palm. Thank God for that.

She reaches into her pocket and pulls out a plastic thimble identical to the one Thom hid in my soy burger and slips it onto her thumb. She presses it against the sensor and, after a moment's pause, the LCD flashes green and the door slides open. She motions for me to follow her inside.

It's a bedroom similar to the one I'd been kept prisoner in. As I step over the threshold, she reaches under the bed and pulls out a length of rope and a few metal clips. She heads over to the glass sliding doors leading to a balcony. I watch, unsure, as she detaches a small black box from her utility belt and presses it against the door. She pushes a button and, without warning, the glass explodes. I duck, hands over my face, to avoid being cut. When I look up, the glass barrier is gone.

"That will have tripped the alarm," the woman informs me, speaking for the first time in a low voice. "We have to hurry."

She steps over the jagged glass and out onto the balcony. There, she tosses one end of her rope over the side and clips the other to the banister. I watch, worried about what she's got planned. We must be four stories up.

She hands me what looks like a rock-climbing harness, and instructs me to slip it around my waist. Then she clicks me into the rope. "Climb over the balcony," she instructs. "And on my word, jump."

I have little alternative. I do as she says, my toes curling against the safety of the balcony as I brace and try to psych myself up for the impending rappel.

My rescuer pauses for a moment, as if listening for something, then pulls the sword belt off her waist and wraps it around mine. "I thought you might like it back," she explains after I give her a confused look. Her voice reveals a smile I can't see under her mask. "I've been keeping it safe for you while you've been gone."

I look down at the sword and pull it halfway out of its scabbard. The blade flashes under the artificial light, almost giving off an otherworldly glow. Did this belong to Mariah? I caress the hilt and something inside me flashes with uneasy recognition. Have I worn this blade before? Somewhere? Sometime? In some other life? I remember the photo in Dawn's living room, and I shiver.

"Uh, thanks," I say, not quite sure what else to do.

The woman's eyes crinkle from under her hood, and I can't tell if she's smiling or holding back tears. "I love you, Mariah, my sister," she says. "Whatever happens, always remember that."

I open my mouth to speak, but the words die in my throat as a sudden pounding comes at the bedroom door. They've found us.

"I jammed the door signal," the woman tells me. "But it won't take them long to break through. You have to jump now."

I glance over the railing at the ground far beneath my feet.

Unsure, afraid. "What about you?" I ask.

"Don't worry about me. Just jump, Mariah. I'll keep you safe. But you must go."

Desperation in her voice compels me to obey. I take a deep breath, send up a small prayer, close my eyes, then step off the balcony. A moment later, I open my eyes to find myself rappelling down the side of the mansion, my feet hitting the outer wall for a moment then shooting out again as my rescuer lets out the rope. I grip the cord tightly, my fingers burning, threatening to lose their grip.

Without warning, the rope goes slack. I tumble out of control, the ground flying at my face at high speed. I reach out—a desperate, stupid attempt to cushion my fall—and land on my hand. My wrist gives way with a sickening crunch.

For a moment, I feel nothing. Then a sharp pain shoots through me and I'm forced to bite down on my lower lip to keep from screaming in agony. I grab at my wrist, pressing it against my stomach. It throbs in protest.

I look up to the balcony far above me, wondering what happened to the rope. The men must have broken through the door. They've likely got my rescuer and are in the process of dragging her away.

Her head appears for a brief moment. "Run, Mariah!" she screams down at me.

I don't wait for a second invitation.

ELEVEN

I sprint across the lawn as fast as my legs can carry me, cradling my swollen wrist against my stomach, pain shooting up my arm at every step. I don't know where to go, what to do; I just know I have to keep moving. Because whoever it was who got to my rescuer is sure to come after me next.

I run down the streets, tryi I run down the streets, trying to remember the route to Luna Park. If only I can get there, find Moongazer Palace, I could try to journey back to Earth on my own. But even as the plan forms in my mind, I realize it won't work. Earth is not the safe haven I want it to be. Not when Duske clearly knows how to find me there. What's to stop him from dragging me back once again? Or sending his goons in to get rid of me once and for all?

No. I can't go back. It'd be a death sentence. But what else can I do?

Find Dawn.

An inner voice, powerful and demanding, thrusts the solution to the forefront of my brain. I try to shake it away; Dawn doesn't even like me. He thinks I betrayed him and his people. He told me he was done forever. That he wouldn't rescue me again, no matter what.

To me, you'll always be a traitor.

But then I remember the pain in his eyes. The wistful glances he gave me when he thought I wasn't looking. He may talk a tough game, but somehow I'm sure, at the end of the day, he'd never allow his precious Mariah to come to harm.

I sprint around a corner and realize I've somehow found the outskirts of Luna Park. I pass the Park Terrace restaurant, the corner Starbucks, the bulletin boards advertising Moongazing. I pass them all, until the façade fades away and the fancy neighborhood begins to deteriorate. At last I come to Moongazer Palace itself, in all its gaudy glory. I stop, panting hard. My wrist has now swollen to the size of a softball.

I give a longing glance at Moongazer Palace, but then firm my resolve and instead locate the manhole cover Dawn showed me my first day on Terra: the rabbit hole leading to the Dark Side. I scramble to my knees and attempt to pry off the cover one-handed, praying it's not locked from the other side. It's not an easy task, but finally I manage to wrench it free, revealing the rickety metal ladder disappearing into the darkness. I crawl down the hole, pulling the cover over my head and begin a one-handed descent. Rung after rung; I wince at every step, straining to see.

I eventually reach the bottom, jump down onto the metal road. I blink a few times, my eyes adjusting to the darkness and dim track lighting, then suck in a deep breath. I'm safe. Well, sort of. Okay, probably not that safe at all. But the immediate threat is gone. I can stop running. Catch my breath. Figure out what to do next.

If only my rescuer had made it out, too. But, in a way, it seemed almost as if she expected to be caught. The way she looked at me. The fact she'd given me the sword. It was as if she knew it was a kamikaze mission.

And yet, she willingly sacrificed herself to get me out. Sacrificed her own life to save mine. Why? Because she thinks I'm Mariah?

I search my brain for some kind of memory, some dim recollection of another life. One where I'm a big-time rebel leader working hard to save her people from an oppressive dystopian regime. But it's no use. No matter how hard I try, I still feel like me—Skye Brown, normal everyday college kid. There's nothing inside me that remotely resembles Mariah.

The Eclipsers are going to be so disappointed. And while it's certainly not my fault that I wasn't born the girl they think I was, I feel a stab of guilt just the same.

I trudge down the underground road, heading in the direction of the Dark Side city where I assume I'll be able to find Dawn. I'm exhausted, and searing pain burns my arm at every step. My kingdom for one of those hover bikes. The road is empty, silent, save for the whirring of the ventilation fans. I walk on.

Finally, after what seems like three forevers, I notice a twinkling light ahead. Relief floods me as I recognize the gates to the Dark Side. I made it. I approach the gate, wondering how I'm going to gain entrance. Then I notice the thumb sensor. Cautiously, I press my thumb against the pad, praying it will work.

A moment later, the doors creak open, welcoming me with giant metal arms. I'm too exhausted to ponder the implications of the gate recognizing my thumbprint. I have to find Dawn.

And so I wander down the twisty antlike passageways until I step out into the town square. The place is bustling, as it was the first time, but a hush falls over the people as they recognize me. A moment later, I find myself once again engulfed by the crowd.

"Mariah! Are you okay?" asks a thin, middle-aged woman with missing front teeth and a second pair of lips.

"What did they do to you?" demands a salt-and-pepper-bearded man with three breasts.

"What happened to your wrist?" a young boy with one leg asks, pointing to my swollen arm.

Overwhelmed, I somehow manage to hold up my good hand to silence them. "Please," I croak. "I need Dawn. Is he here?"

"Go get Dawn!" commands the middle-aged woman to a small boy, presumably her son. "Tell him Mariah needs him!"

The boy takes off. I stare down at my feet, feeling unnerved by all the sympathetic eyes in the crowd. These are good people. They want to help. The nagging guilt returns as I realize I will eventually have to disappoint them. How could Mariah have betrayed these poor people? Sold them out for a better life? It seems inconceivable that someone could do that.

The crowd parts as Dawn approaches. His arms are crossed over his chest and his blue eyes seem to pierce into my soul while his mouth dips to a frown. He doesn't look happy to see me. At least, not as relieved as I am to see him.

"Dawn!" I cry, grateful to lay eyes on a familiar face. "Thank God I found you."

He stops in front of me, staring me down with obvious disapproval. Then he drags me away from the others. I can feel their hopeful stares as we walk to a quiet part of the town square. "So, you've decided to slum it again. Or have you been sent to spy on us by your new friend?"

"What? No! I—" My face falls as I realize he thinks I've sided with Duske and his Circle of Eight once again. Not that I blame him. In a way I did. But how can I explain it wasn't of my own free will?

"Don't you think you've done enough, Mariah?" Dawn continues. "Can't you leave us well enough alone?"

"You don't understand," I say, searching his angry eyes with my own. "They're … they're trying to kill me. I barely escaped with my life."

He snorts. "Please. I'd kill you myself if I didn't think death was too kind a punishment for a traitor like you. You—" He stops short, his eyes falling on the sword strapped to my waist. "How did you get that?" he demands.

I glance down at the weapon. "The woman who rescued me. She helped me escape Duske's house. She saved my life."

"Where is she now?"

I was afraid he'd ask that. "I don't know. They caught her …" I trail off, hanging my head. "I'm afraid she sacrificed herself for me."

"She's an idiot then. You're not worth it."

Anger burns at my gut at his repeated condemnation. I came all this way to find him. A million painful steps. How dare he treat me this way? "Look," I say, incensed. "You can't blame me for crimes I didn't commit!"

He shakes his head wearily but doesn't answer.

"Dawn, she's hurt!" cries the bearded man from across the way. "You must heal her." I glance over at him, gratefully. Thank goodness not everyone thinks Mariah's the bad guy here.

The crowd takes up the cry for healing. "Yes, Dawn. Mariah's hurt!"

Dawn releases a long sigh, then gently picks up my wrist in his large hands, lifting it to get a better view. I can't avoid a cry of agony as burning pain shoots up my arm. He runs a light cool finger across my skin, closing his eyes.

"It's broken," he remarks without emotion. "Pretty badly, too, by the feel of it."

"It really hurts," I admit, a tear escaping the corner of my eye and dripping down my cheek. I hate crying, but the pain, along with the emotional stress and uncertainty, is too much.

Dawn pauses a moment, then seems to come to a decision. "Fine. Come inside. Let's see what I can do for you."

He lowers my wrist tenderly, as if wary of causing me any more pain. I meekly follow him through the crowd, out of the town square, and into the tunnel that leads to his little cave house. Once we're inside, he shuts the door behind us and motions for me to sit down on the futon. I sink down into the cushion, grateful to finally be off my feet.

"They were going to kill me," I repeat, half to myself and half to Dawn. He nods slowly and takes my arm and places it across his thigh. A small tingle tickles my stomach as I feel his heat against my bare wrist. His trousers are soft, cottonlike. His touch is careful. Gentle.

"Close your eyes," he instructs in a low voice. "And imagine something pleasant."

I do as he says, too tired to ask why. A moment later I feel his soft fingers trip up my arm, wispy and slow, trailing a warmth that relaxes and soothes. I try to do as he says, to think of something pleasant. But all I can concentrate on is his touch. Which is, admittedly, pretty pleasant.

A slash of pain jerks through me. My eyes fly open. Dawn has his own eyes closed as he grips my arm in his hands. I stare down at my wrist and watch with horrified fascination as the bone—the one that just a second ago had been bent at a weird angle—slides back into place. The swelling is visibly retreating. My arm still hurts, yet at the same time I feel a strange, overwhelming peace washing over me, almost as if I've been drugged.

A moment later Dawn opens his eyes. He looks at me, his expression one of amused disapproval. "You cheated," he accuses. "You peeked."

I can feel my face heat. "That was amazing," I say. I lift my arm off his lap, flexing my fingers. My wrist still feels a bit stiff, but the bones have somehow knitted together, mended in a way that should have taken six weeks and a cast. "How did you do that?"

Dawn shrugs. "It's a long story. One you used to know." He rises to his feet. "But you should be okay now. While I was in there, I also located the tracking nano they implanted into your bloodstream. That's how Duske and his goons found you so quickly last time. I believe I was able to disable it, but I'm going to activate the house scrambler as well. Just in case."

I look up at him. "House scrambler?"

"Electronic interference. Makes it tougher for the government to locate people. We'll hang out here tonight—we're running too close to curfew to leave now—but tomorrow morning I'll take you to the Eclipsers. One of their doctors should be able to ensure that your nanotracker is deactivated for good."

"Thank you," I say gratefully. "I had no idea I was being tracked. When I went off with Duske, he tricked me. He pretended to be one of the Eclipsers and he told me he knew I was from Earth. He promised me more asthma medication." I give him a rueful look. "I didn't mean to—I mean, I had no idea." I sigh. "Basically I'm a big blind idiot, stumbling around in a world I don't recognize. I don't know where I am, who to trust." I shrug helplessly.

Dawn surprises me with a sympathetic look. "I know," he says, coming over to sit down beside me. "I didn't mean to sound so harsh out there. It's just frustrating, you know?" He rakes a hand through his hair. "I look at you and I don't know if I should kiss you or kill you."

I swallow hard as his eyes meet my own. He looks so sad, my heart breaks for all he must have lost. No wonder he's so bitter and angry. I wish there was some way I could make it all better. But what can I do?

Dawn shakes his head, breaking the moment. "Anyway, enough of that. Are you hungry?" he asks. "I don't have much. Rations were cut again this week—surprise, surprise. But I have a few tins of beans. Some bread. Tea."

"I don't want to eat all your food," I hedge. But my stomach chooses that moment to betray my intended martyrdom with a loud growl. Dawn chuckles, a soft, sweet sound that makes my stomach twist again. Not from hunger this time.

"It's okay," he says, reaching out to ruffle my hair. His fingers, scraping lightly against my scalp, send a tingly feeling down to my toes. What is it about this guy that makes me feel such longing? He's beautiful, yes. But there's something much more than physical attraction. Some kind of deep connection between us that I can't begin to explain. Could I really have suppressed memories of a past relationship buried somewhere deep inside my subconscious? It seems impossible. Yet, how else can I explain the soul-wrenching pain inside me every time I catch a glimpse of his face?

Dawn heads over to the kitchenette, opening cabinets and pulling out drawers. "I have enough to spare. I just didn't want you to be expecting some kind of gourmet adventure. We Dark Siders don't exactly feast like they do in Luna Park." He sets a kettle onto an electric stove. "Then again, I'm pretty famous for my stone soup around these parts."

"Stone soup," I repeat with a small laugh, thankful he's willing to lighten the mood. "Sounds delish. I'd love a bowl."

"Then you, my dear, shall have one. Sit tight. Brother Dawn Grey, Dark Sider chef extraordinaire, is prepared to work his magic." He makes an exaggerated flourish and manages to drop the mixing bowl he's holding. It goes crashing to the floor. "Uh, yeah," he says, reaching down for it. "I meant for that to happen. You may think I'm a bumbling idiot, but really that was a vital part of my very complex and elaborate recipe."

I laugh, clapping my hands like a good audience member. "Of course it was, oh chef extraordinaire." I grin. "I must say, I'm extremely impressed so far, and am waiting with bated breath to see what kinds of wonders you will perform next."

"Likely cutting my finger," Dawn says, and chuckles. "But sometimes I like to mix things up with a burning-my-hand-on-the-stove number. I'm tricky like that."

I lean back into the couch, watching him as he bustles about the small kitchen, pulling out tins and pans, opening packets and adding water. He walks over to the bookcase and pulls the lone book from the top shelf. I realize it's not a real book at all, but a hollowed-out replica containing a secret compartment. He reaches in and pulls out a small sack, holding it up with a shy smile. "Black market herbs," he says, his voice rich with pride. "We might just have a feast tonight yet."

"Awesome." I curl my feet up and under me, feeling warm and cozy for the first time since I got back to Terra. It seems hard to believe that less than an hour before I'd been running for my life. Under Dawn's protection, I feel completely safe.

Dawn wanders back to the stove, and a few minutes later a rich, spicy aroma permeates the cave house. "Smells delicious," I remark. Dawn tosses me a smile, then walks over to hand me a crude pottery mug containing tea. I take a sip, the sweet beverage warming my insides. "Mmm, thanks," I say, wrapping both hands around the warm cup.

He walks back to the kitchen. "Dinner's just about ready."

"Do you need any help?"

"Nah. I'm good." He scoops out ladles of soup into two bowls and brings them over to the coffee table. I dip my spoon into the broth and take a mouthful. My eyes widen at the taste. It's fabulous. Like nothing I've ever eaten. I take another bite as Dawn brings over a small loaf of bread on a plate and sets it before me.

"What is in this soup?" I ask. "It's great."

He beams, the smile bringing a light to his face, making me realize just how beautiful he really is. "Secret recipe," he brags. "It was always your favorite."

My enthusiasm dampens somewhat as reality is shoved back into central focus. I'm not on some first date with a handsome stranger. He believes I am his long-lost girlfriend. *That's* why he's being so sweet to me. Not because he likes me for who I really am.

"Do you really and honestly believe I'm Mariah?" I ask at last, deciding it's time to broach the subject, even if it does destroy the intimacy we're sharing. "I mean, couldn't there be some other explanation as to why I just look like her?"

Dawn swallows his mouthful of bread. "You don't just look like her," he corrects. "You sound like her. You smell like her. You walk and talk like her." He pauses, then adds, "You *are* her, whether you want to believe it or not." He takes a sip of tea. "I mean, just because someone has amnesia, it doesn't mean they're suddenly a different person altogether."

"But I don't have amnesia. I remember everything about my life. Who I am, where I live, what I do. I have family and friends, and memories of birthday parties since I was five years old. If I'm Mariah, where did all that stuff come from?"

"A memory serum, most likely."

For some reason my mind flashes back to my dream. The one where I was running through a tunnel, pursued by uniformed men. I didn't know where I was or who I was or what I was doing there. Then they caught me, pinned me down, injected me with some kind of concoction. Could that have been ...

No. I shake my head. I refuse to believe it. There's no way everything I know and love has somehow been implanted into my brain. My memories are real. My family. My friends. I absolutely refuse to believe they've sprung from some kind of total-recall cocktail.

"Tell me about your life on Earth," Dawn suggests, bringing me back to the conversation.

"Okay," I agree. "Well, I'm eighteen years old and I live in the city of Manhattan. Best city on Earth, really. It's got everything you could ever want." I take a sip of tea. "I go to college during the day and after school I work on this amazing video game we call RealLife. I think it's going to revolutionize games as we know them." I shrug. "Well, who knows, but it's pretty awesome, anyway. My boyfriend, Craig, says that I ..."

I trail off as I catch Dawn's face. Hmm, maybe I shouldn't have mentioned Craig. Now the poor guy's going to think that not only did his precious Mariah betray him by going to Earth in the first place, but once there she hooked up with some random guy while he's been sitting around pining for her.

But what am I supposed to say? I've already told him I'm not Mariah.

"Sorry," I mutter, mostly because he looks so hurt.

He swallows hard. "It's okay. I need to hear it straight. Even if some of it isn't pleasant," he says. "What about your memories? Do you remember growing up on Earth?"

"Well, sure. I grew up in New York. I have a mother and father and older sister. My dad's a doctor and my mom's a lawyer." I trail off, my brain going fuzzy at the edges. Why does my life story suddenly seem so clichéd and stereotypical?

"Tell me a memory you have," Dawn suggests. "A real one. I want to hear about you and your experiences, not just a listing of your family tree."

"Right. Sure. Well, there was one time—" I stop. What story was I about to relate? I try to think of something funny, but I keep drawing a blank. I know we went cross-country as a family when I was seven, but I can't remember any of our specific adventures. I know I broke my wrist when I was twelve, but I can't remember what I did to cause the break. It's like I remember everything about my life on Earth, and yet suddenly it's all feeling like some foggy dream.

"Sorry," I say, shaking my head. "My brain's totally dead tonight. Too much stress most likely," I rationalize, pushing the frightening alternate possibility to the back of my brain. After all, having trouble recalling cute family anecdotes doesn't necessarily mean my whole life was syringe-injected to prevent me from remembering that I'm truly a revolutionary leader who bailed on redeeming a postapocalyptic world.

Dawn reaches over to stroke my head, probably jumping to the same conclusion I'm trying to avoid. He wants nothing more than to believe my memories were indeed implanted. Fabricated. So, how do I convince him it's just not true? Especially when I'm not quite sure of that myself.

"My life's not made up," I insist, knowing my argument sounds weak and unsubstantiated.

"Don't worry," Dawn says. "We'll get this whole mess figured out soon enough. Tomorrow we'll go visit the Eclipsers. I'll take you there this time—no more leaving you alone. They have doctors on staff. Maybe they can tell you what's going on in your head."

He lowers his hand to my cheek, caressing it with light, feathery fingers. I close my eyes, relaxing under his gentle touch, breathing in his musky scent, wondering if I should pull away, resist the tender advance. It feels so good. So right. And yet, I still have a boyfriend on Earth. Would this be considered cheating? Of course it would. Yet for some reason I can't seem to summon an appropriately guilty feeling. Maybe it's because right now life on Earth seems so distant and foggy, while this moment on Terra is richly detailed and real.

I swallow back my hesitation and allow myself to submit to his touch, folding myself into him, hyperaware of his flushed skin against my own. He does not disappoint, wrapping his arm around me so I can cuddle my head in the nook between his shoulder and chest. He strokes my shoulder with a gentle, slow touch.

"Tell me about Mariah," I suggest, after a few moments of comforting silence. "Maybe it'll jog some memory or something." Now that I'm feeling warm and safe, I'm able to broach the topic without an overwhelming suffocating fear pounding through my brain.

Dawn's fingers pause for a moment, then continue their caress, weaving gentle threads of warmth through my entire body. It takes everything inside me not to literally purr.

"Mariah was passionate. Determined. Extremely intelligent. She rallied the Dark Siders effortlessly. She had an uncanny power to convince anyone to do anything, with just a quick smile or wink in their direction," he says. "Hell, she had me wrapped around her little finger."

"But you're angry with her now," I say, opening my eyes to study his expression. His face clouds and I can almost see the hurt wash over him.

"Yes, because you—sorry, she," he corrects. "It's so hard to look at you and say 'she.'" He shakes his head. "Because she—Mariah—betrayed us all. She who started the Eclipsers and the campaign for a better life for Dark Siders sold us out to the Senate and then abandoned us. The very night that should have been our ultimate victory instead became our worst nightmare. All thanks to her."

"I don't understand. What exactly happened?"

"It wasn't an overnight thing. Originally Mariah started Moongazing to figure out what the government was up to. She wanted to find out if it really was the be-all and end-all our glorious Circle of Eight was advertising." He snorts. "She insisted that if they'd really found a Garden of Eden on another world then it should be opened for everyone to enjoy. It wasn't fair that only those with disposable income could pack up and move to paradise while we poor bastards down below were stuck in hell."

"Well, that sounds like a pretty noble cause," I venture, wondering where everything went wrong.

"Sure, I guess," Dawn says. "Until she started getting addicted to the drugs."

I frown. "I still don't get what drugs have to do with all of this."

"You need 'em to 'Gaze," Dawn says. "Something to do with the brain needing a cushion for travel." He shrugs. "Mariah started getting addicted to the 'Gazers the more she traveled back and forth from Earth. It happened slowly. I noticed small things at first. A few white lies as to where she'd been. But then it started getting worse. I soon realized that she was out of control, running away to Earth every chance she could get. And the revolution—all the plans we had started putting into place—began to suffer from her absence."

"What did the Eclipsers think?"

"They didn't know. Stupid me, I covered for her. I didn't want her to lose all she'd worked so hard to get. I told them she was sick. And she was, in a sense. So the Eclipsers pushed on without her, moving ahead with preparations for our Moongazing seminar sabotage. The idea was to incapacitate the guards and change the program—sending Mariah onstage to inform the gathered Indys of all the atrocities the Senate was performing right under their very noses." Dawn sighs. "But Mariah never made it to the seminar. That afternoon she made the jump to Earth and left us all with useless best-laid plans."

"Why couldn't someone else just get onstage and give the same spiel?"

"There was no one else. It had to be her," Dawn says. "After all, she was born of royal blood. Destined to become one of the Circle of Eight. Hearing the message from her would have convinced the Indys of its legitimacy. Rather than just a random Dark Sider spouting off wild conspiracy theories."

"That makes sense," I say. "I suppose that's why the Eclipsers need her back so badly."

Dawn nods. "The Eclipsers refused to believe that Mariah 'Gazed of her own free will. They insisted she must have been tricked or forced by the Circle. And because I was hiding the signs of her addiction, my explanation of what really happened fell on deaf ears."

"But how can you be sure? Maybe she *was* kidnapped or something."

"No," Dawn says firmly. "She went of her own accord. The morning before she disappeared, she came to my house. She told me she'd found happiness on Earth and begged me to come with her. She wanted me to go to Earth and start a new life." Dawn scowls. "I asked her how she was going to pay for this pilgrimage. Moongazing's not cheap, and she'd already used up most of her family's trust fund to start programs to aid the Dark Siders. She just smiled at me—this sick, sad smile—and said it was all taken care of. At the time I didn't know what she meant." He squeezes his hands into fists. "But that night, when the government soldiers swept in at the seminar and stopped us in our tracks, I realized the truth. There was only one way they could have been so prepared for us. Mariah sold them the information in exchange for her trip to Earth."

"Wow, that's horrible," I say, trying to imagine how such a betrayal must have stung. No wonder he's so bitter about his ex.

"Many good men and women died that night. And it set our rebellion back miles. Not to mention morale. We'd been working for almost a year to set up the sabotage. And it was over in one fell swoop because our great and glorious leader decided to betray us."

I considered this; something still didn't make sense. "But if Mariah did all this, why the hell do the Eclipsers want her back?"

"They don't believe it was her. And when I told them what I knew had happened, they freaked out. We got into a huge fight. I've tried to avoid them ever since. I wanted nothing to do with their insane quest to bring you back. It'd be better for everyone if you just rotted on Earth."

I wince, realizing he's gone back to using "you" to refer to Mariah.

"So, you see how it is," Dawn continues sorrowfully. "How I sit here, with you mere inches away, and yet you're not here at all. How I want to blame you for crimes you don't remember committing." He stares off into space, his eyes unfocused, uneasy, pained. "Is there any Mariah still inside, deep down? Or have the 'Gazers completely gutted your brain? Are you really here of your own accord? Or are you some sort of spy, sent by Duske to figure out what we're up to and betray us all over again?"

I frown. How could he think that of me? "Of course I'm not—"

Dawn waves a weary hand to silence my protest. "Don't bother," he says. "Even if you were a spy, what difference would it make? Even if I knew without a doubt that you had been sent here to destroy me, it wouldn't matter. To have you here, sitting by my side in my living room … I'm powerless to turn you away."

He hangs his head, staring at his hands. "I still love you. A part of me wants to believe you didn't have control over what you did. You were sick. If only I'd been able to help you when I first realized it. In many ways, this is all my fault."

He looks so lost and lonely; my heart wrenches in empathy. I reach over and thread my fingers through his, hoping he'll find some small comfort in my touch, since at this moment it's all I can give.

He looks down at my hand, strokes my thumb with his own. He closes his eyes and leans back, head against the sofa. "Do you know how many nights I've lain awake, too tormented by dreams of you to dare close my eyes and sleep? Wondering if I made the right decision by refusing to join you on Earth? We could have been rich, happy—maybe we would even have had a family someday. But instead I gave that all up for an endless fight that we can never hope to win." He gives me a rueful look, his regret sucking the breath from my lungs.

"You don't really believe that," I find myself arguing. "You know, deep in your heart, that what you did was the only real choice. You chose the unselfish path. You refused to run away. To me, that seems noble and brave."

"Does it?" Dawn asks, his voice scarcely louder than a whisper. He looks over, instantly capturing my eyes with his own. They glow blue. "God, Mariah, it feels like I've waited an eternity to hear those words from your lips."

I lower my eyelids, the hopefulness radiating from his stare too much for me to take in. I don't know this man. I don't remember him at all. But his desperate words, his earnest eyes, his soft touch are able to capture me all the same. The power in his look is indescribable, melting my resistances, my willpower, my soul all in one foul blow.

The softness that brushes my lips is so light that at first it barely registers. Then there's added pressure. My eyes flutter open in surprise. Dawn presses his mouth against mine, lips caressing lips, eyes closed, face enraptured.

I close my eyes again, wondering what I should do. This is nothing like the angry kiss he stole in the alleyway. A kiss of violent passion, domination, control. This kiss is different. A fearful tenderness, almost as if he believes pressing too hard will cause me to vanish into thin air.

This is not a kiss of desire. Not a kiss of control. This is a kiss of someone in love.

But he's not in love with me.

I jerk away, pushing past him to rise to my feet. My knees buckle and I'm forced to take a moment to steady myself before managing another step away from the seductive scene. I take a breath, turning to face him and get his reaction to my rejection. Guilt stabs my heart as I catch the pain in his eyes.

He doesn't move. He doesn't protest. He doesn't even question why. He just stares up at me, devastated.

And it's my fault.

But it's for the best.

"Dawn ..." I start, not even sure how to begin. I mean, how do I get him to understand? Deep inside, with every fiber in my body, I want nothing more than to leap back on that futon and throw myself at him with wild abandon. To kiss him senseless, claim his mouth as mine, and never let go. But it's wrong, wrong, wrong, wrong, wrong.

"Dawn," I start again, swallowing back the lump the size of a basketball in my throat. "I'm so sorry, but this isn't right. You know it's not, deep down. After all, you don't want me. You want Mariah. And even if in some crazy way I was once her, I'm not right now. I'm Skye Brown and we ... well, we barely know each other."

Even as the words spill from my lips, I know that I'm protesting too much. After all, even though I barely know anything about Dawn, the connection between us is undeniable. There's a bond so strong it feels dangerous. Which is why, I remind myself, it's best to stay aloof. At least until we figure out what's going on.

Because if I'm not Mariah—that means someone else is. And if I let myself succumb to Dawn's tenderness, fall for him and allow myself to care, then the real Mariah could someday come back to reclaim her boyfriend as her own. And then where will that leave me, the one who freely gave away her heart and soul to a man who loved her only because he thought she was someone else?

I shake my head. It's better to resist.

"You're right," Dawn agrees at last, a slight quivering of his lower lip giving away his unhappiness. "Of course you're right." He rises from the couch, stiff and slow, and heads to a small cabinet at the far end of the living room. He pulls it open by its handle and grabs a pillow and blanket from a shelf. He presents them to me. "It's late," he says. "Let's call it a night. Go ahead and take my bed. I'm fine out here on the couch."

I take the pillow and blanket from him. "Don't be silly," I protest. "I can sleep on the couch. I don't want to take your bed."

"I want you to have it," Dawn says, in a voice that leaves no room for argument.

Reluctantly, I gather up the bedding and head into the adjoining room. Like the rest of the apartment, it's a small cave—and there's no room for anything but the full-sized mattress on the ground. I wrap the blanket around me and lay my head on the slightly musty-smelling pillow. Once still, I can hear Dawn in the next room, shuffling around.

An ache of emptiness fills my stomach and a small fear twists up my spine. If only I could call out to him. Invite him into the bed. No, not for the reason you think. I just want to curl up in his strong arms and let him cuddle me to sleep.

I force my mind away from his imagined warmth. It isn't fair to lead him on. To make him hope for a future that we cannot share. I have to be strong for the both of us. And tomorrow, we'll figure things out. Somehow.

I close my eyes and slow my breathing, begging for sleep to take me quickly. But the goddess of slumber ignores my pleas and so I lie awake, in the dark cave bedroom, and content myself to just listen. Listen to Dawn collapse on the futon, listen to him toss and turn. Listen to his breathing slow until he finally falls into a restless sleep. And eventually, listen to him cry out, as if in pain, over a nightmare from which he can't awake.

And through it all, I lie still, resisting the temptation to crawl out of bed and rouse him from his nocturnal terror. To comfort him and tell him everything will be okay. That he's just having a dream.

"Mariah!" he cries out, anguished and uncensored in his sleep. "Oh God, please, Mariah!"

I sigh and roll over, pulling the covers over my head, feeling helpless and sad and oh so alone.I sigh and roll over, pulling the covers over my head, feeling helpless and sad and oh so alone.

TWELVE

I open my eyes. At least this time I know what to expect, though that doesn't really make the experience any more comforting. Once again, a tiny room. Video screens on all four walls, a nauseating kaleidoscope of color.

"I'm sorry to wake you," he apologizes, "but the Eclipsers are asking for you. There's a major event scheduled for tonight that they've been organizing, and they're hoping to get the day's business squared away first, so they can finish up the party plans."

"What … time is it?" I ask. Besides the artificial light streaming in from the living room, there's no indication. It could be midnight. It could be high noon. Or somewhere in between.

Dawn glances at his watch. "Five o'clock," he says.

"It's early." Unless time in Terra works differently than it does on Earth.

"Actually, it's late. It's five in the evening."

I sit up, shocked. "I slept all day?" I ask, rubbing the sleep from my eyes.

"You slept two days. But you looked so peaceful, lying there. I didn't want to wake you until I absolutely had to."

I gape at him. I can't believe I've been out for that long. Though I guess it's not surprising. After all, it's not like I was getting much shut-eye back on Earth for the last few months. My body must have just collapsed. Thank goodness it picked a place where I was safe. At least, I think it's safe here.

"Did they come looking for me?" I ask. "Duske and his men, I

99

mean."

Dawn shakes his head. "We haven't seen signs of them. I'm sure they'll be here soon, though. Which is why we need to get you together with the Eclipsers so we can discuss our strategy. Then we can get you settled back into your old house. Um, Mariah's house," he corrects quickly. "No one will find you there."

"A house?" I repeat, surprised. I guess I never really thought about where Mariah might live. I wonder what it looks like. A simple cave like Dawn's place? Or something a little more upscale? After all, Mariah was royalty, though she abandoned her birthright. I wonder if stepping through the front door will jog any memories? Or will it seem, as everything else in this world has up until now, completely foreign?

"Mariah needed someplace to stay after she ran away from her parents' house in Luna Park," Dawn explains. "She found a very pretty apartment, well hidden in an old, abandoned building, deep underground in Stratum Three. It's small, but she did an excellent job making it homey and cozy."

"Um, great," I reply, gnawing on my lower lip. He doesn't plan to just leave me there, does he? I mean, homey or not, it's still some abandoned apartment deep underground in a postapocalyptic world. Unless he agreed to stay with me. Would that be weird of me to ask?

I shake my head. Time for those questions later. First I must meet with the Eclipsers, who will hopefully be able to provide some answers as to what the hell is going on here. Though, of course, they'll all be convinced that I'm Mariah. And will be trying their best to get me to remember a life I never led. To convince me that my true memories are nothing more than a drug-induced lie.

She's utterly convinced she's from Earth.

I angrily push Duske's words to the back of my brain and firm my resolve. I'll go to the Eclipsers' meeting, hear what they have to say, ask my questions, then petition to be sent back home to Earth once and for all. Keep a low profile for a few weeks, until Duske and his men have given up looking for me, then go on with my real life and put this nightmare behind me. Renew my relationship with Craig, help launch the video game—hell, maybe I'll even go clubbing with Suzy.

But first I have to convince the Eclipsers to help me. I'm sure they won't be too pleased when I ask to go back. But they'll understand, right? I'll simply explain that no matter how much they wish I was Mariah, I'm not, and that they're just going to have to continue fighting their revolution without me. I mean, what can they really expect from me anyway? Charity only goes so far. And this isn't throwing a couple of quarters in a jar to help save polar bears from global warming. They're asking me to undergo a complete identity transplant and lead a revolution that I don't know anything about.

Dawn shows me the bathroom and explains how to turn on the shower. There's only cold, rusty water drizzling from the showerhead, but really, that's not a lot different from what I'm used to at the dorms. I wash my hair quickly, thankful they at least have sweet-smelling shampoos and soaps. From the black market, Dawn explained when he handed them to me moments before. He evidently went out and purchased some essential supplies while I slept, saying he wanted me to at least have a few comforts to wake up to. The fact that he did that, obviously at great expense, makes the soaps smell even sweeter and the cold shower almost pleasant. He really is a great guy. So sweet and thoughtful. Mariah's a fool to have left him.

After bathing, I wrap myself in a threadbare towel, suddenly realizing I don't have any clean clothes to change into. My one outfit is soiled and caked with blood, reeking of sweat from my narrow escape. I'm so not interested in putting that back on.

"Dawn?" I call out, peeking from behind the closed door. "Um, do you have anything I could wear?"

"One second." He appears in the doorway, a pile of folded clothes in his hands. He averts his eyes from my toweled body as he hands them to me. The consummate gentleman. "I borrowed an outfit from one of my neighbors. She's about your size."

"Thanks. I really appreciate that." The guy thought of everything, didn't he? This really is an alternate reality.

I close the bathroom door and slide the beige jumpsuit up one leg, then the other. It's a bit scratchy and more than a bit ugly, but beggars can't be choosers, right? I wonder what clothes Mariah keeps in her closet. Do we share the same fashion sense? Would she mind me wearing her clothes if we do? After all, we'll be the same size.

"Okay, ready," I say, appearing from the bathroom. I've tied my still-wet hair back in a messy ponytail and am wearing no makeup, but I feel fresh and clean and well rested. I slide on my boots and, on a whim, grab the sword belt and strap it around my waist, feeling more than a bit self-conscious about wearing a weapon. Especially one I have no idea how to use. But then I catch a glimpse of myself in a mirror. The jumpsuit actually fits. And there's a certain primitive style to it, I realize now—raw and powerful.

I can feel eyes on me and I whirl around, catching Dawn giving me a once-over. "You clean up well," he says, a small smile playing at his lips. I can feel my face heat at the compliment.

We walk out of the house and into the cave corridor, Dawn locking the front door with his thumb. It takes me a moment, as we head toward the town square, to adjust my eyes to the dim lighting. I think I would go insane down here long term. It's so depressing without the sun. My body lets out an involuntary shiver, cold. Dawn reaches over and rubs my back a few times, a much appreciated attempt at a quick warmup.

Dawn locates his hover bike behind a Dumpster, hands me a helmet, then gestures for me to climb aboard. I do, no longer uncomfortable with the idea of being forced to wrap my arms around his waist. In fact, I'm sort of looking forward to it.

Dawn revs the engine and the bike lifts off the ground. We float slowly through the Dark Side, residents coming out of their caves to wave to us, their faces alight and hopeful as they watch us fly by. I shake my head. Mariah sure must have been something special to garner this kind of unabashed worship from her people. What happened to make her betray them all in the end?

We pass through the town gates and then pick up speed as we enter the underground aqueduct tunnels. The ride is as exhilarating as it was the first time around—fast, furious, the wind whipping across my face. I scarcely notice the cold as I hug Dawn tight against me, melting into the ride, giving myself over to the sensations of motion and speed, the curve of Dawn's arched back, and me comfortably squashed against it. I shouldn't like it as much as I do.

We zoom down the tunnels, the underground world unfolding in seemingly endless twists and turns. We pass through several other towns identical to the one Dawn lives in. Bleak, brown, tattered. My enjoyment starts to dissipate as I catch the faces of scrawny children and browbeaten adults wandering the streets, without enthusiasm, without hope. My heart aches for them. How could the government let this underground ghetto exist while they thrive and frolic in a gaudy, opulent playground above? No wonder the revolutionaries are simmering with hatred.

"Why are they all deformed?" I ask as we leave the third area's gates. "I mean, what happened to make them that way?"

"There's radiation deep in the rocks that many Dark Siders are forced to mine," he replies. "It's amazing they can reproduce at all."

"Forced to mine?"

"The government needs crystals embedded in the rocks to run their supercomputers. So they keep the Dark Siders down here, work them as slaves to satisfy the needs of the high-tech, luxury-rich world above," he explains.

The bike's motor and the wind blend into a roar as we pick up speed, drowning out any chance of further conversation. I settle back against Dawn, feeling an overwhelming sadness for the plight of these people. I couldn't imagine a life like they led: stuck deep underground, forced to work a job that will poison not only their bodies, but also their children's. How could the government be so cruel? And how can the people aboveground accept the fact that their comfort comes at the expense of others? Are the Indys even aware of what's going on beneath the surface of their world? They can't be. There's no way they could consciously be so selfish, could there?

After about a half hour of travel time and a ride across a colorless and dismal underground landscape, we arrive at a large iron gate looming in front of us with menacing spiked bars. Dawn lowers his bike to the ground and dismounts, walking over to the gate, pressing his thumb against the sensor.

"Dawn Grey. REJECTED," a robotic voice pronounces solemnly. Dawn scowls and kicks the gate with his boot.

"Goddamn it," he grumbles. "The Eclipsers must have revoked my pass when I told them all to go to hell—when they first told me they were working to pull you out." He motions to the sensor. "Try your thumb."

I stare at him. There's no way my thumb will work here. Is there?

I get off the bike and walk over to the gate, fear making my heart pound. This is a test, I realize. A major test to see who I really am. I may look like Mariah Quinn, but do we share fingerprints? DNA?

I press my thumb against the sensor, sucking in a breath, not sure which outcome to pray for. Do I want the gate to open? Or do I want to prove I'm not who they think I am?

I don't have a choice. "Mariah Quinn," the robotic voice chirps, sounding a lot friendlier this time around. "Welcome back." The gates creak open, revealing a decrepit, windowless stone tower embedded into the cliff and stretching up into the darkness.

"Still convinced you're not Mariah?" Dawn asks, eyebrow raised.

For a moment I can't breathe, instinctively searching for my inhaler. Of course I don't have it with me, so I run through my breathing exercises instead while my mind grasps at straws. Maybe we've got some kind of alternate-reality-twins scenario going on here. She and I are different people but share the same fingerprints. Or DNA. Or whatever those thumb sensor things register. That could happen, right?

Keep rationalizing, Skye. Maybe at some point you'll talk yourself into believing.

I shake my head. No use to dwell on such things now. Better to just get to the Eclipsers and hope they can shed some light on this whole mess.

Dawn leads his bike through the gate and releases its kickstand. The gate swings shut behind us, coming together with a metallic clang that causes me to nearly jump out of my skin. I hurry to follow Dawn into the building.

The entrance was once made of glass-paned double doors, but the glass has long been smashed into oblivion and swept away. I'm careful as I step through to dodge the jagged shards still clinging to the frame. No need to accidentally cut myself on top of everything else. Who knows what kind of first aid they've got down here?

Through the doors is a small vacant lobby painted a dismal olive color that only succeeds in sucking out most of the already dim orange light coming from several table lamps scattered throughout. Cobwebs cling to every crevice, and the tables and chairs are covered in thick dust. It looks as if no one's entered this place in years.

I glance down at my boots. They're going to get filthy tramping around here. But wait—I do a double take; they're not dirty at all.

They're still as shiny as when I first pulled them onto my feet. I glance behind me for dusty footprints, but there's no sign I just walked through the lobby whatsoever.

I look to Dawn, head cocked in confusion.

"Optical illusion," he explains. "The floor's actually made out of a thin film screen. They project a dusty floor image onto it to make it look like the place has been abandoned. Really, they sweep every other day."

"Amazing." I crouch down to touch the floor. Sure enough, I can drag my finger through the dust and not get a speck of dirt on my hand. "You guys thought of everything."

"Actually, it was your idea," Dawn informs me. "Smart, too. You can't be too careful these days." He heads over to the antique-looking elevators at the far side of the lobby and presses a black button. "The last thing we need is for the government to start snooping around our headquarters. In fact, only a few people know this place exists."

The elevator doors open with a loud groan, sparking a question of its last safety inspection. But I keep my mouth shut and follow Dawn inside. Who knows, maybe this is another trick to keep the bad guys away. The door slides shut and I watch the mechanical dial counting up the floor numbers, fighting the urge to grab Dawn's hand. Not out of some misplaced romantic gesture, mind you, but simply because this whole place has me more than a little freaked out.

The elevator bings when it reaches the top floor, and the doors slide open. We're greeted by a much cleaner scene: a red-carpeted hallway stretching off into the darkness, dimly lit by small ceiling lamps every few feet. The whole place reminds me of that Tower of Terror ride at Disney World, and I jump off the elevator before it can send me spiraling down thirteen stories.

Dawn smiles and grabs my hand in his, squeezing it. "Don't worry," he assures me. "We're almost there."

"Great," I mutter, not willing to admit how much better I feel with his hand in mine. I grip him tightly as we walk down the nondescript hallway, passing door after door. Finally, we stop at one of them. To me, it's undistinguishable from the other dozen doors we've passed, but Dawn seems to know where he's going. He drops my hand and gestures to the tiny sensor I hadn't noticed by the handle. I press my thumb against it, grimacing as the robotic voice cuts through the silent hallway, addressing me once again as Mariah. Just what I need in this spooky place: a reminder that I may very well be the resident ghost.

The door slides open and we step over the threshold, into what appears to be an old vacant tenement apartment. There's tacky floral wallpaper, faded and peeling from the walls, cheap ceramic frogs and unicorns on the shelves, and cracked red vinyl couches and armchairs.

"What is this place?" I ask, glancing around the room. "I thought we were going to some secret headquarters." This can't be where the Eclipsers meet, can it? I mean, it's so ... tacky.

"Well, you're certainly as impatient as Mariah, I have to say," Dawn comments wryly. He walks across the room and points to a three-foot-high wooden bear statue standing like a sentinel in the corner. "Do you recognize Melvin at least?"

"Melvin?" I repeat, staring at the bear. "Well, back on Earth I have a stuffed bear I call Melvin."

Dawn's eyes light up. "Really? That's great. Maybe there is something left inside you," he says excitedly.

I shrug, not wanting to disappoint him. "It's just a stuffed animal. I mean, I wouldn't read too much into it."

But Dawn's still talking. "You and I went up to the surface once," he says. "We found this old resort by a dried-up lake. One of the crumbly places from back before the war. We wandered around a bit, until we came across an ancient wooden carving of a big brown bear. Obviously a relic of the prewar world."

"But wasn't that a long time ago? How could a wooden statue still remain intact?"

Dawn shrugs. "I don't know. But that's partially what made him so special to us." He looks thoughtfully at the statue. "In any case, we named him Melvin. And you loved him so much that the next time I was aboveground I stole a log and smuggled it back down here. Had it de-radiated and did my best to carve you a replica." His eyes shine as he relates the story. "Since then, Melvin here has always been a symbol of our revolution. A deified bear, if you will. Our symbol of hope. We know that no matter what happens down here, he's waiting up on the surface, withstanding weather, age, and radiation—never doubting that someday mankind will return. He's never given up faith after all these years, and so we decided neither should we."

I watch as he tells the story, his fingers tracing over the wooden bear's head. He's so passionate, so happy in this memory of a time shared with his precious Mariah. I suddenly find myself wanting desperately to be able to share it with him. I search inside myself, trying to imagine a taller version of the bear, trying to remember a love and affection for him. But I come up blank. Empty.

"I wish I could remember Melvin," I say wistfully.

Dawn walks over to me. "But don't you see?" he asks. "You do. You named your stuffed bear on Earth after him. That's too big to just be a coincidence. There must be something there, deep inside your subconscious. On some level you remember him. Maybe soon you'll remember other things too."

Or maybe not. But I can't stand to crush Dawn's glimmer of hope, so I keep my mouth shut.

"How did Melvin wind up here?" I ask, twirling around and gesturing to the tacky room. "Doesn't look like much of a place for a god bear to take up residence."

Dawn nods. "I agree completely. But you insisted. Said there would be no better guardian to keep the Eclipsers' secret headquarters safe." He walks back over to Melvin and presses two fingers into the bear's slightly rounded tummy. The back wall slides open, revealing a secret passageway leading off into the darkness.

"Wow. Melvin's a tricky little bear, isn't he?" I say, impressed.

Dawn grins. "He is a wise and all-powerful bear, indeed." He gestures me to follow him down the passageway. "Come on. We're almost there."

We walk down the hall, the wall sliding shut behind us. But for some reason I no longer feel frightened. After all, Melvin's standing guard behind us. What could possibly happen on his watch?

Dawn pushes open a door and we enter what appears to be a small conference room made entirely of metal. Metal chairs, metal table—even the walls are shiny, slick, polished. Several people stand around the table, all dressed in black high-collared jackets like Dawn's. They look up when we enter, voices trailing off into a hushed silence. They pause for a moment, and then one of them starts to clap. The others join in and soon the room is filled with applause, echoing off the metal floors and ceiling. I hover at the doorway, unsure how to react. Should I bow? Smile? Wave?

I catalog them quickly. Three women, four men, all of varying ages and looks, though a couple have the same glowing blue eyes as

Dawn. I wonder if that's some side effect from living underground. Maybe they have better night vision or something.

Before I can analyze further, I'm rushed by the mob, all of them evidently wanting to be first to give Mariah her welcome-home hug. Each seems determined not to have the others get a coherent word in edgewise, all talking over one another until I'm deafened by unintelligible babble.

"Hey, hey!" Dawn cries, his voice breaking through the cacophony. "Give her a second, okay? Back up! Jeez. Don't you all remember the three-foot-bubble rule?"

The room falls silent and the Eclipsers (for that's who I assume they are) retreat to their seats around the table, offering me precious breathing room and mumbled apologies. Dawn nods approvingly and steps forward to stand at my side. "That's better," he says, addressing the room's occupants as if they're all small children who need to be reprimanded. "I mean, really! I know you're all excited to see her, but you're as bad as the Dark Siders. Remember, the girl doesn't even remember who *she* is, never mind the rest of you clowns."

"Our sincerest apologies, Sister Mariah," offers an apple-cheeked, middle-aged woman at the far end of the table, nodding her head in apology. Her hair is cropped flush to her skull and she wears large golden hoop earrings. "It's just so good to see you. In the flesh. Among your people once again."

"Indeed," adds a twenty-something man with a trimmed black beard. His green eyes glow with enthusiasm as he looks up at me with what can only be described as unabashed adoration. "We weren't sure we'd ever see you again." He throws a self-satisfied smirk in Dawn's direction. "Though *some* of us had more faith than others."

Dawn holds up his hands in protest. "Fine, fine. Mock me if you must," he says with an amused smile. "But even you have to admit—pulling a 'Gazer back from Earth against her will? That's usually a mission impossible."

"Yes, well, that'll teach you to underestimate the Eclipsers!" cheers a teenage male in the back. He sports large silver piercings in just about every visible orifice (and probably some I can't see.) "We don't let some silly alternate reality get in our way." The others whoop in agreement and a spattering of high fives circle the table.

Their extreme enthusiasm sends a nagging sense of guilt straight to my insides. They're all so happy to see me. So excited to think they've finally gotten their long-lost Mariah back. How am I ever going to convince them that I'm not really her? And what will they think when they finally realize that all their hard work pulling Mariah out of Earth was in vain? At the end of the day, they got the wrong girl. One who can't help them—unless they have a video game they need testing. They need a brave, revolutionary leader to step up to the plate and save their world, but somehow got stuck with an incompetent club kid who can't even remember to save the electricity bill by shutting off the lights when she leaves the room.

They're going to be so disappointed when they finally face reality.

"Where's Glenda?" I ask, scanning the room but not seeing the serene face of my personal trainer among the motley crew. "I thought she'd be here." At least Glenda's been to Earth. She's met me as Skye. She'll probably be the easiest person to convince of the truth.

The Eclipsers grow silent. A few of them slump into their chairs. I frown. Was it something I said? Then Dawn touches my arm. "You know the woman who freed you from Duske's mansion?" he asks.

I stare at him, dumbfounded, the blood rushing from my face. "That was Glenda?"

Dawn nods.

I sink into a vacant chair as my mind replays the scene. Glenda, giving me my sword, urging me to jump. The guards dragging her away. She gambled her very life to get me out of that prison, and may have come up snake eyes.

"She was captured," I say, voice hoarse. "Do you think they … I mean, do you think she's …?" I trail off, not able to voice my fears.

"We're trying to get some intelligence on her now," explains a middle-aged Asian man at the left side of the table. "We think she might still be alive. After all, she's got a lot of information on the Eclipsers. Things the government would do anything to learn. Killing her would be counterproductive."

"At least without torturing her first," mutters the black-bearded man.

"Torture?" I repeat weakly, my heart sinking.

"Do not fret, Mariah," insists the apple-cheeked woman. "Glenda did not go blindly into this. She knew her mission was risky from the start, but she truly believed her life was worth sacrificing to save yours."

Guilt mixed with anger slams at my gut. I rise from my chair and lean my hands on the table as I stare at the Eclipsers. "But that's so stupid!" I cry, furious. "My life's not worth crap to you guys."

The room goes silent. The Eclipsers stare at me. Then the pierced teen pipes up. "Are you kidding? Your life is worth *everything*," he insists. "You're Mariah. You're our only hope." The others murmur their agreement.

Oh god, this has gone way too far. I squeeze my hands into fists and suck in a deep breath. It's time for these people to hear the truth. Face reality. "Look," I say flatly. "I don't care what you think. I'm not Mariah. You have the wrong girl. And even if by some weird stretch of psycho imagination I was once Mariah in another life, I don't remember anything about her. Or you. Or the revolution for that matter. I can't help you. I wish I could, but I just can't. I'm not the person you want me to be."

There. I said it. At least I can relieve my guilty conscience and know I've done everything in my power to tell them the truth. Hopefully they'll be able to accept this and no more insane sacrifices will be made on my behalf.

I look around the room, trying to glean whether they're buying my words. The somber faces sap my resolve. I've disappointed them. Crushed their hopes and dreams of getting their Mariah back. I slump back into my chair, scrubbing my face with my hands, feeling guilty and angry and helpless all at the same time. "God, I wish I *could* help you guys somehow. I really do. I mean, you went through so much to get me here. But I'm useless. Utterly useless."

The silence in the room is thick, thoughts heavy, eyes downcast. Then I feel hands on my shoulders. I look up and see Dawn standing over me, still by my side. His touch imparts to me a small strength.

"Don't look so glum," he says, addressing the room in a clear, confident voice. "Even without her memories, Mariah is still a powerful symbol of the revolution. She can still be much help in reinvigorating our people. We can present her to them tonight. Let them see that the news reports were false—that Mariah Quinn has returned to us and is still fighting by our side. Right now, that's all we need." He looks down at me. "Surely you can help us with that."

"I ... I guess so," I say, trying not to sound too reluctant. It's not that I don't want to help—how could I not, after seeing the desperate, hungry faces of the children below? But what can I actually do? I mean, this isn't some video game to test. They're asking me to lead a revolution. I'm so underqualified for this heroine/save-the-world stuff it's not even funny.

Still, they did so much to get me here. I feel I should do *something* before going back to Earth. *Something* to further their cause in some small way. To help those poor people find some sort of hope.

I realize they're waiting for me to speak. "Look," I say. "If you need help, well, I'll try to do what I can. But after that, you need to let me go. I've got to get back to my own life on Earth. There's a lot going on that I can't afford to miss." I decide not to go into detail about what that actually would be, on the distinct suspicion they may think it's less important than the salvation of their world. "Can you promise me that? If I help you, will you promise to send me back afterward?"

The room erupts in murmurs as the Eclipsers debate among themselves. Finally, the apple-cheeked woman turns to me, nodding. "Very well," she says. "We will respect your wishes. After all, we would never force someone to stay and fight with us if their heart lies elsewhere."

"Thank you," I say, surprised that they've agreed without an argument. I expected them to be more like Duske, I guess. Forcing me to stay against my will.

The woman continues. "I don't know if Dawn's told you, but there's a large gathering of Dark Siders tonight. A celebration, if you will—though there is little before now to actually cheer about. Would you be willing to make an appearance? You could simply stand onstage, let the people see you in the flesh." She rises from her seat. "They will likely be so heartened to realize that you have returned that they will scarcely notice you have nothing to say." She turns to the other Eclipsers. "Perhaps Mariah's presence this very night will be enough to invigorate the cause and motivate the people back into action. At the very least they will realize that she did not betray our cause, as the government caused many to believe."

I glance at Dawn, but he says nothing.

The Eclipsers all nod, appearing pretty excited about the plan. I smile, happy that I'm going to be able to help. I may not be a grade-A revolutionary leader, but I certainly can stand in front of a crowd and wave or something. And maybe that really will push their fight forward. Then I'll be able to go back to Earth knowing I've made a difference.

Satisfied, I glance again at Dawn. My face falls as I realize he's not sharing everyone's enthusiasm. In fact, his face remains tight, his expression frosty. My enthusiasm wanes as I realize I've disappointed him. But what can I do? He's asking for way too much. I can't live my life playing the part of his amnesiac girlfriend. In the end, it'll be better if he's able to just let go, to forget Mariah and all the pain she caused him and move on with his life. And me being around only serves to remind him of all he's lost—my presence bursting open the scabs time and time again, and his wounds never healing.

And besides, at the end of the day, no matter how sweet he is, how devoted he seems, he doesn't even want me. He doesn't want Skye Brown, the person I am. He's simply searching for Mariah's soul when he looks deep into my eyes. That's not fair to me. I deserve someone who will love me for who I am, not who he wishes I were.

"Then it's settled," the woman says. "And now, I guess, since you don't remember us, Mariah, some introductions are in order." She pats herself on the chest. "I'm Ruth," she says. "I'm the geographer. You need to get somewhere in Terra, you need a rabbit hole, call me and I'll get you where you need to go."

"And I'm Kayce," the bearded man beside her pipes in. "Techno-geek of the group. You need a gadget, I'm your man."

"You can call me Hiro," says the young Asian man at the back of the room. "I'm the weapons specialist. You want to relearn how to swing that sword on your belt, you come to me."

The others introduce themselves and their roles. Each has a different area of expertise or skill set. Together they seem to form a pretty dynamic group. I can see why they've had some successes, even though they are completely outnumbered by their oppressors.

"So, what was Mariah, then?" I ask. I'm still not able to use the first person when talking about my alter ego, even though they would probably prefer it.

"The inspiration," says Ruth with a small smile. "And the planner. You chose our fights and decided which objectives we would pursue when, and which were best left for another day."

"One of those objectives was Moongazing," I conclude.

Kayce nods. "You were never a fan of any government programs, but after Senator Duske introduced Moongazing, you decided to make it your ultimate crusade. You insisted that if Earth was such a great place, then everyone had the right to go, not only the rich."

I realize this is a chance to get some answers. "So those people—the rich—who Moongaze to Earth—do they all lose their memories?" I almost add *like I did*, but chicken out at the last minute.

"Depends," Hiro says. "If you're just going as a tourist, trying it out, you retain all of who you are. Of course, it's strictly forbidden to run around Earth telling everyone you're from another plane of existence. You've probably heard of people who have tried that— they get locked up pretty quick!" He chuckles wryly. "The idea is to blend. So when you finally commit and buy a permanent relocation package, you're allowed to choose from a variety of new professions. Actress, socialite, artist, stockbroker, what have you. The 'Gazer agents then set you up with a new life, based on your specifications."

"But do you remember your old life?" I ask again, not satisfied with his roundabout answer.

Kayce shrugs. "Supposedly. But who knows? No one making the permanent migration ever comes back. We only get scattered reports from the tourists. And since they always enter and leave from the same point—some nightclub, I guess—most never have time to venture outside the neighborhood they're dropped in. So, chances are they'll never run into the 'Gazing lifers, who are likely spread out all over Earth."

"This is all theoretical," Ruth pipes in. "We're not sure of all the details. That's why you started 'Gazing to begin with—to figure out how it all works. After all, you said you didn't want to advocate something you'd never tried yourself."

"This club," I say slowly, "it's not called Luna by any chance, is it?" It's a needle in a haystack with all the thousands of Manhattan clubs, but somehow I know I'm right.

Hiro snaps his fingers. "That's it," he says. "Why? Have you been there?"

I sit back in my metal chair, stunned. This is why Luna, which had once been a hole in the wall, had recently become the most popular club in town. I had blamed the Guest of a Guest writeup, but maybe that wasn't it at all. Maybe it had become a launching point for denizens of an alternate universe. After all, it *was* the place where I'd recognized the man from my nightmare. And I had blacked out there and woken up on Terra.

"Are the 'Gazers pretty well off when they jump to Earth?" I ask, remembering how the crowd had changed at the club from raver kids to high society practically overnight.

"Oh yes," Hiro says. "You get money. Especially if you're migrating permanently. You see, the government lets you try it out a few times, a few days here or there to see if you like the place. But when you finally commit, you're required to hand over all your Terran possessions to the government."

"And in exchange for giving up all your Terran possessions, you receive a bank account number to be used on Earth," Kayce jumps in. "That's your startup capital. After all, Terrans are essentially homeless, illegal aliens when they first arrive. But the government supposedly takes pretty good care of you, and you're certainly not forced out starving on the streets."

"So when you first get there, you're just wandering around, undocumented?" I ask.

"Yes. That's your first quest, from what we understand," says Ruth.

"Quest?" I scrunch my eyebrows. "What do you mean, 'quest'?"

Hiro shrugs. "Um, like a mission, I guess? From what we understand, Terrans are given a list of tasks to accomplish when they first reach Earth. They're rewarded for accomplishing these tasks with things like driver's licenses, Social Security cards, and money."

I stare at him. "It sounds like a game."

"Well, it is sort of, right?" Kayce says. "The game of life." He laughs. "I think the government is just trying to make things more interesting so 'Gazers will want to stay forever. After all, if they came back, the government would have to return all their money. I doubt they're very interested in doing that."

"They don't have to worry," pipes up the pierced boy who earlier introduced himself as Taryn. "No one ever comes back. Except you. And we had to pull you out by force."

"True," agrees Hiro. He looks a bit resigned. "Anyway, that's about it. The Indys are evacuating Terra on a daily basis. The government is taking over all their assets—houses, land, the works. The Circle of Eight claims the people are migrating to a better world—"

"But if that's true, how come none of them 'Gaze?" finishes Kayce. "That's the question."

"And that's part of what Mariah was trying to find out," I conclude.

"Yes. But if you ever did learn the reason, you never told any of us," Ruth admits. "And shortly after that, you were taken from us."

"What a horrible night," Hiro says solemnly. "The government kidnaps you and decimates our attempts to sabotage their seminar, all in one blow."

"Such an odd coincidence," Dawn mutters under his breath so only I can hear.

"But now we've brought you back!" Ruth crows. "An unquantifiable success for our team. We can only pray that your return—even if it's only temporary—will bring some hope back to the cause."

"Hell, I feel some of mine returning already!" cries Taryn, crossing the room and slapping me on the back. "I can't wait for tonight. I believe you're still you, even if you don't think so!"

I force a smile to my lips, hoping they'll buy the halfhearted expression. How did I get myself into this?

I shake my head. *Don't be selfish, Skye.* It's just one night. One event. And it's for a good cause, too. I'll do my part, help them out with a little inspiration, then head back to Earth tomorrow. Back to normalcy. I can put this whole thing behind me for good.

So how come I'm suddenly not so sure?

THIRTEEN

A few hours later I find myself standing behind a thick red curtain strung across some sort of large stage that's been carved out of solid rock. I can hear the crowd gathering on the other side, a building roar of excited murmurs, shouts and laughter rising above the pounding techno music that blasts from large speakers strategically placed around the cave.

"They sound like they're having a good time," I remark to Ruth, who is attaching a wireless microphone to the lapel of my jacket. Earlier, I was fitted with a new outfit: a sweeping black duster jacket, like the rest of the Eclipsers wear, tight black pants, knee-high boots. I now look the part. Hopefully I can talk the talk.

Ruth nods. "Indeed. The Dark Siders work hard all day, slaving away in the mines and factories. When they clock out, they're in desperate need of stress relief. Actually, it was you who came up with the idea of holding weekly gatherings. To dance and drink and let off steam. By doing this, you believed, it would cut down on the in-fighting and add to the community spirit of the different Dark Sider enclaves."

"And has it worked?" I guess it's not so odd to think of me, former club-kid girl extraordinaire with the DJ boyfriend, coming up with the idea to hold weekly dance parties. Maybe Mariah and I have more in common than I thought.

"Definitely. We've seen a marked decrease in violence since we started holding the raves. People work off their anger and frustration on the dance floor. And they get to know their neighbors better. It's made us into a more cohesive group, rather than a bunch of independent slave pods. And the more we can align, the more power we have to fight against oppression."

"We even have our own alcohol," Kayce says, stepping up with two drinks in his hand. He presents one to me. Clouds of purple steam rise from the glass, as if it's been dusted with dry ice. I take a tentative sip, immediately recoiling at the potency. I think I've just swallowed fire. Kayce laughs. "Yeah, strong stuff," he says. "Total black market. The government has their own watered-down gin they send down with the rations. Just enough to lull you to sleep, not get you rip-roaring drunk like this will. This," he says, taking a swig from his own glass, "will totally kick your ass."

I raise my glass in a salute. I guess there's no drinking age in Terra. "Here's to getting my ass kicked," I toast, then tip the glass backward and swallow the reminder. It scorches my throat and heats my insides. But it's worth it. After all, in a few moments I have to face the throng, pretend I'm their valiant leader, back from an alternate reality prison. A little liquid courage can't hurt.

"I wish you would have gotten a chance to talk to some of the Dark Siders while you were here," Ruth says, taking my glass from me and setting it on a nearby tray. "They're really amazing people. They have so little, and yet they refuse to curl up and die. They have a passion that's truly impressive. And you are solely responsible for it all."

"I wish I could have stayed longer," I say, honestly more than a bit regretful. There's so much here I'd like to learn. It's too bad I couldn't travel back and forth between worlds at will. Go back to Earth, help launch the game, take my finals, then come back here for summer break or something, helping them reinvigorate their cause. It would be nice to meet the people. The ones in town were so sweet. So welcoming.

"Okay, we're going to make the final preparations," Ruth says. "We'll come get you in a minute." She turns on her heel and walks over to another part of the stage, Kayce in tow.

"Are you ready?" Dawn asks, coming up behind me and placing his hands on my shoulders. His touch sends a now familiar tingle through me, but I try to ignore it. Getting all hot and bothered is not going to help me face the masses. Or face leaving Terra for Earth tomorrow.

"As ready as I'll ever be," I say, turning to him. I look into his beautiful glowing eyes. "Though I have no idea what I'm supposed to say. Did you write me a speech or something?"

Dawn smiles down at me and takes my hands in his. "You don't have to say a word," he says. "Just having you standing there onstage will be enough. The people will see that Mariah has returned. That she is leading the Eclipsers again. They will find hope and courage just realizing that."

I laugh self-consciously. It's still blowing my mind that people would see little old me as a symbol of hope. "Okay, if you're sure."

Dawn squeezes my hands. "I want to thank you for doing this," he says. "I can't imagine what it's been like for you. Thrown headfirst into a raging war and being told you're the leader of the losing side. It's got to be a lot to take in. And yet, you've agreed to help us. You can't begin to know what that means to the Eclipsers." He pauses, then adds, "What it means to me."

I can feel my face redden at his compliment. "Yeah, well, I mean, it's not really a big deal."

He catches my eyes in his, and my knees almost buckle at the intensity of his gaze. But he holds me up. "It *is* a big deal," he says softly. "It's a huge deal. So accept my thank you and don't argue."

I laugh nervously. "Okay, okay," I say, admitting defeat. "You're welcome. I'm glad I can help in some small way." And I am, I realize. I feel warm and fuzzy at the idea that I'm able to provide some solace to the masses just by being me, or at least Mariah. These people need a symbol of hope. I'm helping them. And in return, I'm helping Dawn. That's what matters. Thoughts of returning to my real life can be set aside for a bit. Tonight is about the oppressed people of Terra, the Dark Siders. And whatever little thing I can do to help their cause, I should be prepared to do.

"We're ready for you now," Ruth says. She reaches over and straightens my microphone. "Are you going to be okay?"

"Yes," I say, glancing back at Dawn, confidence, which has nothing to do with the alcohol welling up inside of me. "I think I am."

The music fades and I can hear the MC silencing the crowd. He's a pro, and a moment later the chatter and murmuring fades to an almost eerie silence. "It's good to see everyone out and about tonight," he says, his voice echoing through the cavern. "I know with the recent production increase mandates you've been working long, hard hours. And with the cut in rations, it's not been on very much food."

A few boos erupt, the crowd evidently not big fans of hard work with ration cutting.

"But tonight is a special night. And we have a special surprise for all of you."

"Tickets to Earth?" shouts one heckler, prompting a smattering of laughter and appreciative applause.

"Better," says the MC, a smile in his voice. "Tonight we have a very important guest here to see you."

"Is it the Circle of Eight?" another heckler calls out. "And have they agreed to let us tar and feather them?" More laughter. I love that they're able to keep a sense of humor through all they've suffered.

The MC shakes his head. "Even better," he says, then pauses dramatically. A hush falls over the crowd. It's as if this entire room of thousands is holding its breath at once. "Tonight only. Making her glorious return to Terra after months on Earth. I give you the one, the only—"

"Get to the center of the stage," Ruth urges, pushing me forward. The curtain begins to draw back. I take a hesitant step, all of a sudden not one bit ready to meet my public.

"Mariah Quinn!" the MC bellows as the curtain sweeps open. A spotlight shines down on me, blinding me where I stand. The crowd goes silent. I can feel thousands of eyes staring at me in shocked disbelief as I make my way to the front of the stage. Not sure what to do, I give the crowd a little Miss America–type wave. Cheesy, but I can't think of anything else on the fly.

Then it happens. One by one every member of the audience, every Dark Sider in the crowd, gets down on his or her knees. They raise their hands over their heads and open their mouths, one single word leaving their lips, over and over again. Pulsing, throbbing, electrifying.

Mar-i-ah. Mar-i-ah. Mar-i-ah.

The chant starts low, but grows in volume and intensity.

Mar-i-ah. Mar-i-ah. Mar-i-ah.

The sound washes over me. My name. I mean, *her* name, rolling off their tongues in an all-powerful caress.

Mar-i-ah. Mar-i-ah. Mar-i-ah.

I shiver, chills wracking my body with the power their chant invokes. I certainly wasn't prepared for this kind of worship. What could Mariah have possibly done to inspire such loyalty? Could her plans and actions actually have made this much of a difference in these people's lives? I wonder if she enjoyed this: playing the role of goddess. Everywhere she went, people worshipped her. Did she get off on it? Or was she a reluctant leader?

And again, what happened in the end? She left them high and dry? Abandoned them for a happier, richer life on Earth? Betrayed their eternal devotion—not to mention Dawn's love—to look into the moon?

No wonder Dawn hates her so much. She's beginning to strike a sour note with me as well. Not that in a way I'm not doing the same kind of thing, returning to Earth after this night and all. But the difference is, this isn't my fight. I didn't start something I couldn't finish like she did.

Not that rationalizing eases the guilt all that much as I look down at the people on their knees before me.

I open my mouth to speak, not at all sure what I should say, if anything. Still, I feel the need to at least send a few encouraging thoughts their way. After all, it's not every day I get bowed down to and chanted at.

"People of Terra," I begin, my voice quavering. "It has been a long time. I know you've been through some terrible ordeals while I've been away. And I know the government's asked you to believe some horrible things about my departure. But I stand here before you tonight, dedicated to our cause and asking you to renew your faith as well. I understand how easy it can be to settle into your daily existence. To give up and figure it's not worth fighting the good fight. But we all know, deep in our hearts, it is worth it. Every bead of sweat, every drop of blood, every tear shed—it all brings us one step closer to our ultimate goal. To freedom!"

The crowd leaps to its feet as one, cheering and clapping and whooping. I've got to admit, I'm pretty impressed myself. I have no idea where that speech came from. But I'm glad it touched them somehow. I steal a glance at Ruth, who's standing at the side of the stage. She's beaming and clapping. A sense of pride swells inside me. I've not let them down.

But suddenly the cheers are replaced by screams of terror. I look back at the audience and see armed men in silver-colored body armor bursting through the auditorium doors, throwing smoke bombs into the crowd, assaulting the Dark Siders where they stand.

"Stay where you are!" a voice from a megaphone commands. "You are all under arrest for violation of the Terra Code 1-55435-4. Unauthorized political gatherings are not permitted under the law."

Panic ensues, the blinded crowd trying unsuccessfully to dissipate before being knocked down by the gas fumes. It's total chaos—running, trampling, screaming, begging. I watch the scene in horror from the stage, my hands fingering my sword belt, wondering if drawing a weapon I don't know how to use will do any good. I'm so lost in the riot before me that at first I don't feel the hand at my arm, frantically trying to pull me offstage. Then something registers and I whirl around, ready to meet friend or foe head-on.

I realize it's Dawn, his face ashen and his eyes wide.

"They're looking for *you*," he says, his terror clear. "We have to get out of here. Now!" He thrusts a gas mask–like contraption at me and yanks another over his own face.

I don't need a second invitation; I pull the mask over my head.

Dawn leaps off the stage and I follow. My boot heel snaps as it hits the concrete floor and I'm forced to kick off my footwear and leave it behind. We weave into the panicked mob, pushing and shoving our way through the crush, heading for the exit. There's an overwhelming smell of sweat and fear, and the smoke from the bombs makes it nearly impossible to see where we're going. Someone steps on my bare foot, causing me to stumble, falling into the mob and onto the ground. For a moment I fear I'll be trampled to death, but Dawn grabs my hand and yanks me to my feet just in time. Then, without releasing his hold, he drags me down the side of the stage and into the orchestra pit.

We come to a small door cut into the stage, maybe once used as a discreet exit for musicians and their conductor. Tonight, it's a lifesaving portal. Dawn presses his thumb against a sensor and it swings open. We have to duck to make it through the small entrance. As soon as we're on the other side, Dawn pulls the door shut and the LCD lights turn red, letting us know it's been locked.

"Come on," Dawn says. "We can get out this way."

"What about the others?" I ask, looking back at the door.

"There's nothing we can do. It's more important to get you out."

"But we can't just leave them!"

"Mariah—I mean Skye," Dawn cries. "What are you going to do if you go back out there? Take on the entire regiment yourself? You're good with that sword, but not that good."

He's right. I know he's right. But it breaks my heart to think of the Dark Siders out there, being brutally punished for their devotion to me—er, Mariah.

"What if I gave myself up?" I asked. "I mean, if they're looking for me."

Dawn shakes his head furiously. "No. That won't help. And you'll be doing your people a disservice. They need you. They need to believe in you."

I give up. After all, it's not like I want to go turn myself in and face torture and death at the hands of crazed totalitarian government officials. And Dawn's right; there's nothing I can do at this moment to save those people out there. Better to live and fight another day.

"Besides," Dawn adds, "they'll be fine. We get gassed by soldiers on a regular basis these days. It's not pleasant, but they won't suffer any permanent damage."

Knowing this makes me feel a bit better as I follow Dawn down the dark passageway, past dusty trombones and tubas and stage props. At the end of the room there's a door. Dawn presses his ear to it before activating the thumb sensor.

"I can't tell for sure if anyone's out there," he says. "We'll just have to risk it."

He pushes open the door and looks from side to side. Then he motions for me. I step out into the hallway.

"We need to get to my bike," he says. "It's parked outside."

We rush down the corridor, the background of screams sound-tracking our journey. The smell of smoke and fear hangs heavy in the air. We turn a corner and stop short as we see our exit is blocked. Two burly guards, dressed in silver uniforms and wearing swords, are standing in front of the door. They look up and see us, and motion to one another.

"Great," Dawn mutters. "We're going to have to fight."

He's on them before they can pull out their communication devices and report. With strength and speed I've never seen, Dawn grabs the two of them by their necks and effortlessly lifts them a foot off the ground. They claw and kick and choke, but can't break free from his grasp of steel. His eyes are wild as he bashes their heads into one another, skulls colliding with a sickening crack. He releases them, their bodies crumpling to the ground. They're not getting up. Maybe ever.

I stare in disbelief at sweet, gentle Dawn, who has suddenly transformed into the Incredible Hulk right before my eyes. My thoughts fly back to the fight we had in the alleyway over the knife. He must not have been even trying.

"How did you ...?" I start to ask, amazed at his superpowers. But I can't finish my question. Someone grabs me from behind, yanking me by my hair. I whirl, drawing my sword on instinct as I turn and thrusting out my arm. The blade slices through my attacker's middle as if he were made of butter, meeting resistance only at his vertebrae, before completing its journey to the other side. The man's face freezes in a death gaze as his top half slides off his bottom and onto the floor. Blood spurts out like a waterfall, soaking me.

I sway, dizzy and light-headed, my eyes blurred with panic and fear. But I have no time to be sick or afraid. No time to hesitate. A second guard rises behind him, brandishing his own sword. I raise my weapon, hoping and praying I can either channel Mariah or pick up some sword skills on the fly.

"They've jammed the door," Dawn calls out to me, his voice panicked. "Try to fend him off while I decode it."

My katana flashes under the artificial light, almost as if it's shining with an inner glow. My opponent raises his own sword, smiling maniacally. He charges forward, swinging his blade in sweeping slashes—upper left to lower right, upper right to lower left. I stand still, my blade shimmering in the silence, judging his distance, then parrying just at the moment his sword's parallel to mine. The blades clash, and we strain against each other until his slides free. I leap back just in time to avoid his second swing, a calculated slash designed to slice me in half. My heart pounds as I steady my hands and prepare for round two.

He charges again, and I surprise myself with another easy block. Something deep inside me, emerging from some hidden recess in my brain, seems to be giving my hands effective instruction. Have my sword-fighting skills come from a few too many rounds of Mortal Kombat in my youth? Or am I really finding some inner Mariah?

I shake my head. Time to ponder the *why* later. Right now I have a sword fight to win. I check my opponent. Up close, I realize he's a bit overweight and drowning in sweat. His initial attacks have worn him out. Time to make my move.

I parry his weak attempt at a blow, then whirl and stab my sword forward, catching him off balance and off guard. He bellows in agony as the blade slips between his ribs, pinning him to the pillar. Blood soaks his silver uniform.

This time I can't bear it. My stomach heaves and I bend over to be sick. I can feel Dawn behind me, pulling me away. "The door's open. We have to go now!" he cries, yanking my sword out of my victim. It makes a disturbing sound as it's pulled free—a sound I can confidently say I've never heard before. Dawn tosses the blood-soaked weapon to me and I can feel my stomach lurch again. So much blood. So much death. All at my own hands.

But better them than me.

Dawn opens the door and we run down the corridor, jump on his hover bike, and zoom off down the black tunnels as fast as the vehicle can take us. We're really flying. I hold on for dear life, my heart slamming against my rib cage, my whole body shaking. The wind whips through my hair, through my jacket, freezing me to the bone.

We ride for what seems like hours. I can't help but keep turning around, paranoid that we're still being followed by sword-wielding maniacs. Unwanted visions of the invasion still parade through my mind. Both sides are locked in an endless war over a girl who isn't even remotely sure she's who they think she is.

But *am* I Mariah? Am I really? The thought nags and tears at me, unwilling to be ignored. Skye never picked up a sword in her life. I just fought like the bride in *Kill Bill*. How is that possible? I'd love to say I just got lucky, but I know that's not the case. I knew what I was doing. Somehow, some way, I was completely in control of my actions. How is that possible?

An uneasy chill shivers through me. It's not from the bike ride this time. Who am I? It should be an easy question. So, how come I'm starting to doubt the most obvious answer?

Dawn finally slows the bike and it settles back to the ground. He jumps off, then helps me do the same. My muscles are aching, my knees shake, my face is on fire. I look around, assessing my surroundings. We seem to be in the center of a Dark Sider community of some sort, but it appears deserted. At first I have the troubling thought that perhaps this is because its inhabitants are all lying unconscious back in the arena, but then I notice the crumbling buildings are covered in cobwebs. Either it's another illusion, like the tower, or this place hasn't been lived in for a while.

Dawn walks up to a metal door of a tall tenement building and yanks it open. We step into the ruined lobby. There are scuffed, dirty linoleum floors, a crumbling stone concierge desk at the far end. Faded paintings of children romping in the sunshine hang haphazardly from the wall, and a row of elevators stand to the right. It's similar to the lobby of the Eclipsers' secret hideout, but even more depressing, if that's possible.

"What's this?" I ask.

Dawn doesn't answer. He simply motions for me to do the thumb thing to call the elevator. A moment later, the door slides silently open. We step inside and Dawn pushes the button for the tenth floor. We shoot upward, the elevator car creaking and shaking from side to side as we rise.

Dawn and I both stare straight ahead, as if mesmerized by the numbers rising to meet our destined floor. The tension between us is thick. We don't touch, but at the same time, I can feel him just inches away. As I breathe in, his scent fills my nostrils—musky, dark, intense. I squeeze my hands into fists, trying to resist the overwhelming urge to give in to the near-escape adrenaline thrumming through my veins and throw myself into his arms.

The doors slide silently open, revealing a decrepit hallway with peeling wallpaper, pulled-up carpet, and trash strewn everywhere. Graffiti promises the apocalypse is near. Guess the taggers were right.

I follow Dawn down the musty corridor, careful not to step in puddles. Must be plumbing problems here on top of everything else. He certainly picked the most remote building in Terra to hide out in. Which, I guess, is probably best, given the circumstances.

He comes to a door and motions for my magic thumb again. I press it against the sensor, amazed that even here it works as a magical key. The door slides open and we step inside.

I gasp in surprise when I see the cozy apartment that greets me. If I hadn't made the journey myself I wouldn't have believed this well-decorated space was part of the building we just wandered through. There's a plush, cozy couch in one corner, a flat-panel TV hanging on the adjacent wall. A full-service kitchen leads off from the living room, complete with breakfast bar. On the walls are numerous framed photos of people. I take a closer look. Some I recognize as Eclipsers. Others are unfamiliar. But it's the center picture that grabs my attention.

It's of me, cuddled in Dawn's arms, both of us smiling happily into the camera. Dawn's face is so radiant, so unguarded and joyful. It breaks my heart. I glance over at him, standing awkwardly by the door, as if not sure to make himself at home. His fingers twitch by his side. His face is white and his eyes dart everywhere but to me.

Poor Dawn. Poor, poor Dawn.

Something inside me breaks—a thin filament keeping me together, keeping me hanging on to life on Earth and all the decencies that go with it. Blame it on the senseless attack and our narrow escape. Or perhaps it's just some lingering memory deep inside my subconscious.

Whatever. I just have to have him. Here. Now. Mine.

I cross the room in seconds, throwing myself into his arms. Smashing my face against his—seeking, finding his lips, his mouth. I slide my fingers from his cheeks to his hair, digging into the long smooth strands while my body hungrily presses against his.

He's still for a second, as if in shock; then he returns my kiss, opening himself to me fully, sharing all that he has to give without hesitation. He slams me against the wall, pinning my arms above me with one hand. His other restlessly explores, curving around my hip, dragging across my stomach. I shudder and let out a small squeak. The ache he's invoked is nearly unbearable. I twist my calf around his thigh, pressing myself into him. He wants me. Perhaps as badly as I want him.

"Dawn," I moan. "Oh, Dawn."

There's no response. I open my eyes, aware of a sudden emptiness, a sudden vacancy. It's then that I realize Dawn has retreated to the other side of the room. What the hell? Here I am, prostrate against the wall, panting, sweating, barely able to form a thought in my head, and he's gone off to read a magazine?

"But, wait—" I say, not sure what's going on. Why did he walk away? Fear and confusion shoot through me as I fight to regain my senses and figure out what happened. Did I do something? Say something? "Don't you want to … I mean …?" I'm not sure what to say, not sure what to do.

I can see his hands trembling, belying his nonchalance. He does want me. Wants to continue where he left off. But something's stopping him. What?

"Dawn, talk to me," I beg, my voice croaky and concerned.

"This isn't right," he says at last. "We shouldn't do this. After all, as you've told me a hundred times, you're not Mariah. You're not the girl I love."

An aching emptiness floods me as I manage to peel myself from the wall. I feel disgusted at myself. For allowing this to happen. For succumbing to my desire for a man I don't even know. One who's in love with someone else.

I look over at Dawn, at the pain and frustration clear on his face. He squeezes his hands into fists, staring so intensely at the ground I'm half afraid it will burst into flames. He's so passionate. So unguarded and desperate in his love for this girl who betrayed him. A part of me suddenly wishes I really was Mariah. To be the recipient of such intense, powerful devotion from this beautiful boy. To be loved with all of someone's heart, soul, and mind. I've never had that. My relationships have always been more about companionship and fun and hanging out than any kind of deep connection like he's experienced with his true love.

Fearless leader of Terra or no, Mariah must be one stupid girl. She had it all. Had Dawn's unwavering attention and yet she let it slide away. And now I'm the one left to pick up the pieces of this broken boy's heart. A walking, talking empty ghost of the person he once loved. I don't deserve his devotion. His passion. I've done nothing to earn it.

"I'm sorry," I say, though I'm not sure exactly why I feel the need to apologize. Am I sorry I kissed him? Sorry I let him act on that kiss? Sorry I'm not the girl he wishes I were?

"It's like making out with a ghost," Dawn mutters, half to himself, not acknowledging my apology. "To a shell of someone I once loved."

His words stab me in the gut. Just what I want to hear after opening myself up to a guy I'm really starting to like. I'm not good enough. I'm not the one he wants. The encounter between us meant absolutely nothing. Shame wells up inside me and my stomach burns. I feel so dirty, so vile. How could I have accepted his touch, burned under his mouth? Succumbed to a cheap, physical act and confused it with more that that?

I want to be sick.

"I'm sorry," Dawn says, catching the look on my face. "I don't mean it like that. I liked ... well, I mean ... It's just ... what are we doing here? There's no way we should be getting involved. You're leaving tomorrow to go back to your life. I don't want to get attached to you just to have you abandon me all over again."

"Right. I understand," I say stiffly. I sit down on the couch, as far away from him as possible. "I'm sorry. It won't happen again."

We're both silent for a moment, each locked in our own heads, trying to sort out what happened and what can be done about it. I'm desperate to change the subject. "So, um, where are we?" I ask. "Who lives here?"

Dawn releases a long sigh and I realize I've once again said something wrong. "This is Mariah's apartment," he says. Oh. Right.

"It's, um, nice."

He snorts. "Yeah, sure. You should have seen her parents' house."

"Oh right," I say, remembering Duske's story. "She was of some kind of royal blood, right?"

Dawn nods. "If Mariah had continued on the path she was born to take, she would have been one of the Circle of Eight by now," he says. "And probably married to Senator Duske."

I raise an eyebrow. "But he's so old."

"He's twenty years older than her. But that doesn't change how he feels about her," Dawn replies. "That's probably why he allowed her to Moongaze to Earth instead of killing her when he had the chance."

"Interesting." No wonder he'd been staring at me like that back at his house.

"In any case, the Circle of Eight consists of four men and four women, and the positions are passed down from generation to generation," Dawn explains. "The idea is that unlike the democracy we had before the war, no appeal for votes or campaign contributions will force the governing official to be swayed in policy. The Circle will always be in power, and therefore there is no threat to them ruling fairly and decisively." He shakes his head. "That's the bull they feed us, anyway. In reality, the Circle is probably more corrupt than any democracy ever was. And because you can't vote them out of office, they are able to do anything they please."

"Absolute power corrupts absolutely," I murmur. "So, what made Mariah decide to rebel?"

Dawn is silent for a moment, staring at the blank wall in front of him. "She met me."

"Ah. So it was like a postapocalyptic Romeo and Juliet kind of thing? Indy and Dark Sider?" I'm almost amused at the cliché.

Dawn snorts. "Not exactly." He fiddles with a ring, pulling it off and on again. "I wasn't always a Dark Sider either."

I raise an eyebrow. This I did not expect. Though I guess I should have—after all, he doesn't have the deformities of the others. "So you were an Indy as well?"

"It's a long story."

"I don't think we're going anywhere tonight."

Dawn gives me a rueful smile. "It's also a big secret. If word got out about who I really am, I would be killed on sight."

I remember the identification card back at his apartment. "So, what? Are you on some ten most wanted list or something? I kind of figured all the Eclipsers were anyway."

"The Eclipsers are a nuisance to the government, yes," Dawn says. "But I'm a walking, talking liability. And the Senate doesn't exactly like to leave loose ends like me wandering around."

"What do you mean?" I'm beyond curious.

"Look," Dawn says, turning to me. His blue eyes are earnest and concerned. "What I'm about to tell you can't leave this room. If they find out who I really am, they'll track me down and kill me without a moment's hesitation." He rakes a hand through his hair. "I'm trusting you here. Am I right to do so?"

"I'd never betray your secret," I assure him. I lean forward on the couch, eager to hear what he has to say. What secret could be so big?

"The surface of our world, as you know, was made unlivable after warring nations decided to bomb each other into oblivion," Dawn explains. "The types of bombs they used allowed for the decimation of life without destroying the infrastructure. So there are a lot of treasures up there on the surface. Stuff the government would kill to possess."

"I can imagine."

"In any case, my birth wasn't the result of two people making love," Dawn continues. "I was an experiment by the government.

Egg, sperm, and a boatload of cybernetics—all mixed together in one big genetic soup. A few semiconductors in the brain, lead/titanium plates under my skin, and the pièce de résistance—a palm implant that emits special radioactive nanoparticles, which allow me to heal people." He stares down at his hands. "I don't know all the details. Never got to see my own blueprint. But the idea was to create superhumans who were immune to radiation. Beings who were extra strong and able to go up to the surface and labor for long hours, looting old buildings and bringing their treasures back below."

"So you're a ..." I'm not sure what word I'm looking for.

"Nothing awful," Dawn assures me. "Just a genetically enhanced human. I'm flesh and blood like you. I can feel. I can think. I have all the emotions a regular person would have. Only more."

I nod, feeling a bit relieved that I hadn't just been making out with a robot.

"That's how I healed your arm," Dawn adds. "I was created to be a surface medic. To take care of the others when something went wrong."

"That's a pretty useful skill," I remark, glancing down at my wrist. You could never even tell it'd been broken. "So, what happened? Obviously you're not working on the surface now."

"The experiment was a failure. No matter how hard they tried, they couldn't create a radiation-proof neuro-Terran—or nT, as they call us. Eventually, just like any human, we'd get sick. But did the government decide to stop the program when they learned this? No." He shakes his head, disgust twisting his mouth into a frown. "The treasure retrieval is too valuable to their operations. So they continue to use us. Once we become too sick to work, they dispose of us and create new nT workers to fill our slots. Luckily for them, we're cheap to manufacture."

I stare at him, horrified. "They'd dispose of you? Like, kill you?"

"They call it 'retiring.' But yeah, it's pretty much just murder. Though by the time they take someone off the job, they're so sick with radiation poisoning, it's almost better to die and get it over with."

My stomach churns with nausea. How can anyone do something like that to another person? "How do people stand for that? How can they just sit back and watch it happen?"

"Easy. The government tells people that the nTs are nothing more than mechanical creations. That we're metal monsters with no feelings."

"And people believe that."

"Some do. Some don't care either way. They choose to stick their heads in the sand and ignore all the atrocities. The government pacifies Indys any way they can—alcohol, drugs, little luxuries, and nowadays, Moongazing. When life is good and you're feeling happy, people tend to ignore what's going on, as long as it's not in their faces. Indys figure it doesn't involve them. They don't know any nTs, so they simply don't care what happens to us. Just like they don't care what happens to the Dark Siders."

I screw up my face in disgust. "I can't believe they'd just look the other way, enjoy their lives, sponsored by the labors of the exploited classes."

"In their defense, some don't know the truth," Dawn amends. "They believe what the government tells them. That the nTs are manufactured worker robots without feelings or family. If you think of it that way, the fact that we're supposedly disposable doesn't seem all that bad. I mean, would you feel empathy for a burned-out toaster oven? No. You'd be happy it was useful while it lasted and quick to replace it once it wore out."

"So that's where Mariah came in," I conclude. "She learned the truth about the nTs and decided she wanted to help."

Dawn nods. "We met accidentally. I had escaped my work crew, broken a tunnel seal, and shot down a rabbit hole. Dazed and confused and lost, I wandered into Luna Park. I didn't know where I was or what I was doing. Mariah found me hiding in a ditch. She felt bad for me, I guess, and took me into her home and fed me. Risked her life to save mine, to hide me when my platoon came looking. No matter what, I'll always be grateful to her for that."

"And then you fell in love."

Dawn smiles, his eyes far away. "We did. She was so passionate. So angry when she learned the truth about what the Circle was actually doing to people. She decided then and there that it wasn't enough to save only me. She wanted to save all of us."

"And so she started the Eclipsers."

"First, she went around trying to garner support among her own friends. Other wealthy Indys and Circle members. They mostly just laughed at her. They said she should give up her silly crusade and get back to her training. Take her chosen position in the Circle of Eight and then she'd be free to voice any concerns she had there."

"That does seem like a reasonable idea. I mean, she would have had the power."

"Not really. It is a circle of *eight*, remember. Each member still must accede to the majority. And Mariah realized very quickly that she'd never be able to gain support from within. The Senate is too set in its ways. Too greedy. Without the Dark Siders and nT slave labor, the economy would collapse. No one was interested in their extravagant lifestyles being taken from them just to relieve the daily drudgery of a working class they never even met."

"So then, what did she do?"

"Well, she did manage to drum up some support from a few sympathetic Indys. And so, with their help, she formed the Eclipsers. She set up secret meetings and laid the seeds of our eventual revolution. At first her ideas were small, but as she grew into her new role, she began to implement major initiatives designed to improve day-to-day life for the Dark Siders."

"They must have been thrilled to have her," I remark, remembering the throng chanting her name.

"Oh yes. The would-be senator who lived down in Stratum Three, getting her hands dirty while helping the Dark Siders? No one had seen anything like it. And the people fell in love with her. She was so well-spoken, so strong in her belief that they could really make a difference—she quickly became a symbol of hope for the people. She gave them something to live for."

"It must have been so satisfying. To see them start to dream again."

Dawn nods. "It was great. But it was also really hard. The pressure was a lot for Mariah to handle. The Dark Siders began to see her as some kind of demigod, and made their demands accordingly. And she was just a girl. No magical powers, no enhanced DNA. By the end of each day she was exhausted—not to mention an outcast among her former friends and family. She couldn't return to her home. Her own mother, Senator Estelle, denounced her as a traitor and a threat to the Circle. She swore up and down it didn't bother her, but we all knew she was lying."

I consider this. No wonder Dawn's not interested in me. He's got this super ex-girlfriend, able to leap social injustices in a single bound. And here I am, a silly gamer geek from Manhattan. I'm nothing compared to the great, illustrious Mariah Quinn. Nothing at all.

"She sounds like an amazing person," I comment quietly.

"She was," Dawn says, staring down at his hands. "Until she succumbed to addiction."

I cringe. "That must have torn you up inside. To watch her start to slide away like that."

"It did," he admits. "But still, I never dreamed she'd go so far as to actually betray us to the Senate—her own archenemies. I guess I underestimated the extent of her problem." He shakes his head. "I still remember that night, clear as if it were yesterday. The soldiers rushing in, brandishing weapons, cutting down the Eclipsers where they stood. Watching as all of our great plans were decimated in one fell swoop." He fists his hands. "We had the opportunity to show the population what atrocities the government was inflicting on the Dark Siders. A chance to sway them to our side once and for all. Instead, because of Mariah's betrayal, that night became just one more atrocity and the Indys still have no idea what's really going on in Terra. But I've told you all this before. You don't need to hear it again."

The pain in his voice is tangible. I can't imagine how he must have felt that night as he realized what was happening. To have the person you love more than anything turn on you and destroy everything you've worked for—it must have been devastating.

"We fought back, of course," Dawn adds, unable to let it go. "But we were greatly outnumbered. In fact, it was a massacre. And I just remember thinking over and over again, *Oh Mariah, what have you done to us?*"

"You're *sure* it was Mariah?"

"Think about it. She was a strung-out junkie, wanting to make that last migration to Earth. She had no money—she'd emptied her savings to help fund the revolution long ago. How did she get to Earth? She had to pay somehow."

"Right. I can see where you would think that." Still, something wasn't adding up. How could someone be so passionate about a cause one day and then abandon it and sell out her friends the next? There had to be some missing piece to this puzzle.

"So," Dawn says, "the next time I saw her—you—was in that alleyway on the outskirts of Luna Park. Obviously I was more than a bit confused at that point. I'm sorry about my reaction."

"It's okay. I understand completely, given the circumstances."

Dawn rises from his seat and stalks the length of the room. He takes the photo of him and Mariah off the wall and studies it closely. "It's still not easy," he says, looking back at me for a moment before returning his focus to the portrait. "You look like her. You smell like her. You walk and talk and have all of her mannerisms. But you don't have her inside you. You don't remember me. Our life together. You don't remember all we had—what you threw away without ever telling me why!" His voice breaks on the "why," and he slams his fist into the wall, punching easily through the plaster.

Empathy consumes me as I watch him lean his head against the wall. It's impossible to comprehend what he's feeling. His true love, discarding him like an old habit, betraying not only him, but everything they'd fought for. No wonder he'd acted so hateful toward me. I'd hate me too.

I approach him slowly. He's shaking, hands still in fists. His face is crimson. His eyes narrow, and he's still seething with anger. I'm half afraid that if I touch him he'll hit me, knock me across the room with his superstrength. But at the same time, I know he needs me. On some base level, he knows it, too. And so I risk it, coming up behind him and wrapping my arms around his waist, burying my head in his back, squeezing him tight, not saying a word.

At first he's stiff, resists my touch. Refuses to accept my offer of comfort. But then he breaks. His muscles relax under my hold. I can feel his hard swallow, and a moment later he turns to face me. His eyes are rimmed with angry tears.

He reaches up and brushes the back of his hand against my cheek. A shiver flitters through me. "I should kill you," he says. "For what you've done to me. For what you've done to the Dark Siders. And yet, I can't manage to hate you. No matter how hard I try."

His words break my heart. I can't bear it—all this pain, all this hurt. If only there was a way to take it away. To draw it into my body and leave him with nothing but peace. Instead, I stand uselessly. Holding him. Giving him as much comfort as I can.

We stand there for what seems like hours, barely moving, just looking into each other's eyes. The connection between us, the bond, is so strong it makes me want to cry.

"It's late," he says finally. "And you've had a big day, if not a long one. It's best if you get some rest. I'll take the couch."

He breaks away, and emptiness consumes me once again. I want to run across the room and throw myself back into his arms, beg him to hold me for just five more seconds. Or minutes. Or hours. Or years. Instead, I head reluctantly to the bedroom and collapse on the bed, not bothering to flip on the light.

I'm so exhausted I assume sleep will take me immediately. But there's too much swirling around in my mind. And it's too hard to hear Dawn breathing in the other room. He's way too far away for my liking. I contemplate my options for a moment, then give in to my desire.

"Dawn?" I call out. My voice sounds plaintive and hesitant.

In half a second, he's in the bedroom. "Do you need something?" he asks, shifting from one foot to the other.

I swallow hard before nodding. "Yes," I say at last. "Would you mind ... I mean, I'm feeling a little uncomfortable and scared in here by myself. So much has happened. This is all so strange and—"

"Anything. Name it."

"Could you come in and sleep next to me?"

I see his silhouette in the doorway; he both enters and retreats at the same time. "I ..." he starts. "I don't know if—"

"Look," I say. "I don't know about the past or anything, or all the things you think I did. But I do know that whoever I am, I need this. I'm not asking for anything. Just—I need a friend. I don't want to be alone."

He enters the room, shirtless, dressed only in a pair of flannel pants. His chest is as powerful as I'd imagined, all sharp planes of muscle, taut and toned. A few harsh scars mar the otherwise perfect flesh, but they only serve to make him more fascinating. He crawls into bed behind me, wrapping his arms around my body and spooning me close. He nestles his face in my hair and I can feel his hot breath gently tickling my earlobes. I snuggle closer so that our two bodies touch as much as possible, feeling warm, safe, protected. There's a part of me that wants nothing more than to flip around, kiss him full on the mouth. Find out what it's like to make love to this beautiful man. But I know this is not the time for that.

Right now, this is enough.

FOURTEEN

I wake up, still wrapped in Dawn's arms. For a moment I don't move; I just lie there, enjoying his warm body snuggled against mine. It's so strange. I barely know this guy, yet I already have such a deep connection to him. I should be feeling overwhelmingly guilty, lying here in another guy's arms. But right now, my Earth relationship with Craig seems so distant. Almost unreal. As if it were a dream I once had.

It's going to be hard—torturous—to go back to Earth, I realize. To leave Dawn and all he's beginning to mean to me. But in the long run, what choice do I have? We each have our own separate lives and destinies. And while, for a brief moment, the stars aligned and we shared something special, that's where it has to end. An alternate reality one-night stand, I guess. And now, as morning breaks, it's time to say good-bye.

I shift in his arms, rolling over so we're face-to-face. He opens his eyes, mere inches from mine. A beautiful, sleepy blue, they sparkle like crystal from under his long sooty eyelashes. He smiles a shy smile and reaches up to brush a lock of hair from my face. My heart breaks at the simple gesture. How am I going to say good-bye to him?

"Good morning," he whispers, kissing me lightly on the nose.

"Good morning," I say. Wishing I could wake up this way every day for the rest of my life. But that's impossible. I know it. He knows it. And we both need to stop pretending and face it.

After a few more minutes.

We lie there together, legs and arms intertwined, stroking each other softly, neither person very interested in moving away. At last, he grins sheepishly and sits up, running a hand through the long strands of his tousled hair. "Would you like some breakfast?" he asks. "I could go stand in line to see if they're doling out egg-synths this morning. It's a long shot, but you never know."

I shake my head. "No, it's okay. I'm not hungry." I'm actually starving, but I can't bear the thought of making him go wait in line. Or even get out of bed.

"It's probably for the best anyway. That fight last night—when I was bashing those guards' heads together. I'm afraid one of them might have realized what I really am."

My cozy thoughts fade as I remember all that had happened the night before. "What will they do if they figure it out?" I ask.

"Work to kill me, probably," Dawns says with a shrug.

I sit up, horrified, worried. "No! They can't! That's … that's …" I don't know how to appropriately express my horror.

What difference does it make? a voice jeers in my head. *Dead or alive, after today you'll never see him again.*

My heart pangs and I want to cry. I need to get back to Earth. I have to. But how can I leave Dawn behind? And I already know he won't come with me. If he wouldn't leave for Mariah, there's no way he'd leave for Skye.

Dawn looks at me, a thoughtful expression on his face, then he rises from the bed. "Bathroom," he says. "Then we get dressed and head over to HQ to assess the damage."

"But what about …" Did he forget? Great. That's going to make this whole thing even tougher.

Dawn stops at the doorway, shoulders slumped, frozen in place, obviously remembering. "You still want to go back," he realizes aloud.

"Well, I mean, um, yeah," I say, stumbling over the words. It's hard to talk when everything inside me is begging that I reconsider. But no, it's impossible. I have a life on Earth and I need to go back. I have responsibilities, commitments, family, friends. I can't just abandon them all, can I? After all, isn't that the same thing Dawn condemns Mariah for doing, going the other way?

Is what you have on Earth really so special? the voice inside me nags. *Don't you think you could do a lot more good by staying here?*

"Fine," Dawn says, leaning against the door frame. "I'll drive you to Moongazer Palace instead. Let you get on with your life. Sorry to have kept you here so long." But he doesn't sound sorry. He sounds angry.

"Thanks," I say, trying to shake off the ache that's settled into my bones. "I'd appreciate that."

Dawn stalks out of the room. A moment later, I hear the bathroom door slam shut. I curl into the fetal position on the bed, wracked with guilt. How can I do this? Just leave him? Leave the Dark Siders. Go back to my life and never return. Never even hear how their fight ends, if they eventually won equality or were resubjected by the government.

I try to remind myself of all that I'll be going back to: RealLife—finally released to the public. Craig—poor guy, I've been so vacant of late. School, homework, my family. Why does it all suddenly seem empty and meaningless?

My troubling thoughts are interrupted as Dawn returns, standing silhouetted in the doorway. "Well?" he asks, his voice cold. "Let's get a move on. I have a lot to do today after I drop you off."

I crawl out of bed, the cold air biting at my bare legs as I abandon the blanket. Dawn steps aside as I walk out of the bedroom, but I can't help catch a glimmer of hurt in his eyes as I pass. It makes me ache inside, to recognize the pain he can't completely mask. Obviously deep inside he's been hoping, praying, that somehow, some way, I'll magically transform into the girl he loves. The girl capable of leading a revolution.

But, I remind myself, even the illustrious Mariah left in the end. And now, through me, Dawn has to relive her betrayal, her exodus to Earth, all over again. Not that it's fair, really, to compare the two scenarios. Not totally. She left her world. I want to return to mine. But for some reason, that doesn't make me feel any less guilty.

"Before you go," Dawn says slowly. "May I show you a few things?"

"Sure," I say—probably too quickly, too eagerly, desperate to spend a few more minutes with him. But life on Earth has waited this long; it can wait a few hours longer.

"Okay. Go shower and get ready." He sounds more cheerful already. "We'll make a few stops before heading to Moongazer Palace."

I shower and change, finding a closet stuffed full of clothes.

Mariah's clothes. I choose something simple: a plain pair of black pants, corset top, and trench coat. No need for frilly skirts and platform boots today, no matter how cute they are.

We head out of the apartment, across the water-soaked hallway, down the creaky elevator, and through the dismal lobby to where Dawn parked his hover bike. We get on the bike and zoom through the tunnels. I want to ask where we're going, but I don't feel much like shouting over the roar of the bike.

We stop at a small building, its metal facade built into the rock. Once inside, I recognize immediately that it must be some kind of one-room schoolhouse. A couple dozen Terran children of various ages sit cross-legged on the floor in front of a teacher who is reading from a tattered book. The children are dressed in rags and some of them wear soiled bandages wrapped around their arms or heads. All are terribly mutated. Extra fingers. Third eyes. Humped backs. They're hideous in appearance, yet the light shining on their faces as their teacher reads makes them somehow more beautiful than a playground full of Gap Kids models.

"The government doesn't allow the Dark Siders to go to school," Dawn explains. "They figure a little education can be dangerous, so they banned it. Kids are supposed to go to work in the mines as soon as they're old enough to carry rocks. But Mariah felt everyone should learn to read and write. She said the more knowledge we could acquire, the less helpless we would be."

"That makes sense," I say, taken aback by the sight of a child with an extra arm trying to write on a clay slate.

"So we rotate them in and out. One week mining, the next learning. That way there always appear to be children in the mines if the government comes down to check up on us," Dawn says. "The problem is getting teachers. That's one of the reasons Mariah was so desperate to bring more Indys to our side. Sister Anne here is one such instructor. She's retired from her headmistress job in Luna Park and risks her life daily to come down here to teach. If the government knew of her behavior, she'd be punished for sure."

I look at the teacher with newfound respect. "So, some of the Indys do help?"

"A few. Not enough. Not by a long shot. Most Indys are too blinded by whatever the government dangles in front of them. They spend their lives enjoying the restaurants and alcohols and shops. And now there's 'Gazing. Why help the people in your own world when you can hop over to a better one?"

Once again I feel that pang of guilt stab at my gut. Here I am, judging the Indys, when really, aren't I just as bad? Wanting to go back to Earth, refusing to help these poor people, these destitute children whom I could easily teach to read and write if I wanted? When I'm back, will I be able to forget their faces? Or am I in for a lifetime of guilt, knowing I turned my back on them?

Bet you wished you chose the blue pill, Neo.

This wasn't fair. At least Neo was given a choice. He wanted to know. I never asked to be dragged into Terra. To learn the truth of its world. I would have been totally content living out my days in the Matrix, innocent and unaware of it all.

But now that I've seen it, what can I do?

The teacher looks up from her book. Her face brightens as she sees us at the back of the room. "Mariah," she cries. "Oh my goodness, children, look who's here! It's Sister Mariah!"

The kids break into applause and I can feel my face heat at the oh-so-undeserved praise. Here I am, standing, wishing I'd never met them, and they're gazing up at me like I'm their savior.

I give a weak wave. What else can I do? I'm not cruel or selfish enough to disappoint a room full of poverty-stricken, mutant children.

"Mariah used to come here and read," Dawn whispers. "Even with her busy schedule, she always made time to do it, at least once a week. And she brought the best stories with her. Stolen from the Indy libraries above."

I nod, suddenly realizing what I should do. I take a step forward. "Well, guys," I say. "I didn't bring a book today, but if you like, I can tell you a little story."

The kids cheer. Sister Anne smiles gratefully, standing up so that I can take her seat. I walk to the front of the room and sit down, facing the kids, letting their radiating joy beam onto me like sunshine as they wait with bated breath.

I smile back at them. "Once upon a time ..."

I tell three stories—each taken from adventures created for the RealLife video game—my rapt audience begging for more each time I finish. Finally Sister Anne laughingly waves them down, saying that obviously Mariah has more important things to do and they need to let me get on with my day. I reluctantly agree, though I'd have stayed for another hour or two if she hadn't intervened.

I've never had such a captive audience.

I rise from my seat, wave good-bye to the children, then head to the back of the room where Dawn stands waiting, a small smile on his face. One of the children, a blond pigtailed pixie, runs over and throws her arms around my legs, squeezing me with a tiny fierceness.

"I knew you'd return, Sister Mariah," she murmurs, refusing to let go. "I just knew it."

Her words are almost too much. I shoot a look at Dawn, feeling the tears well in my eyes. He smiles at me, looking a tiny bit smug. So, this was his plan when he said he had to "show me a few things"? His clever way to convince me to stay?

He certainly is making it harder.

"What's your name?" I ask the little girl.

"Crystal," she says, then sticks a dirty thumb in her mouth.

"Well, Crystal, you study hard in school and someday you can grow up to be an Eclipser, too," I tell her.

She grins from ear to ear and prances back to her classmates. "I'm gonna be an Eclipser," she brags. "Sister Mariah told me so."

We say our good-byes and exit the schoolhouse. I give one more longing glance as we board the hover bike. Those children, their faces so full of hope. What lives are they destined to lead?

"Can I show you one more thing before we go?" Dawn asks.

"Sure," I say, giving in easily this time. The last thing I want to do right now is leave.

Our second destination turns out to be a secret underground greenhouse. The workers take the time to show me how they carefully cultivate plants and give them the artificial sunlight they need to survive underground. The greenhouses, like the schoolhouse, are illegal. The government doesn't allow Dark Siders to grow their own food—they're supposed to only eat rations grown on government-sanctioned farms. But rations are always being cut, the gardeners explain, and the old and sick Dark Siders are often left out completely. The government doesn't seem to have a problem with starving their slave labor force once they've become superfluous.

"So Mariah decided it would be good if we created our own food to supplement rations. We stole the technology from the government-sanctioned places—after all, Dark Siders usually make up most of the labor—and started our own," Dawn tells me.

"Maybe someday we'll be able to completely feed ourselves and not be dependent on them for food. That'll be a major step toward our independence."

"I'll bet," I say, walking up and down the rows of plants. "I can't believe you can grow all this stuff underground."

"They're specially bred plants that don't need as much light for photosynthesis."

"Next thing you're going to tell me is you have a whole hidden underground farm. With cows and horses."

Dawn beams. "Now that you mention it ..." He reaches for my hand. I hesitate a moment, then slide my fingers into his. "Come with me."

We get back on the bike and zoom down another tunnel, this time going deeper underground. Finally, we come to what appears to be a dead-end, the passageway blocked by crumbling rubble, as if there was a cave-in long ago. Dawn parks his bike and motions for me to follow as he weaves through the boulder field. I keep up, wondering what on earth—make that Terra—he's going to do when he arrives at the dead end.

"Where are you going?" I ask.

"You'll see."

He stops right in front of the massive wall of rubble. Then he turns around, winks at me, and steps right through! The rocks shimmer a moment, and suddenly I'm alone on the wrong side of the wall.

"Another optical illusion?" I ask, wondering if he can hear me on the other side.

He pops his head back through. The effect is more than a bit disconcerting. "Something like that," he says. "Gotta hide our most valuable treasures any way we can."

I take a deep breath, put out my hands, and take a step toward what looks like solid rock. Sure enough, my hand slides through easily and I manage to step to the other side with no effort at all.

"Huh," I say, looking back. On this side, it appears as if there's no barricade whatsoever. I can even see Dawn's bike, parked down the road. "You guys really have thought of everything."

"Well, Mariah believed if you have secrets as important as we have, we'd better do a damn good job hiding them," Dawn says. He steps up to a massive steel door set into the wall, complete with a high-tech combination lock.

"No thumb sensor?" I ask, raising an eyebrow.

"No," Dawn says. "Only a handful of people know the combination to this safe, and we change it every few weeks so that no one can give it away, even under torture. After all, a thumb can be amputated." He turns the combination lock a few times and the door squeaks open. "Here we go." He bows. "After you, m'lady."

I step through the door and gasp as I realize what's on the other side: a series of metal cages, cut into the caves. Each contains animals. Cow, goats, chickens. It's a regular Old McDonald's farm.

"Nice," I say, wandering from cage to cage. "I haven't seen an animal since I got to this place. Duske told me they were practically extinct." I reach my hand between the bars to pat a docile pinto horse on the nose. "Hey, baby," I coo. "Sorry I don't have any carrots."

I can feel Dawn come up behind me. "This was Mariah's pride and joy," he says. "Far beyond any of the petty tricks we'd play on the government. This is our real future here. Our own little Noah's Ark."

"Where did you get them?"

"We stole embryos from the government labs and grew them. They're clones. One male and one female of each species."

"But Duske said the animals are impotent. That they can't breed."

"Funny, that," Dawn says, pointing to a tiny snow white lamb in one pen. "We haven't had that problem. I think perhaps that's just another one of the government's lies. Another way to control us."

I crouch to my knees to pet the lamb's soft wool coat. "So, you're breeding them?"

"Yup. We have six cows, fourteen sheep, and twenty-two goats. It's not enough milk by far, but it does help with orphan babies who don't have a wet nurse. And we're widening the facilities in hopes to someday accommodate all of our children. Our ultimate goal is to someday have enough animals to use them for daily necessities—leather, food, that kind of thing."

"It's funny," I say, getting up off my knees. "When you first said stuff like 'rebellion' and 'revolution,' all I could think of was *Star Wars* or something. You know, guns and battles and, well, light sabers and stuff."

"Maybe someday," Dawn says with a small smile. "But we're

not there yet. We've been stockpiling weapons, training soldiers, and creating complex computer defense barriers for Strata Two and Three. But we can't let on to any of this before we're fully operational. The Circle would simply send in their army and stamp us out—like they did the day Mariah disappeared. They set us back pretty far. But we're still going. If we keep working as we have been, in a couple years perhaps we'll be ready for the real action."

He says the last bit with such intensity that I suddenly feel sad to think I won't actually be here to see that day come. I bet the battle will be spectacular, with the dedicated, downtrodden Dark Siders rising up to finally take back their world.

"In the meantime," Dawn continues, "we're also putting effort into bettering the day-to-day lives of the Dark Siders. By introducing education, growing our own food, and raising animals, we can create a more habitable world that's less dependent on this government. Healthy, happy, educated Dark Siders will be much better equipped when the final showdown does come."

"You really have it all figured out," I say with admiration.

Dawn nods. "But none of this would have ever happened without Mariah."

"She must have been an amazing person."

"Yeah. It's easy for me to forget that sometimes. I've been so angry. But she really did do wonderful things for the people here. Set this whole revolution in motion. It's just a shame it had to end as it did."

Our discussion is interrupted by two Dark Siders dressed in belted tunics and loose cotton pants. They enter the room carrying a large crate, and set it down in the corner. They nod to us and then exit.

"New shipment," Dawn says excitedly. "I wonder what they were able to steal this time."

I look over at the cage, straining to see through the slats. I catch a tuft of grayish hair and hear a distinctive whimper. "That sounds like ..."

A mournful howl echoes through the room.

"A dog!" I cry, running over to the cage. Dawn is right behind me. I get down on my knees and peer inside. Sure enough, a sweet-faced, blue-eyed Australian shepherd looks up at us, tongue lolling from his mouth.

"Wow," Dawn exclaims. "I've never seen one of these before."

I look up at him, surprised. "You've never seen a dog?" I ask, trying to keep the incredulity from my voice.

He blushes. "Well, in movies, sure. But never in real life. I figured they were wiped out during the war. Extinct."

I can't believe Dawn's lived his whole life without the joy of a fuzzy nose nuzzling at his face, the friendly wag of a tail to greet him as he arrives home from work.

Definitely time to change that.

"Let him out of his cage!" I instruct, trying to hide my smile.

Dawn hesitates. "Well, I'm not sure that's such a good idea," he says. "We don't really know what this animal is capable of and—"

"Trust me."

He shrugs and complies, lifting the latch and freeing the Aussie. I stick two fingers in my mouth and whistle. The dog pads over, jumping up to put his forepaws on my shoulders, and starts licking my face with wild abandon. Poor thing. He's been totally starved of attention.

"What is he doing?" Dawn asks, incredulously, staring at us.

I laugh. "Kissing me!" I gently set the dog back on the ground and glance around the room. I locate a small piece of rope lying in one corner. "Watch this." I grab the rope and hurl it down the corridor. The dog runs after it, grabbing it in his mouth and bringing it back to me. He drops it by my feet. For a dog that's been stuck in a government lab, his fetching instincts are evidently still very much intact.

"That's incredible!" Dawn says. "How did he know to do that?"

I shrug. "He's a dog. That's what dogs do."

Dawn grabs the rope and gives it a throw. The dog scampers after it, retrieving. But instead of dropping it at Dawn's feet, he tosses the rope up in the air, letting it hit the ground, then grabbing it again for another toss.

"He wants to play tug-of-war," I explain.

Dawn grabs the rope's other end and pulls. The dog gets into a fighting position, teeth bared, defending his rope. Dawn drops the rope immediately, taking a leap back in surprise. "Er, I think I'm making him mad."

I laugh. "No, no! He's playing! That's just play growling. Trust me."

Dawn hesitantly grabs the end of the rope again. "I'm holding you responsible if he bites off my hand or something," he warns.

"He won't, I promise."

A fierce tug-of-war ensues, the opponents seemingly evenly matched. Finally Dawn manages to wrench the rope away and throws it down the corridor. The dog bolts after it.

Dawn turns to me, his eyes shining. "I think I'm in love," he says with a laugh. "This is better than I imagined."

"What is his name?"

Dawn glances at the cage. "Um, they call him C-1-045-3."

I wrinkle my nose. "That won't do. We should name him." I crouch down to scratch the pup's ear. He drops the rope and leans his head against my hand, tail wagging happily. "Hmm," I ponder.

"How about Noah?" Dawn suggests.

"Noah?"

"Yeah. Noah was in charge of the ark, right? Our Noah can watch over our underground one."

I smile. "Perfect. Noah it is." I ruffle the dog's head.

"Want the rope?" Dawn asks the dog, grabbing it off the ground and waving it in the air. Noah's eyes light up and he bounds forward. I watch Dawn watch Noah retrieve, my heart warming. There's nothing like a boy and his dog.

We play with Noah for a while longer, alternating between fetch, tug-of-war, and wrestling. The dog is a complete goof, and soon we're practically dying of laughter.

"I hope we can find Noah here a girlfriend," Dawn says at last. "It'd be great if all Dark Siders could someday have a dog to play with."

I nod. "That would be awesome. Talk about a morale booster."

"So," Dawn says, straightening up, his smile fading. "I guess that's the end of the tour. I should take you back to Moongazer Palace. Unless," he adds hopefully, "after this tour you've changed your mind about leaving us?"

My heart wrenches at the hopeful look on his face. "Look, Dawn," I say, "I think you're doing amazing things here. I really do. I'm impressed beyond belief. But that doesn't change things for me. I still have to go home. I still have to return to my own life. I just can't abandon my world, the same way you can't abandon yours. I mean, what if I asked you to come back with me to Earth? Would you do it?"

He scowls. "That's not a fair question. You know I'm needed here."

"Well, I'm needed there. I know you don't think the cause is as noble. Hell, I'd be the first to tell you that. But it's still my role. My life. My existence. My destiny. And I need to fulfill that."

"But it's not your world and your destiny. You just think it is because of the drugs."

I sigh. Here we go again. No matter how he plays it, at the end of the day, he really, truly still thinks I'm Mariah. "Dawn, as much as you want to believe that, it's just not true. I'm not sure what happened to your girlfriend. But I know that I'm not her." I pause, then add in a choked voice, "as much as I'd kind of like to be."

His face falls. He crouches down to pet Noah, seeking comfort from the animal just as Earth people have been doing for generations. Noah licks his face, perhaps in an attempt to cheer him. But the kiss does nothing to lighten the atmosphere this time. My stomach aches as I watch the scene, wishing there were some other way, some method to split myself to live two existences. But even as I wish it, I know it's no use. And the sooner I rip off the band-aid and resolve myself to just go home, the less difficult it will be for everyone.

Dawn nuzzles his face up to Noah's and my heart lurches. I can't believe I'll never see him again. "Dawn—" I start. But he waves a hand to interrupt.

"Save it," he says, rising to his feet. "I'll take you to Moongazer Palace. Sorry to have wasted your time."

I cringe at the pain in his voice. The bitter hurt. "No, no," I protest. "It wasn't a waste of time. I'm so thankful you showed me all you did. I'm so impressed by your work. But don't you see? It proves that you don't really need me. Mariah's just a figurehead. You've done all this on your own, and you can keep it going as long as you want."

"Right. We'll be fine without you. Whatever eases your conscience at the end of the day," Dawn mutters. He ushers a reluctant Noah back to his pen. "Come on. Let's go."

"Bye, Noah-boy!" I cry, looking back at the Aussie. The dog whimpers in response, looking as abandoned and lost as Dawn.

*

Dawn slows his bike next to a ladder that leads up to Stratum One. Time for me to emerge from my rabbit hole and head back to

Earth. Alice, no longer in Wonderland. I jump off the bike and shake myself off, then look over at Dawn. He stands still, one foot on the ground, one on the gas pedal, as if more than ready to take off into the night.

Even under the dim track lighting, I can see his face is cold, stone, ashen. Either he's glad to see me go or he's hiding his sadness well. I'm not sure I'm doing quite as good a job. The lump in my throat, the quiver in my jaw, both make it hard to throw on a brave smile.

What's wrong with me? I'm getting what I want. The chance to return to Earth. To be back with my family, my friends, even Craig. But I feel only emptiness gnawing as I stare at Dawn. Why do I have the overwhelming urge to throw myself into his arms and beg him to let me stay?

"Well, I guess this is it," he says. "Have a nice trip."

I drop my head, feeling the tears coming. I can't let him see how his blasé statement crushes me. "Thanks," I say. The word seems so empty, so useless to profess the gratitude I feel toward him. For needlessly risking his life to save mine. For holding me close last night, even though the thought of me as someone else probably broke his heart.

He pauses for a second, as if considering something, then reaches into his pocket and pulls out a wad of paper that appears to be some sort of currency. He thrusts it in my direction. "Here," he says. "Pay with these. If you use your thumb, the government will know you've gone. It'll make it easier for them to find you if they want to."

I accept the bills gratefully. "Thanks," I say. "I really appreciate that."

Dawn shoves his foot onto the pedal and revs his bike without responding. My heart breaks as I realize this is good-bye. Forever good-bye.

"Dawn …" I try to grab his shoulder, but he jerks away, hand up to stop me.

"Enough," he says. "You've made your decision. Just go." He yanks the bike's handlebars and starts down the road, leaving only billowing smoke in his wake. He doesn't turn around once. I stand under the rabbit hole, watching the bike's lights fade into the darkness until there's nothing left but a blackness.

I sigh. I slip the wad of bills in my pocket. Then I start to climb.

A few minutes later I emerge on Stratum One, down the street from Moongazer Palace. The gaudy neon lights are buzzing, still on their (evidently very sturdy) last legs. Wind from a nearby fan whips up debris and I hurry to enter the building, creeped out by the desolation.

Inside, the place is packed with young Indys eagerly sucking on their 'Gazer inhalers and getting ready to vacation on Earth. I now realize that some are going for a short visit, a quick lark to another land. Others are here for permanent migration, weeping as they say good-bye to loved ones, begging them to join them on Earth as soon as they possibly can.

The old Asian proprietor I met during my first few minutes here greets me with a low bow. He's still wearing the same old-fashioned suit. It seems so long ago, and at the same time as if I never left. "I've been expecting you," he says. His chuckle is low and guttural. "Ready to go back in?"

Go back in. The choice of phrase causes my heart to stutter. "I'm ready to return to Earth," I correct, pulling the cash from my pocket.

"One way or round-trip?" he asks, walking over to the computerized cash register.

"One—" I stop, something making me reconsider. I hand him my wad of bills. "Is this enough for a round trip?"

He counts it. "Yes," he says. "Exactly enough. One way costs more. Also, you'd need your official migration permission papers from the Circle."

I remember now how the Eclipsers said a permanent migration to Earth cost an Indy's life savings. Something I certainly didn't have at my disposal. Did Dawn know I'd be forced to buy a round-trip ticket? He must have. Sneaky bastard didn't warn me.

"I guess I'll take a round-trip," I say with a shrug, resigning myself to figuring out the whole thing once I get back to Earth. Maybe I can hide out somewhere and just never take that return 'Gazer bus back, whenever and however it comes.

The proprietor nods, giving me a once-over. "Let me get you your charm," he pronounces, walking over to the cabinet and pulling out one of the many. He drapes it over my neck. "And here is your 'Gazer," he says, handing me the inhaler.

I stuff the inhaler in my pocket. "Um, what's the necklace for again?" I start to ask, but he's already turned away to help another guest.

"You push the button here," a blond elfish girl next to me says, reaching over to flip the necklace's charm around. "It'll indicate you're ready to return to Terra."

"Ah cool. Thanks," I tell her. So that's how the tourists get back. Interesting.

"The return's only good for one week," she informs me. "And they'll totally charge you huge late fees if you stay overtime. Best to get out with an hour or so to spare, just to be safe."

"Okay," I say, not that I really expect to ever activate the thing. I'm going back to Earth, and this time I'm staying there for good. No matter what I have to do.

She looks at me oddly. "Aren't you Sister Mariah?" she asks.

"No," I say quickly, before she starts alerting the others. "But sometimes people say I look like her."

Luckily, the girl seems to buy this. She wanders back over to her friends and plops down on the couch next to them.

"Remember," the oldest-looking one in her group, a guy, is saying to the others. "Once you're there, you're supposed to pretend that you're, like, from Earth. It's called role-playing. You don't go just to be your same old boring self. When you're on Earth you're like a rock star or an actor or something."

"What's it like on Earth?" asks a pig-tailed girl. "Is it really as cool as they say?"

"Cooler," the guy affirms. "In fact, it's like one big, never-ending party. Lots of food, lots of booze, and lots of …" He trails off as he eyes the younger members of his group. "Lots of dancing," he finishes, though I'm pretty sure that's not what he's really looking forward to. "Well, you'll see for yourselves."

"Let's do it!" cries a redheaded boy in the back. "Let's go look into the moon!" He says the last bit exactly like the guy in the commercial, and the other members titter.

Their leader nods and pulls out his inhaler. He raises it up as if he's toasting someone's health. "To the moon!" he cheers, putting the inhaler to his mouth and taking a chuff.

The others follow suit. "To the moon!" they chorus.

I realize I'm just standing there, watching them, totally stalling my own trip to the moon. As if I don't really want to go back. Stupid. I take a deep puff from my inhaler and head down the hallway and toward the 'Gazing booths. I remember my first time walking through this corridor. How lost and confused I had been. I had no idea where I was. Or even who I was. Has it gotten any clearer?

I square my shoulders as I approach room 12. Clarity doesn't matter at this point. I'm through with Oz. I'm clicking my ruby-red heels three times and returning home.

So why do I suddenly feel more like the cowardly lion than the heroic Dorothy? And just who is the wizard behind the curtain?

FIFTEEN

I woke up in my bedroom, not screaming from a nightmare, no cold sweat soaking through my clothes, no anxious roommate by my side. Just a dark room with a glowing clock illuminating the hour of 9:00 P.M. At least the Moongaze machine had dropped me off safe and sound in my own dorm. How it was able to pinpoint where I lived and send me there, I had no idea, but I didn't want to know. I was just glad to be home.

Though, the whole thing did make me wonder: How did it work for real Terrans? Were they allocated an apartment or house before they 'Gazed? That seemed unlikely, especially for the ones who were just visiting. Maybe they got assigned hotel rooms to wake up in. Or was there an arrival platform somewhere? A Grand Central Gazing Station perhaps? But then, why would I wake up here and not there? Were all Terrans dumped in NYC for that matter? Or were they spread out around the country? Or the world, even. I guess it wouldn't be a bad thing to end up in the Big Apple. Here they wouldn't have to worry about not fitting in, as no one knows their neighbors anyway. And what were a few extra bodies in a city of eight million? The cash the government gave them on arrival probably really came in handy. Did they get identification documents as well? A black market immigration operation just for Terrans? Were there Terrans living and breathing and working among us? I wondered if any of them worked at Chix0r.

I shook my head. It didn't matter. I was back and supposed to be concentrating on my real life from here on out. The

Moongazing Terrans would have to take care of themselves. Their reality was fading, even now.

I slipped out of bed and padded around the dorm room, taking in all my treasures that I'd left behind. I picked up my teddy bear, Melvin, and hugged him against my body, triggering a memory of me buying him on a trip to Tahoe. But for some reason now that trip seemed distant. Almost generic. I could remember going, but I couldn't recall any of the details of what happened. No quirky anecdote to share.

I glanced over at the posters hanging on my wall. *Star Wars*, *The Matrix*, *Blade Runner*. My eyes caught on the last one, squinting in confusion. *Blade Runner*? But the movie was *Phaze Runner*. I'd seen it a thousand times. There was no way I'd confuse the title. Did I buy the wrong poster? Some Japanese import or something? But no. The last time I was in my bedroom it was definitely *Phaze Runner*. I'd bet my life on it.

What was going on here?

Unnerved, I dropped Melvin back on the bed and headed to my bookcase, pulling a book out at random. I knew I'd read the fantasy epic in my hands a hundred times. I could see my ink-stained fingerprints at the page edges, the folded corners where I'd left off for the night. But while I had an overall impression regarding what the book was about, it wasn't in any greater detail than what was written on the back cover.

I set the book down, a panicky feeling fluttering through my insides. Everything in my room, all my precious possessions tied up with memories and meaning, suddenly seemed fake and altered, flat, one-dimensional, almost an obscene parody of a character I was supposed to be playing. I was in a cliché bedroom of a college geek girl. I had the sci-fi posters, the fantasy epics, the killer computer. It could have been a movie set.

I grabbed my photo album, plopping into a butterfly chair and flipping through to find pictures of my parents and quell the fear bubbling to my throat. I took a deep breath and forced myself to focus on the people in the pictures. Smiling. Waving. But were these shiny, happy people really Mom and Dad, or just some random folks that came with the album?

I felt sick. I threw the album across the room and jumped from the chair to make a dash for the bathroom. My stomach heaved and I barely made it to the toilet in time. I threw up violently.

Hacking. Coughing up something I didn't remember eating. Then I sank to my knees and leaned my head against the porcelain seat, sobbing my eyes out.

What was I doing? Why was I freaking out like this? I knew going back to reality might take a little adjustment, but I had no idea it'd be this hard for my brain to accept. Was I losing my mind? I should be dancing around my apartment, overjoyed to be back, instead of doubting all the things I'd trusted throughout my life.

This was my stuff. My reality. My life. It was Terra that I didn't remember. Terra that I should mistrust. So how come memories of Terra suddenly seemed so solid and real and those of Earth so fake?

A vision of Dawn, of his beautiful glowing eyes, his comforting smile, his warm embrace, flooded my consciousness. If only he were here. If only he had come back with me and could comfort me in my terror, tell me everything was going to be all right. But Dawn was gone from my life forever. That was my choice, and now I had to live with it. I had another guy here on Earth who would be overjoyed to have me back. My real boyfriend, Craig. A popular techno DJ at a Lower East Side club.

The club-kid gamer and her DJ boyfriend. My life really did seem like a cliché.

Desperate, I rummaged through my pocket and took a whiff of my inhaler. After all, the medication supposedly helped bond the body with the new reality of Earth. The more I puffed, the more real Earth would seem. Maybe that's what I needed. I took a second dose, breathing in deeply, just in case.

A few minutes later, the medication kicked in. My breathing slowed and my heart stopped racing. The panic receded to the back of my brain and I rose to my feet to, once again, take stock of my surroundings. My reality.

I stepped back into my dorm room. I was home. Everything was as it should be. I was just having a panic attack from the transition. But I was okay now. All that I owned was here and familiar. My teddy bear, my family photos, my well-worn books, my computer. They were all suddenly teeming with resonance. Feeling better, I crawled into bed and stuck my feet deep under the quilt my aunt had made me. Snuggled into my pillow and closed my eyes.

Everything was going to be okay. I was safe. I was home. I was me again.

So why did it take sucking down a drug to make me feel that way?

*

I slept for nearly twenty-four hours. When I woke, I was still feeling out of sorts—itchy and uncomfortable in my own skin. I sucked down more asthma medication. It was the only thing keeping me from going completely insane. I lay in bed for hours, staring up at the ceiling, wondering if I'd made a huge mistake. I should be happy to be home, but all I could think about was Dawn. His hurt, pained eyes, his cracking voice as he said good-bye. Sure, I wanted my old life back, but being so distant from him—knowing I'd never see him again—it was tearing me apart.

I slept. I woke. I ate a few random things I found in my drawers. Then I slept again, skipping classes, ignoring the emails from my boss at Chix0r. At times I wondered what happened to my roommate and then wondered whether I had a roommate at all. Like everything else, I really couldn't be sure.

I felt sick and weak and drugged, and I missed Dawn with every fiber of my being. It wasn't till my third day back that I finally forced myself out of bed. My answering machine was blinking madly with messages from Craig, each invoking a pang of guilt for disappearing on him as I had.

I firmed my resolve; I had to find some semblance of control over my life. My *real* life. Or else I was going to end up a ghost in a shell. And so, that night, I decided to head down to Luna. Craig would be spinning and I could meet up with him between sets. Apologize for all I'd put him through and, if he would still have me, promise to be a better girlfriend in the future. Then we could live happily ever after and I'd forget all about Dawn.

I hoped.

I threw on some clothes—skinny jeans, slouchy boots, a long black belted sweater—and walked out of my dorm. As I locked my door behind me, I noticed a discarded bag of moldy Japanese take-out sitting outside my place. My heart sank as I remembered I'd invited Craig to come over right before I'd gotten pulled back to Terra. Poor guy. Here he'd been waiting for me and I was off in some alternate universe, throwing myself at another guy. How long did he stand out here knocking before giving up and going home? I really had to find him and make good.

I headed down the elevator and into the lobby. "Good evening, Skye," the doorman said as I stepped out.

I startled. We didn't have a doorman. And wasn't this dorm a walkup the last time I was here? Or were there always elevators? I tried to remember, but my head remained foggy and unclear.

I stepped outside. The night was warm, and a full moon shone down on the streets of Manhattan. The sky was so bright, in fact, you could even manage to make out a star or two. Unusual in the city. People hustled up and down the sidewalks, eager to get to the next restaurant, the next bar, the next place to see and be seen. All living empty existences, I realized glumly—just like the Indys back on Terra. I reached into my purse and handed a homeless man on the sidewalk a ten-dollar bill.

Heading down into the subway, I readied myself for the normal ridiculous wait. To my surprise, the train came immediately, pulling up just as I stepped onto the platform. What luck! And it wasn't even packed like the normal can of sardines. Unheard of for a Friday night. But no one else seemed to notice the change.

I emerged just south of Alphabet City and headed straight to Luna. As usual, the club was packed and the line wrapped halfway around the block. At least some things never changed. I found myself staring at the club-goers more closely this time, wondering which ones were Terrans and which were regular Earthlings. All I could tell was that the eighties look had caught on big time. Nearly everyone sported legwarmers, long sweaters, and leggings. I caught a few teen girls pointing at me and whispering. Probably Terrans recognizing Mariah. Super.

I headed to the front of the line, where Bruno was attending to the door. "Hey, baby!" he said, wrapping me in a huge hug. "Where have you been all my life?"

"You wouldn't believe me if I told you, Bruno," I said, forcing a casual laugh. "But I'm back now. For good." For some reason the words made me sad.

"Well, I'm glad to hear it," he said. "Craig's been going nuts without you, and the crowd's starting to pick up on the bad mixes and skipping records. You guys have a fight or something?"

"It's a long story. But I'm here to make it up to him."

Bruno nodded approvingly and unclipped the velvet rope.

"Enjoy the makeup sex," he said with a knowing wink. "That's the best part."

I laughed, waved off his suggestion, and stepped inside. The thought of sex was too much for me to even consider at this point. Not with me hanging on to reality by a thread.

You just would rather have it with Dawn, the now familiar inner voice jeered. I shoved it to the back of my brain. That might have been true, but it wasn't a thought I was prepared to deal with at the moment. What brief closeness I had with Dawn, that was over forever. It was time to leave the dream behind and bond with reality. Get closer to Craig. Renew our relationship. Find happiness with the guy I was supposed to be with. Not the one I had left behind.

I pushed my way through the club and soon found myself in the center of the room, lights flashing, bass pounding, people dancing. I knew I should head straight to the DJ booth, find Craig, and work it all out, but I realized I wasn't quite ready to face him just yet. I'd dance a bit first, I decided. Then I'd go talk to him when he was on a break. After all, I always felt better after dancing, after letting thunderous jungle beats flow through me, losing myself in the rhythm.

And so I danced. Became one with the others on the dance floor, swaying my hips, swinging my arms, nodding my head, trying to find my true self somewhere in the music. Trying to seek out even a moment of peace.

It used to work wonders back in the day; on the dance floor I could shut off my mind and allow the music to take me to a higher plane of existence. But tonight, my mind wasn't surrendering that easy. Instead of retreating to a high mountain of unconscious bliss, it chose to stay firmly on the ground, rehashing images of Terra. The Dark Siders. Dawn.

I stopped short as a vision slammed through my consciousness: Dawn's tortured eyes, as clear as if they were blinking right in front of me. I smelled his fear. Felt his horror. Heard him call my name—Skye, not Mariah. He was begging for my help.

It was as if the wind had been knocked out of me. Was this some kind of premonition? Was something wrong on Terra? Had the government done something? Were people being hurt? Was it because of my leaving?

I shook my head. I had to give it a rest. I was back on Earth. I had to forget Terra. It wasn't my world. It wasn't my fight. I had my own crap to deal with. An angry boyfriend, a ton of unfinished schoolwork—the last thing I needed to be worrying about was Terra.

But something inside me wouldn't allow me to let it go. I couldn't dry-swallow the blue pill now that I'd partaken of the red. Now that I knew about Terra, I realized, I'd never be able to forget. Those people—how they suffered. My mind flashed back to the little schoolgirl, Crystal, who'd wrapped her scrawny arms around my legs and thanked me. How could I have left her behind? And for what? I looked around the room. For this empty shell of a life? Clubbing, video-gaming, shallow relationships with people who didn't mean anything. I was just as bad as the Indys.

"Sister Mariah!" A girl's voice cut through the loud music. I turned, suppressing a grimace. Two teenage girls, dressed in matching short skirts and thigh-high stockings, stood behind me. At first glance, they could be club kids. But I realized they must be Indy teens out for a night of 'Gazing.

"Now you've done it," the second girl said, kicking her friend. "We're supposed to be staying in character, remember? What if she tells on us?"

"Please. It's Sister Mariah. She's not going to tell on us. Are you?" She looked up at me beseechingly.

"No. I won't tell," I assured her. "But maybe you two should run along—"

"Wow," interrupted the first girl, her eyes glistening under the flashing lights. "I had no idea you'd be here. All the news feeds said you were kidnapped by the Dark Siders and being held prisoner."

"Yeah, the government has been doing everything to find you, Mariah!" said the second girl, who sported long dark braids. "There's, like, a huge reward and everything."

"There is?"

"Yup. And the Dark Siders are getting punished for stealing you away," added the first girl, tossing her long blond ponytail over her shoulder.

"Which is totally short-sighted," complained the second girl. "I mean, no offense, but if the Dark Siders all die, who's going to mine the tellurium so we can all 'Gaze? I'd simply die if I couldn't 'Gaze anymore."

"Duh. They'll just get the nTs to do it," proclaimed her friend.

I held up my hands to slow them down. "Wait a second," I said. "Did you say the Dark Siders are dying?" I waited, breathless, for their reply.

The girls nodded in sync. "Yeah," said girl number two. "I heard it from my friend. They've been pumping in some kind of poison gas through the ventilation fans. You know, to motivate them to set you free."

I stared at them in horror. Could it be true? Could the children I met in the little one-room schoolhouse now be gasping for breath, the senior citizens collapsing in the market square? Could my leaving Terra have put everyone's life in jeopardy?

And what about Dawn? Could he be suffering too?

"Wow. Mariah Quinn." The blond girl gazed at me in awe. "Our friends will be so impressed when we tell them we hung out with a legend like you. Do you want to party with us tonight?"

"Sorry. I've … I've got to go," I stammered. "Um, are there … Moongazing booths around here somewhere?" Or was I supposed to use the necklace? I should have asked more questions.

"Yeah, up in the VIP lounge," said girl number one. "Well, they don't look like the booths back in Terra, though. They're just chairs. Sit in a chair and activate your necklace. You'll be back in no time."

"But do you have to go now?" whined girl number two. "Can't you hang with us first?"

"Yeah, hang with us!" begged girl number one. "Supposedly Paris Hilton is going to show up tonight. And she might dance on tables. How cool would that be?"

"I think it's Paris *Milton*," I muttered, but suddenly I wasn't so sure.

"Sorry, girls," I said, backing away. "It was great to meet you." I turned and made a dash for the VIP section. The chairs? Of course. That's exactly where I was sitting when I was transported to Terra the first time. I ran through the club, pushing past sweaty bodies, ignoring the protests of the jostled dancers. No time for apologies; I had to get to the lounge.

My body stopped short as it slammed into something solid. I looked up, realizing that I'd just smacked into the very person I'd first wanted to find but now sought to avoid. Craig looked down at me in a mixture of surprise and annoyance. He grabbed me by the shoulders, his eyes piercing.

"Where the hell have you been?" he demanded.

I didn't have time for explanations. For excuses. He wouldn't understand anyway. He wouldn't believe. I suddenly realized that, Mariah or no, Terra had become a huge part of me. And he couldn't share that. There was no use wasting any more time on this superficial relationship built out of attraction and convenience.

"Long story," I muttered. "Let me go."

"I'm on my break. I have time for a long story. Let's go to the back room and you can tell me."

"I'm sorry," I said, and I was, in a way. "But I don't have time right now."

He didn't let go of me. "Why?" he demanded. I looked down at his hand gripping my arm. How come I'd never noticed he had one of those weird moon tattoos? "Got a hot date?" he asked. He was bluffing, of course, not having any idea how close he was to the truth. "You know, usually it's custom to break up with someone you don't want to see anymore, instead of just disappearing off the face of the earth, leaving them standing at your door with a bag of Japanese takeout."

I cringed a little, feeling his disappointment, his anger. He didn't deserve the treatment he'd gotten from me. He'd been a decent boyfriend, always treating me right. Just because I didn't share the connection with him that I did with Dawn didn't mean I should hurt him.

But this was an emergency. I couldn't waste any more time. If what the girls said was true, then Dark Siders were dying and it was all because of me. I had to get back there and figure out a plan to stop the government from killing them. And I needed all the time I could get.

I reached up, kissed Craig on the cheek, and said good-bye forever. I felt terrible, especially after catching a glimpse of his hurt face, but I saw no alternative. My life here was trivial and unimportant, and I was wasting valuable time. I had to help the people who needed me.

"I'm sorry," I said one more time, really meaning it.

Then I pushed past him and raced up to the VIP room before he could stop me and plopped down in a chair. Out of the corner of my eye I saw that he was running after me, taking the steps two at a time. I had to act fast. I grabbed for the necklace, fumbling with it for a moment before my fingers located the tiny button.

I pressed down hard, closed my eyes, and readied myself to go back to hell.

A hell that was feeling more and more like my real home.

SIXTEEN

I open my eyes and find myself in a familiar, swirling, technicolor Moongazing booth. I let out a sigh of relief. It worked. I'm back.

I remove the shades, find the handle, and step outside the booth and into the hallway, feeling a bit freaked out at what I've just done: left my home, willingly, and perhaps, a nagging thought at the back of my brain reminds me, for good this time.

I shake my head. I can regret this all later. Right now I have to find the Eclipsers and get an update of what's going on and how I can help. I have to find Dawn.

I dash down the hallway and burst out into the lobby of Moongazer Palace. It's completely empty now, save for the ever-present proprietor.

"Short trip," the Asian gentleman notes coolly from his position behind the counter, looking me up and down with his spectacle-covered eyes. Does this guy ever take a break? A day off?

"Long enough," I reply, realizing how oddly good it feels to be back. The weird, displaced vertigo I'd been suffering on Earth has totally disappeared, and I'm almost getting this strange home-sweet-home vibe. I feel like me again. Which doesn't make any sense, I realize, but there you go.

Without bothering to ask permission, I grab the phone off the counter and dial Dawn's number.

"Hello?" he answers a moment later, his voice low and sleepy sounding.

I let out the breath I hadn't realized I'd been holding. "Oh my

163

God, Dawn," I cry, relief and happiness flooding through me just from hearing him answer. "I'm so glad you're there."

"Mariah?"

I wince, consider, then force myself to correct him. "It's Skye."

"Um, right. Sorry," he stammers, sounding a bit out of breath. I remember the Indy girls' tales of the poison. My heart quickens. Is Dawn down there, literally asphyxiating as we speak? "Where are you?" he asks, finding his questions. "I thought—aren't you on Earth? How can you be calling me from there?"

I guess an explanation is in order. But not with the nosy proprietor nearby, obviously eavesdropping while pretending to sweep the floor. "It's a long story. I can't explain now. But I'm at Moongazer Palace. Can you come get me?"

"I'll be there in five minutes. They've got sensors to alert them if the rabbit holes are activated from the inside, so you'll have to come down to me. I'll meet you at the bottom of the ladder. But be careful, Skye. The government's looking for you. And they'll pretty much stop at nothing to get you back."

"I know," I say. "Please hurry."

I head outside and down the street till I find the rabbit hole. It's the one Dawn and I used on my first trip to Terra. That day seems like a lifetime ago, and my heart thuds in anticipation of seeing him again. I've missed him, I realize. Even in this short time of being apart, I've missed him dreadfully.

I climb down, deeper into the darkness, the air becoming thicker and sickly sweet the further down I go. My lungs struggle to take it in, and panic swells. But I force myself to practice my breathing exercises. As long as I stay calm, there's plenty of air. At least for now.

I step off the ladder and onto the road. The air is still and quiet. The fans unmoving, just as the girls had described. A moment later, Dawn pulls up on his bike, parking it and jumping off, throwing his arms around me and squeezing me so tightly it's even more difficult to breathe. "Oh, Skye," he cries, burying his face in my hair. "Oh, sweetie, I thought I'd never see you again."

I nestle my head against his chest, feeling his rapid heartbeat against my ear. He feels so good. So solid, warm. I breathe him in, his musky scent tickling my nose. He's so beautiful, so wonderful. So passionate and loving. How could I have ever thought to leave him, to abandon all that he is for a shallow existence on Earth?

Never again, the voice inside me whispers. *You belong with him. And you should do everything in your power to stay by his side.*

Dawn pulls out of the hug, cupping my face in his hands, looking down at me with loving, desperate eyes. "Why did you come back?" he asks, his voice fraught with concern. "I mean, don't get me wrong, I'm happy to see you. But it's not safe here. The government, they've ..." He trails off, gesturing weakly to the fans. "We'll be dead in a week if they have their way."

"I heard," I say, standing on my tiptoes to kiss him lightly on the mouth. His lips tremble as they meet mine. "That's why I came back. You need me."

"I'd rather you were safe," he says, pointing at his bike. "But go ahead, get on, we'll go to headquarters. Everyone's already gathered. We're trying to work out a plan."

After a short trip, we arrive at the Eclipser headquarters and go through all the bells and whistles to obtain admittance. Inside, all the usual suspects are gathered. Their faces are drawn and anxious, and none of them look like they've eaten or slept for days. The air inside is even thicker and staler, if possible, and I'm finding it very difficult to breathe.

They look up when we enter, concern etched on each and every face.

"Sister Mariah," Ruth greets me, rising from the table to walk over. Her movements are slow, probably to conserve air. "We thought you left. That you went back to Earth."

I accept her weak hug, feeling the guilt rise all over again, even though there was no condemnation in her voice. "I did. But then I heard what the Circle had done. All because of me. I couldn't just stay on Earth and let you guys suffer for my sake."

Kayce frowns. "At least there you were relatively safe. I don't think you realize how dangerous your situation is here. They'll wait until we're half dead and too weak to fight back, then charge in here full force, leaving no stone unturned until they locate you." He sinks back into his chair. "On Earth, at least they wouldn't have found you."

"You don't know that. And besides, what good would that do? You'd all be dead. What good is it for me to be safe for the revolution if the revolution has been reduced to a pile of bodies at the bottom of a pit? That's stupid." I realize I'm being harsh, but what else can I do? They've got to see reason here.

"They're bluffing," suggests Hiro. "They wouldn't really kill us all. They need us for mining."

"Unless they're planning to use nTs instead," I remind him.

Dawn cringes. In fact, they all do. I guess none of them really wants to admit this could be one act of mass genocide, taking care of a troublesome population once and for all.

"No," Kayce says finally. "I refuse to believe it. This will all blow over. We just have to stay strong. In the meantime, we need to get you out of here."

Dawn nods. "Yes, Skye. We need you to go back to Earth."

I stare at him, mouth open. "*You* want me to go back?" I can't believe what I'm hearing.

He nods. "You know I'm still not a fan of Moongazing, but it's better than the alternative. They'll find you and kill you if you stay." He shoots me a pointed look. "And I'm not going to stand around and let that happen."

The room erupts in murmurs as the Eclipsers discuss the situation at hand. I grab Dawn's arm and drag him to the back of the room. "Are you crazy?" I hiss. "You really want me to hide out on Earth while you guys suffer here?"

"Yes," he says simply.

"But you think 'Gazing is dangerous. Addictive."

"Addiction is better than annihilation."

"But I can't just leave you guys."

He grabs my hands in his and squeezes hard. "I appreciate your loyalty," he says. "More than you could know. But there's another thing to consider here. If we're found harboring you, maybe they really will kill us all. If you're not here when they raid, maybe they'll conclude they made a mistake. They'll stop the siege, hand out antidotes …" He looks miserable, knowing his excuses sound far-fetched and ridiculous. As if I don't know what he's really saying. Grasping at straws in an effort to keep me safe. I love him for that. But this time I can't obey.

In the center of the room, Ruth raps her gavel against the table. "We'll take an hour recess," she announces. "And then make our decision."

The Eclipsers file out of the room one by one, slowly and deliberately, so as not to use up excess air. Soon Dawn and I are the only ones left. I climb up on the table and plop myself down.

"Skye, it's the only way you'll be safe," Dawn says, joining me.

He reaches over and threads his fingers through mine. "And I can't bear to lose you again."

"But you will lose me," I argue. "I'll be on Earth. Not here with you."

Dawn pauses for a moment. "You *will* be with me."

I look up, uncomprehending. "What? What do you mean?"

"I'm going to go with you."

"To Earth? You're going to 'Gaze?" I cry, disbelieving. "I don't understand."

"It's simple. As I said before, I won't lose you again. You offered me a choice the last time: go with you or stay to help the Eclipsers. I stayed. I thought I was doing the right thing by doing so. But maybe I was just afraid. Maybe I should have trusted you. What would life be like now if we'd just gone? Said good-bye to it all? We'd be happy on Earth. Wandering the parks, playing with the dogs, cooking fabulous meals, and kissing under the moon."

"You can't mean that."

"Why not?" he asks, jumping off the table, looking at me with desperate eyes. "I'm sick of living like this! Like a rat in a cage, worried every day that one of us will be killed. And for what? Have we really made a difference?" He scowls. "I don't know. Seems to me the Dark Siders are worse off than they ever were. At least before we had simple things like air to breathe and food to eat. Now, because of our rebellion, their very existence is in jeopardy. It would have been better for everyone if I'd just gone to Earth and stayed there."

"No!" I cry, sliding off the table. I grab him by the shoulder and pull him around to face me. "You're wrong. The reason the government is so up in arms is because we're succeeding. They're scared by our victories. They're threatened by our success. We've accomplished so much. We've given the people new hope. A reason to live. The Eclipsers have worked hard, scraping their fingers to the bone for every small victory. And I'm not about to give up now. Screw Earth. I'm a Terran. An Eclipser. And I'll never run away from my destiny, no matter what they try to do to me."

I pause for breath, but get none as Dawn's mouth clamps down on mine. Kissing me as if there's no tomorrow. And maybe there won't be. But that doesn't stop my body from igniting as his lips sear my own, his hands digging through my hair as he pushes me against the wall. I wrap my arm around him, pulling him close. So close. I'd crawl inside of him if I could.

"I love you," he says against my mouth, his voice breathless and husky and not just because of the lack of air. "God, how I love you."

My heart soars at his words; his tone leaves no question that he means them. "I love you, too," I whisper back. "And I'm glad you understand."

He pulls back so that he can meet my eyes. His face is flushed but serious. "Of course," he says. "I was a coward and selfish to suggest we run away to Earth. I just wanted to protect you. But you're right. We can't turn our back on the people. We have to continue the fight. It's what Mariah would have wanted." He smiles down at me. "I wish I had your strength. Your courage. I wish I wasn't afraid to die."

"Don't think I'm not afraid to die," I tell him. "I just can't be afraid to live."

Dawn smiles, leaning down to kiss me again.

"Um, sorry. Did you two need more time?"

We break apart from our embrace and my face burns as I realize Ruth and Kayce have reentered the room. I can see Ruth holding back a smile. Dawn grins sheepishly.

"I think we're good," he says.

Ruth widens the door and the other Eclipsers file in. "So, it's time to take a vote," she says, after everyone's settled. "Should Mariah go back to Earth?"

"There's no need for a vote," I interject. "I've already made my decision."

"She's not going," Dawn adds. "No one is. We're going to fight back."

SEVENTEEN

"Fight back?" Hiro echoes skeptically. "How do you propose we do that? What can we possibly do to defend ourselves against this kind of siege?"

"Well, first off, let's talk about the poison. How is it being piped in?" I ask, ready to get down to business. It's what Mariah would have wanted.

"Up on Stratum One, there's a top-security bunker that serves as both a physical plant and a high-tech headquarters," Kayce explains. "It's a huge sprawling complex that houses almost every project the government's got its mitts on; the controls for everything from traffic lights to Moongazing are all inside. I'm positive this is where they'd run the fan operations."

"So could we go in and somehow stop the poison flow?" I ask. "Reroute the air or something? Do we have that kind of technological expertise?"

"Sure," Kayce says. "It'd be no problem at all if we had access to their systems. Just hack in, recode the ventilation program. Maybe even throw in a little computer virus to prevent them from taking back control once we do it."

"So, that's what we'll do then," I say, proud of my plan.

"If it were that easy, we would have already done it," Ruth interjects.

"As Kayce said, it's a top-security place. We've already tried to hack into their computers to get the thumbprint needed to unlock such doors, but you need a thumb of the highest security clearance imaginable to gain admittance to this place. And those thumb codes aren't listed on regular government files."

"What about the people who work there?"

"They never leave," Hiro explains. "They're nTs. They're grown to work in the building and spend their entire lives inside—eating, working, sleeping. You go in, but you don't ever come out."

"Talk about job security," I mutter. "Okay, so basically what you're saying is that we need to create a copy of one of the high government official's thumbs. Like a member of the Circle of Eight, perhaps."

"Yes." Ruth nods. "That would do it. But there's no way—"

"I'm on it."

Dawn cocks his head, looking at me with suspicion. "What do you mean?"

"Easy. Duske wants me back, right? He has the thumb we need. I'll simply go pay him a visit, tell him I was kidnapped by you guys the entire time and finally managed to escape. Now I want to go home. Once I get him to start trusting me, I'll get his thumbprint."

"No way. It's too dangerous," Dawn says. "You. alone in that ... house?" He shakes his head. "I won't allow it."

"I won't be alone," I argue. "You have Thom working on the inside. Probably a slew of others, too. They can help if I get into a jam. And once I have the thumbprint, I'll have security clearance to walk right out the front door if I want to."

Dawn frowns. "And what if he doesn't believe you? What if he decides to kill you on sight?"

I think for a moment. "He won't," I tell him. "He still needs me to be part of his Moongazing seminar. To convince the Indys that Moongazing is a worthwhile venture. Besides, the guy has a thing for Mariah, remember? He was even supposed to marry her. I bet if Mariah shows up, all ready and willing, he'd be good to go."

"Not a bad idea," Ruth says thoughtfully. "Get him close and he'll be putty in your hands."

"I don't like it," Dawn interrupts. "Him, putting his hands on you. I can't—"

"Dawn, it's the only way," I say, laying my own hand on his arm. His muscles are hard, tensed. "What alternative do we have? Stay down here until we're weak from hunger and dying of slow poison? If I'm going to die, I want to die in an attempt to save our people."

And I mean it, too, I realize. I've lost my chance to go back to Earth. Probably forever. But for some reason I don't feel the least bit of regret. My old life now seems nothing more than a very long dream, a halfhearted excuse of an existence where I never accomplished anything meaningful. Who cares about a video game, about school and clubbing and all the rest? It's all empty and useless when standing beside an opportunity to save a world. Today I'm alive as I've never been. I have a reason to live. To fight. I have a cause and people who need me. And I alone have the power to help them.

I gotta say, in a weird way, I love being Mariah.

"She's right," Ruth says in an effort to stop Dawn's continued protest. "It's a good plan. The best chance we've got right now. And Mariah's the only one who can really carry it out."

"We'll put a tracker on her," suggests Kayce. "So we'll know where she is at all times. If she gets in trouble, she can just hit the panic button and we can figure out a way to storm the house."

"And Brother Thom's a great swordsman," Hiro adds. "I trained him myself. He can always break cover and help her, if need be. It's not like there'll be much point of cover if we all die."

Dawn slumps his shoulders. He can't argue with everyone. "Fine," he says. "I can see you're not going to be dissuaded. I don't like it, but I won't stand in your way."

*

"I still think you're crazy," Dawn tells me as we walk through the door and into my apartment. He heads over to the couch and sits down, scrubbing his face with his hands. "What if Duske isn't fooled? What if he kills you?" He looks up at me, his eyes hollow and full of shadows. "I can't bear the idea of something bad happening to you."

"I know," I say, taking a seat beside him. I wrap my arms around him and cuddle my head to his shoulder. His body feels warm and taut against mine. Solid, strong. Only the smallest tremble gives away his fear. "I'm scared, too, believe me. But it's a good plan. It can work. And once we get the high-security clearance thumb mold made, we can not only stop the poison, but maybe we can figure out some other government tricks. Imagine what secrets are being held in that building."

"You're right, I know," Dawn relents. He turns to kiss me on the forehead. "It is a good plan. And you're extremely brave to volunteer." He shakes his head. "Enough talk now. I have one night with you and I don't plan to waste it by worrying about the future."

His lips brush against mine. Soft. Reverent. And I realize something's changed between us. Some barrier that prevented us from becoming close has now melted away. Perhaps it's due to me giving up my life on Earth, giving up all the baggage I've been carrying around and accepting my role on Terra. Whatever the reason, there's no longer anything standing in our way. Tonight we will experience each other fully, accept the bond between us, and become one.

He stops for a moment, capturing my face in his hands, sliding his calloused palms up my cheeks, finding my eyes with his own. His gaze makes my breath hitch in my throat. He smiles at me. A completely unguarded, vulnerable smile. His face is so beautiful I want to cry and laugh all at the same time. Instead, I smile back, hoping he sees the expression for what it is: an offering of everything that I am. Everything I can be.

If I die tomorrow, at least I know I've lived today.

EIGHTEEN

I hover on the ladder, just below the rabbit hole. My knees are knocking together so hard I'm half convinced they'll buckle out from under me, causing me to fall to my death. More than a small part of me wants to play the coward, to turn and flee and never look back.

But then I remember Dawn's face. The love shining from his glowing eyes as he kissed me good-bye and sent me on my mission impossible. The pride in his voice as he praised my courage and told me that, Mariah or Skye, now I really would be the savior of the people. The one they would sing about for generations to come.

How could I possibly deny my new destiny?

I draw in a breath, trying to quell my nervous energy as I push open the rabbit hole, emerging onto Strata One. *Here goes nothing.*

It doesn't take long for the guards to grab me. And soon I'm being carted off in a squad car to Duske's mansion. When they drag me inside, Thom is standing in the foyer. When the guards aren't looking he gives me an imperceptible nod. I nod back; at least I'm not entirely alone, even though I know he won't break his cover unless the situation gets dire.

"Sister Mariah," he cries, keeping in character. "We have been looking everywhere for you. Let me tell the master you are here."

I shuffle my step. I'm now at the point of no return. Inside the belly of the beast. Let's hope he's hungry.

Thom leaves me, heads up the sweeping staircase, and disappears down a hallway. The guards continue to flank me at either side. Was I crazy to think this plan would work? What will Duske do when he sees me? What if he decides I'm worth more dead than alive? Will he simply kill me on sight, never giving me a chance to accomplish my mission?

"Well, well, well." A booming voice above interrupts my racing thoughts. I look up. Senator Reginald Duske is standing at the top of the stairs, dressed in an old-fashioned black suit. His hair is slicked back and his face is cold and unreadable. "It appears the prodigal sister has returned."

Time to earn that Academy Award.

"Brother Duske!" I cry, breaking free of the guards and rushing up the stairs. Before he can react, I throw my arms around him, squeezing him in the most enthusiastic hug I can muster. I press my whole body against him, hoping to spark some heat in his cold, unyielding frame. "Thank God you're here!"

The senator lets me hold him for a moment, then steps out of the embrace. He looks me over, eyebrow raised.

"You seem happy to see me," he observes.

"Of course!" I say, practically bouncing with enthusiasm. "You have no idea what I've been through. This gang of rebels—I think they're called Eclipsers or something—kidnapped me from your house and dragged me underground. It was horrible."

"Kidnapped, huh?" Duske repeats slowly "And here I was sure you'd left of your own free will."

"Are you kidding me?" I give him a disgusted look. "Do you know where they took me? Some horrible underground ghetto with these crazy mutant freaks. They kept insisting I was that girl named Mariah, their rebel leader or whatever. And they wanted to use me somehow to unite the people against the government." I shake my head, as if reliving the horror. "So, I'm like, 'Dudes, I'm so not Mariah. I'm Skye, and I'm from Earth and I need to get back.' But did they believe me? No! They locked me up and only took me out when they wanted to show me off like some kind of prized cow." I allow my voice to crack. "Oh God, Duske, I thought I was going to die down there. I was so scared." I throw my arms around him again, sobbing into his shoulder, hoping it's not overkill.

Duske stands still for a moment, then awkwardly pats me on the back a few times. I try to gauge his reaction. Does he believe me? Even a little? I step away and study his face. It's hard to tell.

"An interesting story," he says.

"Interesting?" I screw up my face in disgust. "Horrible is more like it. All I want to do is get back to Earth. To my real life. Please. You've got to help me."

"How did you escape?" he asks, ignoring my request.

"There's something going on down there," I explain, glad Dawn and I had role-played this encounter last night so I knew exactly what to say. "The fans have stopped and the air has become poisoned somehow. It's made everyone weak. I saw my opportunity, and when they were transporting me, I acted. I attacked my two captors and went up one of the hatches. That's where your men found me and brought me here." I shudder. "You can go look, if you want. Their bodies are probably still there, right under the rabbit hole by Moongazer Palace."

This was a small insurance the Eclipsers had arranged to make my story more believable. The bodies in question were two asthmatic Dark Siders who had succumbed to the poisoned air a day before. Hiro and Kayce had worked on the two bodies and laid them by the exit to provide legitimacy to my tale.

Duske turns to the guards at the bottom of the stairs. "Return to Luna Park," he says. "Go down the rabbit hole by Moongazer Palace. See if there are bodies there."

The guards bow low, then exit the building to carry out their orders. Duske turns back to me. "I'm sorry not to take your story at face value," he says amicably. "But these days we cannot be too careful." He claps his hands again and two more guards show up. He instructs them to pat me down. Luckily, we'd envisioned this kind of scenario and so I'd come without weapons.

"I totally understand," I assure him as the guards search me. "But soon you'll believe me and we can move on. Did I miss your Moongazing seminar? I'll still do it if you want. I'll do whatever it takes. I just want to get back to Earth—like you promised." I'm crying now. Easy to fake tears when I'm this terrified. "I'm so sick of this creepy place. All I want to do is go home. To see my family. My friends."

Duske's face softens. He reaches out to stroke my hair. "Shh," he says. "Don't cry. It'll be okay. The nightmare is over. You're safe with me."

I breathe a sigh of relief. He's buying it. He's actually buying it.

"So, can I go to my room?" I ask. "I'm dying for a bath. And then maybe we could go to dinner tonight? I loved that place you took me originally. What was it called again? The Park Terrace? The ravioli is divine."

Duske scratches his chin, studying me with his piercing eyes. "All in due time," he says. "But first we must take a little trip." He turns to walk down the hall, beckoning me to follow.

I cock my head. A trip? What kind of trip? Does he believe me or not?

"Come along," he says, and I realize I have no choice but to follow him.

We walk down the hall until we come to an elevator. He presses his thumb to call it, and a moment later the doors slide open. We step inside and Duske selects a bottom floor. The doors close and the elevator shoots downward. We travel for what feels like a long time. I wonder how deep we're going. My heart pounds so hard and fast I worry it'll burst. I steal a glance at Duske, trying to read his expression. He simply stares at the descending numbers flickering above the doors, his face inscrutable. Finally, the elevator shudders to a stop and the doors slide open.

We step out into a long corridor, highly guarded by thumb-sensored doors, seemingly every few feet. This place is more secure than Fort Knox. But Duske's thumb works magic on every lock. I so have to get a copy of it, no matter what it takes. I consider jumping him now—after all, we are alone—but then reconsider. At present I have no means to get his thumbprint. I must wait for Thom to slip me my supplies.

"Where are we going?" I ask, praying this is not some trick— some one-way trip to a high-security prison he plans to throw me in.

"Bunker twelve," Duske says, stopping in front of a small golf cart. "Get in."

I obey, joining him in the cart as he activates the hover controls. Soon we're floating down the corridor at low speed, and about ten minutes later we come to another door. This one's flanked by human guards in addition to thumb-sensor locks.

Duske steps out of the cart, nods to the guards, and waves an identification card at them. They step aside, pressing their thumbs against matching sensors, and Duske does the same with his. The locks click simultaneously and the door swings open.

We step into a long, featureless hallway, illuminated by dim fluorescent lighting lining the ceiling. I follow Duske down the hall, trying to memorize each twist and turn. The place is like a maze. An industrial catacomb. There are a million doors dotting the myriad of hallways.

Finally, we come to a door at the end of one corridor. Duske presses his thumb against the sensor and the door slides open. We step inside, into some sort of prison, though it certainly wouldn't meet Geneva Convention standards. The smell of decay and rot permeates the air, and I have to resist a nearly overwhelming urge to block my nose with my hand. The floor is strewn with debris, and behind each iron-barred cell there's a prisoner, dressed in rags and lying on the ground, covered in her own filth. There are no beds, no toilets, not a single creature comfort to be seen.

I steel my expression, not wanting him to see my revulsion. It's all I can do not to lean over and puke. "What are we doing here?" I demand instead. "I thought you would take me to my apartment."

"All in good time, my dear," Duske says, patting my arm. Then he turns to one of the cells and gestures. "Do you recognize this prisoner?" he asks.

I peer in, unable to stop the gasp escaping my lips as my eyes fall on the woman inside.

Glenda. She's barely recognizable as my former personal trainer back on Earth. Her always lithe frame is now skeletal, her face gaunt, and her eyes blackened. She's shivering in her thin slip dress, and her arms and legs are riddled with sores.

Horror slams through me, and I struggle to keep my composure. So, they didn't kill her. She's been here this whole time. Starved, probably tortured—all for rescuing me. My stomach heaves as I turn away, unable to look at her bruised face.

Oh, Glenda, I'm so sorry. I'm so sorry you had to suffer like this for me.

"That's Glenda," I say, calling upon every molecule of strength inside me to keep up the charade. Every fiber of my body yearns to turn around and attack my host. To kill him for what he's done to this poor woman who only wants to better her world and save her people. But I can't act now. There are guards everywhere, armed with heavy artillery. I have to wait. Bide my time. Play selfish Skye from Earth for a little longer. "That's my personal trainer. What is she doing here? Is she a Moongazer too?" I ask, turning to Duske, mostly to avoid looking at the disappointment radiating from Glenda's hollow eyes. If only I could send her a signal. Somehow relay to her that I'm only acting. That her sacrifice was not in vain.

Duske shakes his head. "This woman only pretended to be from Earth to lure you into the Dark Siders' trap. She's actually one of the head Eclipsers. She was the one who broke in and attempted to kidnap you the day you left us."

"Really? That was her?" I turn back to throw her my most disgusted look. "So it's her fault I'm stuck in Terra? That I was dragged underground and forced to live with those disgusting mutants?"

Glenda whimpers from inside her cell. A knife to my gut.

Duske nods. "It is," he says. "All her fault." He reaches down, pulling up the hem of his trousers, and producing a knife banded to his ankle. He unsheathes the blade, stands back up, and holds it out to me. "Obviously, she needs to pay for her crimes—for what she did to you." He smiles a sick smile. "Go ahead. Take this knife and kill her."

I stare at him and then the knife, horrified beyond belief. Oh God, this is like what always happens in the movies; the hero's supposed to prove his loyalty to the villain by killing someone from his own side.

But I can't be that hero! There's no way I can take a knife and slice up an innocent woman—one who risked everything to save me. There's just no way! But if I don't, then Duske will doubt my story. He'll likely turn the knife on me instead. If I don't kill Glenda, I'll die. And everyone else will, too. The Dark Siders, the Eclipsers, Dawn.

What am I going to do?

I try to swallow, but my throat's too dry. I try to think, try to remember back to the day the Eclipsers told me that Glenda had been captured trying to rescue me. They told me that to her, the cause was more important than life itself. Did she still feel that way? Would she want me to kill her if it meant saving the others? How close was she to death already? Would I only be putting her out of her misery?

"Go on," Duske goads smugly. He's obviously enjoying my indecision. "We don't have all day, you know. I mean, you do want to get back to Earth, right?"

I stare at Glenda, cowering in the corner, hands over her head, not so brave anymore. My mind races with indecision. She's weak. It'd take one blow. She'll probably die anyway. She'd want me to do it. I have to do it. The cause is more important than one life.

How many times have the Eclipsers told me that?

I grab the knife from Duske, step into the cell, raise the blade. I stand above Glenda's quivering skeletal body, drawing in a breath, garnering every ounce of resolve within me. If only I had Mariah's strength. She'd be able to do this. She'd be able to act decisively if it meant furthering the cause.

"Do it!" Duske commands. "Now!"

But I can't. I drop the blade. It clatters uselessly to the stone floor.

"No," I croak, resigning myself to the fact that I've likely signed the death sentence for all of the Dark Siders and myself. But what else can I do? I just don't have it in me to kill a defenseless human being. "I'm sorry. I know you guys have different rules on Terra, but on Earth we don't go around killing helpless women for no reason. I was already forced to kill once today—in self-defense. But this would just be cold-blooded murder. And I am not a murderer."

Duske reaches down and scoops up the blade. He shoves it back into its sheath. "Very well," he says. "Let's head back to the house. We're finished here."

I stare at him, not understanding. "B-but," I stammer. "I thought—"

Duske shrugs. "It was a test," he says. "If you were really working for the Eclipsers, you would have killed her to keep up your act. That's how they work. Sacrifice one person to save all the others. To them, their silly cause is more important than individual life."

Realization hits me with the force of a ten-ton truck. I made the right decision. My weakness actually proved my character. He was testing me to see if I acted like Mariah. And she would have done it. By refusing, I've effectively proved myself to be Skye.

"So you believe me," I stammer, praying it's not too good to be true.

"In my position, I'd be a fool to believe anyone," Duske replies. "For all I know—"

A burst of static interrupts him. He reaches down and pulls out his communication device. "Yes, what is it?" he asks impatiently.

"We found the bodies, sir," says the voice on the other end. "Just where you said they'd be."

"Did you test them?"

"Yes. They appear to have been beaten to death with a bat that we found discarded a few feet away. Fingerprints on the bat appear to belong to one Mariah Quinn. There are also a few blood splatters on the body that appear to belong to her."

Phew. And here I thought Kayce and Hiro were crazy when they insisted on me giving a blood sample before I left.

"Very good," Duske says into the device. He switches it off, shoves it in his back pocket, and turns to me with a thoughtful expression on his face. "You're either telling the truth," he says, "or you're really, really clever." He shrugs. "I guess in the end it makes no difference."

"I'm telling the truth. I swear to God," I cry. "Please, just let me go back to Earth. I can't take this anymore."

Duske frowns. "Let's not get ahead of ourselves, Sister," he says. "Even if I do believe you, which I'm not saying I necessarily do, nothing has changed. I still need you to speak about Earth at one of my seminars. Only then can I allow you to return."

"Oh yeah," I say. "And you're still going to give me a million and a half dollars, right?" I try not to grimace as I ask the question. Is it possible to believe someone would actually be so shallow? To be more concerned with her burgeoning bank account and free trip back to Earth than the plight of the poor woman languishing in this cell? The plight of the people down in Stratum Two?

Of course it's possible, I realize, feeling a bit sick to my stomach at the thought. In fact, it's not only possible, but exactly how I had been acting only days before. Imagine what Dawn must have thought of me, those first days in Terra. For him to have to stand by and witness the only woman who had the power to save his people prattle on about a meaningless video game and a shallow, pointless life on another plane of existence. Refusing to step up to the plate, face her destiny, and do something meaningful with the life she'd been given. It must have been completely unbearable. No wonder he'd been so hesitant to let me into his life. Into his heart. I must have come off as the most selfish bitch in the universe.

Well, no more. From now on I'm promising to live my life for a higher purpose. Even if that purpose ends up hastening my ultimate demise. Whether I was born Mariah or Skye, right now people are depending on me. I'm holding thousands of lives in my hands. And I can't turn my back. No matter the danger.

But Duske can't know this. He has to see Skye—greedy, one-track-minded Skye.

"'Cause, like, a million and a half dollars would totally rock," I add. "I can get a new computer. And my own car—no more taxis for me. How awesome would that be?"

Duske smiles and pats me on the back—as if I'm some silly child he can patronize. Perfect. I've got him completely buying this act. "Truly awesome," he returns. "And you will get your money. As soon as you take part in the presentation."

We walk out of the cell. I try to block out Glenda's whimpers. I wish I could do something to help her. But at least she's alive. I only wish there was some way to relay a message to her: *Just hold on a little longer and we'll get you out.*

We head back to the main house. As we're walking down a hallway, we come across Thom, heading in the other direction. He's looking down at a list in his hands and slams into me, as if he hadn't been looking where he was going. I fall backward, as planned, and he reaches down to pull me to my feet.

"Watch where you're going," I grumble.

"I am so sorry, Sister," Thom says, brushing me off.

"Yes, yes. Be more careful, Brother Thom," Duske says—but not before Thom manages to press a small object into my hand. He continues on and I slip the object into my pocket. It's what I need to complete my mission. A razor.

At first I'd been horrified when they told me the plan. Me, cut off a guy's thumb? But then they'd said I only needed the print. That was gruesome, but more manageable. I didn't want to think of anyone—even Duske—running around with a bloody stump.

"Are you taking me to my room?" I ask. "The one I was supposed to stay in that first day?"

Duske nods. "Of course. Then you'll have a chance to bathe and change."

"Thank God for that." I scowl down at my outfit. "This thing stinks to high heaven."

"And if you like, I can make a reservation at the Park Terrace for this evening," Duske continues. "It's last minute and they are usually at capacity, but I'm sure I could pull a few strings."

"Sounds like a plan." I throw him a grin. "Thank you so much for taking me back. I owe you more than I can possibly say."

"It's my pleasure. I'm just sorry you had to spend time with those barbarians down below," Duske says, his voice getting a sudden soothing, seductive tone. "Now, if you'll follow me, I'll show you to your room."

I draw in a breath and finger the razor in my pocket. God, I hope this works. It has to. There's no plan B.

We arrive at my room a few moments later. It's just as I left it. All perfect and princesslike with its canopy bed and big-screen TV. I can't believe this is a spare bedroom to someone like Duske while the people down below live in such squalor. Maybe he does deserve to lose his thumb.

I force thoughts of injustice from my head and concentrate on my mission, sending up a prayer to whatever Terran gods are listening that that this will actually work. It had seemed so perfect while discussing it down in the safety of Eclipser headquarters. Now it seems impossible. Crazy, even. How the hell am I going to pull this off?

I step inside the room, and Duske hovers at the door. I frown. I need to get him inside if this plan is going to work.

"So, um, is this it?" I ask, swaying my body slightly from side to side. "Are you going to go off into that big house of yours and leave me all alone now?" The forwardness feels out of character, but I pray Duske's obsession with Mariah will blind him.

The senator raises an eyebrow, interest and confusion warring on his face. He's not sure where I'm going with this line of questioning, but he's not shutting me out, either. That's a start. "Well, I figured you'd want a shower," he says hesitantly. "To freshen up before dinner."

I shrug and wander over to the bed, slowly brushing the pastel-colored comforter with my hand. "Yeah, I suppose I'd like to get clean—eventually," I say, throwing him a glance past lowered eyelids. I bat my lashes once, hoping it's not overkill. But the hungry look on Duske's face makes me realize that I've hit my mark. He's wanted Mariah for a long time, and now he's thinking he may finally have his chance.

It won't play out exactly as he hopes.

"Is there something you require?" he asks, stepping into the room. *Yes.* He's taken the bait. Now it's time to move in for the kill. Here goes nothing.

"Require?" I repeat, cocking my head to one side. I catch his eyes with my own wide, innocent ones. "I'm not sure about that. But there is something that I want." The words sound so cheesy coming from my lips. Will he buy them? I suck in a breath, waiting for his reaction.

Duske steps forward—he's only inches away. *Oh yeah, baby. Come to Mama.* I let out my breath, not sure why I'd been so worried. He thinks he has *me* brainwashed. Why not take advantage?

"Yes, my lady?" he asks gallantly. "What is it that you want? Be it half my kingdom, you shall have it."

Yuck. He's so cheesy. "Forget the kingdom," I say sultrily. "I just want you."

"I think that can be arranged." He reaches up to trail a hand down my cheek. "Because I didn't really mean it about the kingdom."

Of course you didn't, jerk-off. But I have a few jokes of my own up my sleeve. You're going to love them.

I stand on my tiptoes to press my lips against his. His mouth is cold and clammy. Disgusting. He responds to my advance, however, flicking his tongue at my lips. It's like being kissed by a snake, and I have to resist the urge to jerk away and ruin everything. I remind myself that this slimy kiss is for all the people of the Dark Side.

I part my lips, allowing his slithering tongue entrance. He groans and presses his body against me. So much for foreplay with this guy, I guess. At least he's going for it. I love that, at the end of the day, evil government leader or no, he's just a horny old man.

I realize it's time to make my move before I throw up all over him. I lower myself to my knees and slowly begin to unzip his pants. He moans in delight.

"Wait," I say. "We'd better close the door."

He agrees, shuffling over and slamming it shut. He presses his thumb against the sensor to lock it up from the inside. "There," he says. "Now no one can disturb us."

"Excellent," I say, though not for the reason he assumes. I smile coyly and beckon him back to me. He complies eagerly, putty in my hands.

I pull his pants down to his ankles, leaving him fully exposed. Then I rise to my feet and kiss him again, trying not to gag. As he leans forward to deepen the kiss, I bring up my knee and slam it as hard as I can into his groin. He doubles over in a mixture of shock and pain. I follow with an uppercut to his jaw and his head flails backward. He trips over his pants and crashes to the floor. I slam my heel into his stomach, and he bellows in rage. Luckily, as he so proudly told me during my first visit here, the walls are soundproof.

I grab a vase off the dresser, ready to slam it over his head and render him unconscious. He's too quick, rolling to one side to avoid the blow. He grabs my ankle and pulls it out from under me, knocking me onto my backside. Before I can scramble to my feet, he's whipped out his knife. My element of surprise is gone. He's ready now. It'll be a fair fight from here on out. I hope the preliminary injuries slow him a bit; otherwise I'm outmatched.

"I knew this had to be a trick," he growls, waving the knife at me. "I'm going to gut you, bitch," he says. "And crucify your body for every Dark Sider to witness before I kill them all."

I jump to my feet, assuming a battle stance, hands in front of my face. "Go ahead," I challenge. "I'd like to see you try."

Luckily, he appears more interested in personal revenge than calling for backup. He's sure he can best me; after all, he has the weapon. I wait for him to charge, which he does, bellowing in rage, then roundhouse kick with my back leg, making contact with his hand. The knife he holds slices the side of my foot, but the impact causes it to go flying. Now he's unarmed.

At first I think he'll dive for the weapon, but instead he comes after me—throws his entire weight into it. I lose my balance and crash to the floor. He pins me there, clamping my neck between his hands and squeezing down on my carotid. I can't breathe. I grab his wrists, desperately trying to pull his hands away, but I'm not strong enough, especially with my breath cut off. My vision starts to grow spotty; I'm going to pass out. I struggle to stay focused, to remain in control—to black out will be to sign my death warrant.

It's then that I remember Thom's gift. I drop my hands, grab the razor from my pocket, and use it. I manage to slice into my attacker's stomach. He bellows in surprise and pain, staggering backward and thankfully letting go of my neck. I pull my knees out from under him and kick my feet forward, slamming them into his chest and knocking him back. I leap forward, on top of him now, straddling him, my razor inches from his face.

"Don't move," I tell him. "Or I will stab this blade right into your eye."

"Killing me will do no good," he growls, but he drops his hands to his side.

"I'm not going to kill you," I say. "I'm going to take your thumbprint."

His eyes widen as he realizes the meaning of my words. I grab his thumb and take a deep breath. I remind myself that, gruesome as this is, the bastard will live and the skin will heal. He likely deserves much worse.

I swallow hard and ready the blade. Then I slice. Blood covers the razor, pooling, making it difficult to make my cut. I have to be accurate, the Eclipsers warned, or the function will be cancelled. Duske's writhing body increases the difficulty.

"Stop squirming," I command. "Or I'll kill you and take this anyway."

He stops his movements, his face white. I take the opportunity, before he changes his mind, and I slice fast, hard. A moment later I have the invaluable flap of skin separated from his body. I take the other thumbprint too, rendering him unable to leave the locked room. Then I crawl off him. He sits up, looking dizzy, trying to stop the bleeding by pressing his bloody thumbs into his shirt.

"It'll heal," I say. "You're lucky I'm so merciful."

"You won't get away with this," he growls.

"You keep saying that," I note. "But I don't really see how you're going to stop me." I scramble to my feet, grabbing his knife off the floor. "I'm leaving now," I inform him. "Perhaps at some point you'll be rescued. Though it's a shame this house is so big and no one knows where you are. It may take them a while to find you."

Duske spits at me. I shake my head.

"Such manners," I tsk at him. "And here you're supposed to be the politician." I press his bloody skin against the sensor. It beeps and the door slides open. I throw Duske a grin. "Thank you so much for loaning me your keys," I say as I exit the room. "I'll be sure to put them to good use."

NINETEEN

Back at the Eclipsers' underground headquarters back on Stratum Two, I triumphantly present my souvenirs to the rebels. I'm the big hero, as you can imagine. But no one's more excited than Dawn. Though I get the feeling that it's nothing to do with Duske's thumb.

He scoops me up in his strong arms and twirls me around, then sets me down and plants an enthusiastic kiss on my lips. "I didn't breathe the whole time you were gone," he whispers fervently.

"Trying to conserve air?" I tease. "That's very noble of you, Brother Dawn."

He laughs. "You know what I mean."

I do. And it warms me inside to realize how much he cares. We're a team now, fighting for a cause bigger than us. It's exhilarating.

"I still can't believe I pulled it off," I comment as we join the rest of the Eclipsers at the conference room table. I'd handed off the thumb to one of the Dark Sider technicians who was now working to upload the print data into the computer and craft a less bloody simulation.

"But you did. And now we can fight back. Get the clean air flowing again," Ruth says, her voice bursting with pride.

"We'll show the Circle they can't mess with the Eclipsers," Hiro chimes in. Everyone applauds.

"So, what's the next step?" I ask, after the cheering fades. "Once the simulation is done?"

"Long ago, one of our spies managed to steal blueprints of the bunker," Ruth says, pulling a set of prints from a metal tube and rolling them out on the table. "We've had them on file forever, with no way to make use of them." She looks up at me. "But thanks to you, that's all changed."

I study the prints. The place is huge, bigger than I'd imagined. Full of twisty passageways, seemingly without rhyme or reason. Ruth points out the physical plant, where the mechanisms needed to restore the fans are located. "That's where you need to go," she says.

"Got it," Dawn says after a few moments of study. "I'll head out as soon as the technicians are finished with the key."

I look at him in surprise. "You're going?" I ask, suddenly realizing I'd never thought about who would actually do the rest of the dirty work.

He nods. "It only makes sense. I'm an nT, just like the guards inside. I'm the only one with the strength to overpower them, if need be. Plus, I have the skills to reprogram the ventilation system and recode it."

"But ..." I stammer. "But I don't want you to—"

"Risk my life for the cause like you did?" Dawn finishes my sentence with a pointed look. "Sorry, but there's no other way."

"Well, then, I'm going with you," I say, determined. No way am I letting him risk his life alone.

"No." He shakes his head. "It's too risky."

"Tough luck. I'm not letting you out of my sight again, Dawn Grey," I say. "And besides, I can be useful. You need someone as a lookout while you do your reprogramming thing."

Dawn scrubs his face with his hands. "You've been in enough danger already—"

"And look at me! I'm completely unscathed. Don't be pigheaded. You know we have a better chance doing this together."

"She's right, Brother," Ruth interrupts. "And you should know better than to let your personal attachments interfere with the cause."

"Besides, with her sword skills, she'll be very useful to have," adds Hiro. "After all, back in her school days she was a legend. No one could touch her."

Dawn releases a sigh and holds up his hands in defeat. "Fine, fine," he says. "I can see I'm not going to win. As usual." He turns to me. "It's not that I don't admire your bravery, you understand," he says. "I just can't bear the thought of anything happening to you."

I lean over to kiss him on the cheek. "I'll be with you," I remind him. "You can keep me safe."

He smiles and kisses me softly on the mouth. "That's true. And I promise to protect every little hair on your head."

"I'll hold you to that."

Ruth clears her throat. We jerk apart, red-faced. I giggle, for once not at all embarrassed by the PDA.

"Brother Thom was able to obtain a couple of uniforms," Kayce adds. "Like what the nT workers wear inside. So as long as you keep a low profile, you should be able to fit in."

A knock sounds on the door and a technician steps inside. He presents the thumb simulation to us. "All done," he says proudly. "You're now in possession of the most powerful key in all of Terra."

"Great," I say, grabbing the simulation and affixing it to my thumb. "Let's go save the world."

*

I swallow hard as the bunker door slides shut behind us, sealing us in with a loud, echoing clang. We're in. I grab for Dawn's hand, needing to draw from his strength, to hold on to something steady and solid and unwavering for at least a moment before we begin our quest.

But I realize even Dawn is shaking.

It'd been easy to enter the place. Almost too easy, in fact. Using the thumb imprint, we were able to deactivate the sensors to get up to Stratum One and to the bunker itself. Once there, we neutralized the guards at the back entrance with injections Kayce had cooked up. Once they were rendered unconscious, we dragged them back behind a nearby trash bin and then used the thumb simulation to activate the lock. Security seemed almost lax, especially for a building of this importance. But I guess when you only have a few thumbs in the whole world keyed to enter, you don't need an army to guard the door.

Dawn points to security cameras slowly panning back and forth every few yards down the long hallway. Thank goodness we have uniforms. I've also drawn a rough rendition of the blueprints on my palm. Last thing we need is to get caught whipping out a map.

I study my hand for a moment, then point down the hallway. "This way," I whisper to Dawn. "We'll take our third left."

Dawn nods and follows me down the hall. We walk slowly, our faces turned downward, to minimize risk of recognition by whoever's monitoring the cameras. Of course, according to Ruth, everyone in here is an nT, born and raised on the inside. They've never seen a news feed and thus would never be able to recognize Terra's most notorious rebel and her boyfriend. But you can never be too careful.

We turn left, into an identical featureless hallway stretching off into infinity. A few uniformed workers pass us, nodding a slight greeting and mumbling "Brother, Sister," as they walk by. I exhale. Our costumes and demeanor are evidently passable to the worker drones.

"These are newer models—much less human than I," Dawn observes. "I'd heard this was happening. The government's replaced the reasoning center in their brains with a superior work ethic. They can't think for themselves. They only have time for their work."

"How sad," I whisper back. "Though, I guess they aren't thinking enough to feel sadness. Maybe they're completely content. But still …"

"I guess it makes sense that the government wants to replace the Dark Siders with these models," he says. "They'll produce more and never demand fair treatment. Never fight back, never rebel. They're dream employees."

"But to massacre people and replace them with drones?" I say, cringing at the idea of it. "It's just not right. We can't let that happen."

"We won't," Dawn says, stealing a glance at me. "That's why we're here."

I throw him a small smile, hoping he's right. It all seems so big, so elaborate. How can a ragged band of rebels stop a government as cruel and powerful as this?

I shake my head. No time to think of the big picture. Not now. Win the battle before taking on the war. If we pull this off, it'll be a major coup—a victory for the Dark Siders and a way for them to regain some independence. We must stay focused, accomplish our mission, and arrive home safe. Then we can worry about the rest.

We trudge farther down the passageway, following my hand-drawn maps, making various twists and turns until we finally come to the room we've been searching for. The place is filled with high-tech machinery, and monitors everywhere are blinking with red, green, and yellow lights. I'm glad Dawn's here with me; I wouldn't even know where to begin.

"Go for it," I whisper, poking him in the side. "Work your magic."

Dawn nods, keeping his head down, so as to not alert the drones inside the room. Luckily, as the others had, they barely acknowledge our presence as we head to the back of the room. Dawn locates an unattended computer and takes a seat in front of it. His face is tense, anxious, as his fingers swiftly dance across the keyboard. His brow furrows.

"What's wrong?" I whisper.

He shakes his head. "Nothing. It's just a little more complicated than I thought it would be." He types a few more command lines. I scan the room. We haven't been noticed yet. That's good. Though, odd, really. Eerie. I mean, I know there's a skeleton crew on because it's nighttime, and I know that the crew is made up of nearly mindless bioworkers, but still. There's just something strange about two people being able to waltz into a high-security government facility and mess with whatever we want with little interruption.

"Hurry," I hiss at Dawn as he slips a small flash drive into a terminal. A horrifying thought occurs to me. What if they know we're here? What if they're watching us as we speak, lulling us into a false sense of security before they pounce? I glance up at one of the cameras that silently scans the room. Who is on the other side of the lens watching?

"Okay, okay, I've almost got it. There!" Dawn hits enter and the screen flashes twice. He looks up at me with a grin. "The air should be not only rerouted through a cleansing filter, but completely under Eclipser control. I programmed in new authorization codes and rerouted the control center to one of the megacomputers back at headquarters. I also successfully inserted a virus into their server that should make it extremely difficult to wrest control back from us."

"Great," I say. "Mission accomplished. Now let's get the hell out of here."

"Sounds like a plan."

We head out of the room, the drones still going about their work, barely registering our intrusion. I glance back at them one more time, pity stirring in my heart. I'm so glad Dawn escaped before they did that to him.

We wander through the low-ceilinged passageways, guided by my hand map. The building is so big and the passages so twisty it's hard to tell if we're going the right way. Soon, I realize in dismay, the map doesn't line up at all.

"Which way?" Dawn asks as we stop at an intersection.

I scan one direction, then the other. "I hate to say this, but …" I throw him an apologetic look. "I think we might be lost."

"Great." He grimaces. "That's just what we need."

"Well, let's keep going. Maybe something will start to look familiar again," I suggest, not seeing any other options.

We continue on, taking random lefts and rights in a seemingly endless maze of tunnels. My heart pounds. What if we never get out? What if they find us wandering here? At least we accomplished our mission, I try to remind myself. We may die, but others will live.

It's not as comforting a thought as I'd like.

"What's this?" Dawn asks suddenly, stopping. I come up behind him to see what's got his attention. It's a set of metal double doors with a single sign affixed: MOONGAZING CONTROL ROOM.

"This must be where they developed the astrophysics program to send people to Earth," I exclaim, scarcely able to draw a breath. An insatiable curiosity overwhelms me. Maybe I can finally find out some answers about the program. And more importantly, about who I really am. "We should check it out," I say, trying to keep my voice nonchalant.

Dawn narrows his eyes. "That's not on the agenda," he reminds me. "We're supposed to be in and out."

"I know, but …" I trail off, not knowing exactly how to explain.

Luckily, Dawn recognizes my need. He reaches over and squeezes my hand. "You want to know whether or not you're really Mariah," he concludes.

I nod. "It's important to me."

"Okay," he agrees. "We'll check it out. But just for a minute. Then we've got to get out of here before we end up setting off some alarm."

I run the thumb simulator over the sensor and the doors swing open. I suck in a breath as we step inside, nervous beyond belief. I want to know. But at the same time, I'm scared to find out the truth. What if it's something I'm not ready to hear?

I steal a glance at Dawn. Beautiful, wonderful Dawn. He loves me, I tell myself. And he will love me no matter who I really am, right? Skye or Mariah. He cares for me. I have to trust in that.

Somewhat reassured, I look around. Confidence fades as I recognize what we've stepped into. The room is like a football-field-sized warehouse, with row upon row of computers. Black boxes with blinking red and yellow lights are stacked one on top of the other from floor to ceiling, with only narrow passageways allowing access between them. Wires rope the floor and metal-beamed ceiling, all leading to the back side of the room. A few nTs wander the aisles, checking the computers. They ignore us, as the rest have, thank god.

I throw a confused look at Dawn, wondering what all this machinery, all this major computer power amassed in one room could possibly be for. I mean, I know what the computers are. Chix0r has a server room just like this, though ten times smaller. This is definitely a central command center for some kind of massive network.

We walk toward the back of the room, stepping over wires in our path and avoiding the nTs. We come across a door labeled OPERATIONS. Dawn glances at me. I nod and open the door with the thumb simulator. We step inside.

The room we enter reminds me of NASA's Ground Control. nTs man rows of terminals, all facing a wall-sized computer screen with a satellite map of ...

I scrunch my eyes. Is that Manhattan?

"Wow," I whisper. "That's ..."

"Earth?" Dawn concludes.

"Well, it's a map of one city on Earth. New York. Where I'm from."

As if on cue, one of the nTs types a command into her terminal, and the screen zooms in. I can now see people bustling up and down a busy midtown street, as clearly as if I were watching a movie or a live video feed, or just simply looking out a window.

"They must be monitoring Earth or something," I reason, trying to make sense of it all. "Keeping an eye on the Terrans who 'Gaze."

"Yeah," Dawn says, sounding doubtful. He sits down at one of the computer terminals and starts typing in commands. "Look," he says, "other feeds."

I peer over his shoulder, fascinated. "You're right," I exclaim. "This one's the Upper West Side where I live. Lincoln Center. See, I sometimes go sit by that fountain and read." I look at the next screen over. "And that's the East Village," I say, pointing. "Outside Club Luna. That's where the 'Gazers all hang out." I scratch my head. "I wonder if they just sit here and watch all the places 'Gazers visit. To make sure they're safe or something."

But even as I say this, doubts niggle at my brain. Something's not quite adding up here. How could the government monitor an alternate reality from Terra? How could they place cameras on the streets and somehow send the live signal back to headquarters? My interdimensional physics training is spotty—okay, nonexistent—but this doesn't make sense. And even if they could monitor everyone, why would they bother? Why would they care what their citizens are doing on Earth?

And, most troubling, what are all these servers for?

"Skye, check this out," Dawn says, typing a few commands on the keyboard. He pulls up a 3-D architecture program that's currently busy rendering a skyscraper. I stare at the screen, unable to comprehend what I'm saying. "But that's the new graphic arts building at my school," I say, gulping. "They're supposed to open up next semester."

Dawn looks at me. "They're building it *here*," he says slowly. "Skye, I think I understand what's going on now. You might want to sit down."

His words might as well be a truck barreling me over at a hundred miles an hour. I sink into a chair, crazy thoughts pinging all over my brain. It can't be, can it? No. This is impossible. But, the massive servers. The map rooms and rendering programs.

I dive for a computer and latch on to a keyboard, typing commands as fast as my fingers can handle. The network is surprisingly simple to navigate, nearly identical to my game back on Earth. I open directories, scan folders, read files. A dawning horror consumes me at each turn as I recognize people, places, objects. It's all here. Everything about the Earth I know.

I find a folder listed *PATCH CONTENTS* and click open the READ ME file.

Notes to Earth Patch 11.09.02

Major subway upgrade. System Users will no longer have to wait twenty minutes for a train.

Doorman NUCs added to several apartment buildings. New celebrity NUCs added to Luna locale. Several cultural and historical name inaccuracies fixed. Fashion update: We've introduced a 1980s retro wardrobe players can choose from, including legwarmers, horizontal striped tops, and leggings.

New goals added: In order to keep visiting Terrans involved, they will be approached and offered a variety of new objectives when they interact with NUCs. Each objective will reward the User in a new way.

"What are you reading?" Dawn asks, coming over behind me. "What's a NUC?"

"Nonuser character," I guess, my voice choked, everything falling into a sick sort of place. "An NPC is a video game term for a computer-generated character. They look like regular players, but they're actually just computer programs, designed to assist or distract players from their goals. I think a NUC is something very similar."

"So, why would there be those on Earth?" Dawn asks.

That's the sixty-four-thousand-dollar question. I stare at the screen, trying to make sense of it all. Trying to come up with some logical explanation besides the very obvious one right in front of me.

I think back to my last trip to Earth. The doorman, my poster, the express subway, the change in club clothes, the whispers that Paris Hilton was hanging out at Luna. My stomach churns. My vision grows spotty. I want to be sick.

It can't be. This has to be some kind of awful joke. Some kind of mistake. I'm reading it all wrong. I'm drawing conclusions that shouldn't be made. This is impossible. Absolutely impossible.

And yet.

"What if Earth isn't another world after all?" I ask slowly. "What if 'Gazing is really just a game?"

Dawn sits down beside me, face solemn, stroking my back with a gentle hand. He's already figured it out, I realize. He knows it's true.

"Oh God, it's all here," I say, choking out the words past the huge lump in my throat. "Maps, people, objects, quests. All the tools game designers need to create a virtual reality. Terrans aren't being transported to another world at all. They're just being uploaded into some freaking video game!"

Desperate to be wrong, I open another folder. One labeled NUCs. Inside are 3-D renderings of people and data. Some characters I know. Bruno, the burly bouncer from Luna. Suzy. My boss, Madeline.

And Craig. My own boyfriend.

" 'Computer-generated nonuser characters shall enhance the world, provide a more realistic atmosphere to the game, and offer quests to eligible players,' " I read quietly. " 'They can be identified by moon tattoos on their hands or necks.' " I think back to Suzy. To Craig. To the tattoos they sported. I thought it was a new trend. Stupid, stupid me.

I lean back in my chair, trying to absorb it all, to take it all in. My mind feels like it's going to explode. It's been hard enough coming to terms with the fact that maybe I'm actually someone I don't know, that I could be Mariah from Terra and not Skye from Earth. It's quite another to realize that not only am I definitely not from Earth, but Earth doesn't exist, except in a room of computer servers and the imaginations of some very creative programmers.

No wonder Earth is so much like Terra. Terrans created it. That's why we have the same pop culture references, the same Starbucks on the corner, the same fashion sense, the same language. Not because of some ridiculous parallel universe theory. But because everything on Earth was literally created by Terran game designers. They've simply taken a snapshot of their prewar past and expanded on it. Made it cooler, better, nicer. Added some sunshine. Some moonbeams. And there you have it: a pleasing diversion for bored Indys.

Just like the RealLife video game. Chix0r designed the game to be an escape from everyday life, allowing players to become someone more interesting for a few hours. To free themselves from the stresses and annoyances of real life.

A game for people to get away from a game. Oh god.

"Are you okay, Skye?" Dawn asks, peering at me with worried eyes.

"Skye?" I repeat bitterly. "Skye? I'm not Skye. Skye's just a made-up persona created by a video game designer. Earth doesn't exist so that means Skye doesn't exist either. You were all right all along, Dawn. I'm Mariah. Obviously I'm Mariah."

Dawn pulls me into a hug, squeezing me tight. I try to relax in his arms, but my body is trembling too hard. I bury my face in his shoulder and sob. It's all too much to take. I can barely breathe.

My whole life has been a lie. My every memory obviously implanted, just as Dawn warned. My parents, my boyfriend, my very world? Not only will I never see them again, but in reality I've never seen them at all. They don't really exist.

"I'm so sorry, Skye," Dawn murmurs.

I pull away from his hug. Angry. Hurt. Confused. Alone. *This must be hard?* Please. *Hard* doesn't even begin to explain the pain, the anguish, the horror at what I've just seen. How can I deal with this? How can I just accept the fact that my whole reality exists solely on a freaking computer server?

"So, what does this mean for the Eclipsers?" I demand, my voice harsh. "I mean, the fact that Earth's a computer program instead of another world? Will that help or hurt their cause? What does this mean?"

Dawn looks at me helplessly. "I don't know," he says. "I hadn't thought about it, really. I'm more worried about you."

His words bring a small comfort. I remind myself that I am not facing this horror alone. I've had a great shock, sure, but at the same time, I'd already long ago given up my world in exchange for a life here. I belong on Terra. With the Eclipsers, with the Dark Siders—with Dawn, who loves me completely, no matter what. So, as horrifying as it is to realize my whole past has been a lie, at least I can be assured that my future is true.

"It does prove a point, I suppose," Dawn adds. "Now we know for sure that the government is just trying to steal the Indys' money and land."

"We need to find a way to let the Indys know," I say, pulling out my camera and taking a few snapshots of the room. I'm desperate to focus, to push down the panic growing inside me. "For proof," I explain.

Dawn looks at me. "Are you okay?" he asks again. "You don't

have to be strong here. You've just been through a horrible shock. It's okay to be upset."

I swallow hard, loving him so much at that moment I can barely stand it. "I know," I manage to say without choking. "I'll deal with it later. Right now, we have to focus on our mission."

I finish taking photos and we step outside the room. My legs feel like lead, making it nearly impossible to walk. My brain won't calm down, reeling at top speed. I'd like nothing more than to find a quiet room and just sit down and process it all in my head, alone. But analysis will have to wait until we're safe.

We head back through the server room, my chest hurting as I see the whirring machines, knowing my whole life is stored somewhere on those hard drives. Everything that means anything to me could simply be deleted at a moment's notice. A simple patch to fix a bug could wipe out my whole existence.

Still, I'm a real person, I try to reassure myself. Most of my memories may be fake, but I'm real. I'm Mariah. A revolutionary leader. A savior to the downtrodden. The girl Dawn loves. I've got to hold on to that.

We go back out into the hallway to continue our search for the exit. We come to a dead end with a locked door that I open with the simulator, praying it's a way out. Instead, it opens into a room filled with large file cabinets against the walls. Curious, I walk over to one, peering at its label.

Rupert Smith 11-01-2107

I pull open the drawer, to see what kind of files they might have on old Rupert. To my surprise, the drawer actually contains Rupert himself. Or what's left of him, anyway. His corpse lies white and stiff on a cold metal slab. I put two and two together and realize what this whole room must be.

"A morgue," I exclaim. "Dawn, come look at this."

Dawn walks over to my side, peering down at poor Rupert, a former middle-aged Indy by the look of it. His corpse is swollen, naked, drained of blood, and pasty white, a pair of dark shades over his eyes. I reach down, slowly pulling the dark glasses off his face, wondering why he's wearing them and nothing else. But what's behind the shades makes me stumble backward in shock. Dawn catches me, propping me up, looking as horrified as I feel.

And here I'd thought it couldn't get any worse.

"Oh my God!" I murmur, desperate but unable to look away.

The sockets where Rupert's eyes should have been are now hollow, blackened pits; charred remnants of his former peepers. "How strange." I hurriedly replace the sunglasses. "It's almost as if he gazed into the sun too long. But that's crazy. You guys don't even have sunshine. So, what could have burned out his eyes?"

"Maybe the moon."

I whirl around, eyes wide. Will this day ever stop surprising me? "Moongazing," I whisper in shocked realization. "Do you think? I mean, could it really?" I gesture helplessly to the corpse.

Dawn shrugs. "Seems entirely possible. If Earth really is just a computer-generated game, then that obviously means you're not really traveling to another world when they lock you in one of their rooms. You're stuck twenty-four-seven in a video game simulation. And the visuals are intense, right? So intense you believe they're real. What if, after wearing these glasses long-term, they end up literally burning up your eyes?"

"And kill you, evidently, as well," I add, shoving Rupert's corpse back into the cabinet and slamming the drawer. I lean against the wall, sucking in a breath. "I guess that's not something they'd put in the brochure."

Dawn screws up his face. "All along you're thinking you've just traveled to a whole other plane of existence, a brave new world that you and your fellow Indys are populating. You're ready to start a new life," he says. "But in reality, you're stuck in a box, lost in a drug-induced hallucination until your brain crumbles and your eyes are literally burnt out of your head."

"And the government pockets all your assets," I say. "This would solve the population problem to boot. It's brilliant in a way. Sick, but brilliant."

I stare at the rows upon rows of boxes, each labeled with a name and date. All these people went willingly to their deaths, lambs to the slaughter, with no one the wiser. Rupert's friends, his family, his coworkers—they all assume he's now living a perfect life on a better world. No one has any idea of his real new digs: a nine-by-three drawer in a government fridge.

I pull out the drawer again and take a photo of the body. Then I go to the next drawer, slide out the dead Indy there, and take another. I repeat this over and over, taking photos of corpse after corpse. Each looks exactly the same: naked, bloated, blackened pits for eyes. My stomach churns with nausea, begging me to stop, but

I ignore it. This is too important to be queasy.

"The dates of death," Dawn observes, scanning the drawers, "are all recent. These are all labeled from the last week." He walks to the other side of the room. "These are a bit older. It looks like these people died a few months ago."

I cross the room to join him, yanking open a drawer of one of the less recently deceased. I take a photo. The body still has the telltale blackened eyes, but it looks yellowed, shrunken.

"Why do they keep them?" I wonder aloud. "Why not just bury them or something?"

"Who knows? Maybe they don't want them found. Or maybe they're experimenting on them, trying to discover why they die prematurely. Or perhaps they even harvest their organs. I mean, if it's only their minds and eyes that go, they die with healthy livers and kidneys and hearts, right? Perfect for the fat-cat government officials to use to prolong their own miserable lives."

I shiver at the thought. "That's disgusting. But it does make sense."

I head to the back of the room to another set of drawers. Just a few more pictures and I'll have enough evidence to rally the Indys and get them to force the government to shut down the Moongazing program for good. It won't save these poor people, but at least it will prevent others from dying the same horrible way.

"I wonder how long it takes for someone to die," Dawn says, pulling out another drawer. "It must be a while. After all, you were inside for a few months before the Eclipsers pulled you out."

"Thank God they did," I say, scanning the drawers. I've shot a lot of male bodies. I'd like a woman this time. "Or I'd have ended up—" The words die in my throat as my eyes focus on a name on one of the drawers. My camera falls out of my hands and crashes onto the floor. "Dawn," I cry, my voice scratchy and hoarse. "I think you'd better get over here."

I stare at the name, hoping, begging, praying that I'm somehow reading it wrong. But no. It's there, clear as day. The name I never expected in a million years to read on a drawer in a morgue: *Mariah Quinn.*

TWENTY

"What is it?" Dawn asks, instantly appearing at my side. But my throat's closed up and I can't speak. I point a shaky finger at the drawer. Dawn stares, his mouth gaping, then turns to me, an uncomprehending look on his face.

"What the hell?" he whispers. "How can that—how can that be?"

I shake my head. I have no idea. I really thought nothing could top the shock of learning that Earth was just a virtual reality video game. But if Earth is a game, then by all rights I have to be Mariah. And if I'm Mariah, I'm obviously not a corpse. Which leads us to the ultimate question. Who's in the drawer?

"Maybe it's empty," Dawn reasons, not sounding all that convinced. "Maybe they're saving it for you, hoping to kill you and then put you there."

I swallow hard. "Right," I agree. "That must be it. The drawer's probably empty."

We fall silent, staring at the drawer, neither one ready to test the theory.

"Should … should I open it?" I ask at last. "I mean, so we have proof that there's no one inside?" I really would rather not, but how can I just walk away not knowing? I've come this far. I have to know the truth, no matter what it turns out to be.

"I don't know," Dawn says, sounding at a loss. He reaches down and grabs the camera on the floor, fingering the lens. I stare at the drawer, my heart thudding painfully in my chest. What to do, what to do, what to do?

I take a deep breath and yank it open.

The drawer isn't empty. There's a corpse lying on the slab. The body of a girl. A naked girl with glasses who looks exactly like me.

I stumble backward, then fall to my knees, unable to catch my breath. I double over and throw up, sickly yellow bile spewing from my lips and pooling onto the stone floor. Dawn grabs me, pulling my hair from my face and rubbing a hand over my back. He's saying something, something soothing, but the blood pounding in my ears makes it impossible to hear what's coming from his lips. I take a deep breath and pull myself to my feet, vision blurry with unshed tears. I shiver, my body suddenly freezing cold. I realize I'm likely going into shock and I try to break free from the darkness, pull myself together. Losing it now could end very badly.

"Wow, its not every day you get to see your own dead body," I mutter, going for gallows humor. Or 'Gazing humor, I guess, as the case might be.

Dawn grabs and pulls me into a fierce, smothering hug, squeezing me tightly against him. I realize he's shaking, too, as terrified and confused as I am, but trying to be strong for the both of us. I bury my face in his chest, sobbing.

"I don't understand," I blubber. "I'm not dead. How can my body be in this morgue?"

"I don't know," Dawn answers helplessly. "I just don't know."

"It's definitely me, though, right? It's definitely Mariah?" I can't bear to take another look.

Dawns shifts in my arms for a second glance. "Yes," he says after a pause. "It's definitely Mariah. And it appears she's got the burned-out eyeball thing like the rest of them." He takes a few pictures of the corpse. "I'm going to upload these photos and send them back to headquarters," he says, pressing a few buttons on the camera. "They have to see this. *Now.*"

I nod, barely listening, my whole world spun off its axis. "So, if that's Mariah, then who am I?"

"You, my dear," pipes in a voice from across the room, "are not exactly a 'who' at all."

Dawn and I whirl around. At the entrance to the morgue stands Duske, flanked by six heavily armed guards. He's dressed in a severe black suit, and his thumbs are swathed in white cotton bandages.

Without giving reason a second thought, I rip my sword from its sheath and charge forward, blinded by rage and madness. My vision is red. This man must die. Die for what he did to the people. Die for what he did to Mariah. Die for whatever the hell he's done to me. Whoever I am.

The guards step in front of him, pulling out their own swords and effectively protecting their master. I stop my advance, sword still held high in the air, glowering at the man who is responsible for so many broken lives. Duske grins and gestures for the guards to withdraw. He pulls out his own sword. "This is excellent," he says. "I've wanted to see you fight ever since I created you. After all, you were programmed with all the top training."

I squint at him. "Programmed? What the hell is that supposed to mean?"

Duske shakes his head. "Fight first," he commands. "If you best me, I will tell you everything."

"If I best you, you will be dead and thus unable to speak."

"No, no, my dear," Duske says laughingly. "My guards will not let me die. Don't be stupid. We'll simply spar until there is a clear champion. But we must agree not to shed any blood. I will not kill you if you agree not to kill me."

"From what I saw in the drawer over there, it appears I'm already dead. And why should I believe even for a second that you won't just have me killed later?" I glare at him, not wanting to play games anymore. I should have killed him back at the house. Not doing so was a big mistake.

Duske shrugs. "Because you know I am a man of honor?" he suggests. Then he laughs. "No, I guess that could not be it. How about because you need to know the truth? You're desperate for answers and you know I'm the only one who can give them to you. If you're going to die anyway, wouldn't you prefer to die knowing the truth?"

He's got me there. There's no way I can even pretend the truth doesn't concern me. After seeing my own face dead in a drawer, realizing the world I thought I was from is just a virtual dream, it's now vitally important I find out who I really am.

I raise my sword again, the blade flashing under the lights. "All right," I say. "Let's do this." Maybe he'll be weak. After all, how does one grasp a sword with cut thumbs? But then I remember Dawn healing my wrist. He probably just went to an nT medic and had the skin grown back in minutes.

"Skye—" Dawn interrupts my racing thoughts. "You don't have to do this."

"Actually, I think I do," I reply, feeling an inner power swell inside me. It's a growing strength and retreating fear. This is a fight for the truth. And I have to win.

Duske brandishes his blade and steps forward. I launch into an attack, swinging my sword expertly in one hand. I don't remember learning to fight, but somehow, something inside me knows how to do it—as if I were born with the knowledge.

You weren't born at all, an inner voice nags. I push it aside.

Our swords clash, the blades singing high-pitched squeals. I slide my sword downward, freeing the blade, then swing upward. Duske catches it again easily. He's good, I realize. Maybe too good.

Back and forth we flurry, blades coming together, separating, then meeting once again. Sweat drips down my forehead, between my breasts, as I dance around him, looking for a sign of weakness. But he seems to effortlessly predict my every move. I'm not sure he's even trying that hard. He certainly doesn't seem winded.

Thinking I see an opening, I lunge. He parries with a twist of the wrist, tossing me a self-satisfied grin. He's toying with me, I realize. If I want to win I can't do it this way. I have to try something he won't expect. Something that's not "all fair in love and swordplay." It's then that I remember my character Allora's finishing move in RealLife. The one my boss, Madeline, criticized for being without honor. *Chivalry is based on a code,* she had lectured. Everything is based on rules. But she was just an NUC, a computer-generated character.

And I'm done playing by the rules.

I drop to my knees, swing my blade, and slash at his ankles. He screams in pain as the sword makes contact with his Achilles tendon. He stumbles backward, bellowing in rage. I leap to my feet and point my blade at his now unprotected throat.

"You bitch," he snaps. "You weren't supposed to hurt me."

"You'll live," I snarl back. "Unless I decide to kill you." I press the blade against his throat, just enough to draw a tiny droplet of blood. One step forward and I can drive the weapon straight through and no number of guards can save his life. But, I realize, then I'd never find out the truth. And the guards will simply kill me and then Dawn after their master is dead.

Reluctantly, I lower the sword. The guards step forward and disarm me, then tie my hands behind my back. They do the same to Dawn, roughly shuffling us both to one wall.

Duske reaches down and wraps a strip of cloth torn from his suit over his wound, still grumbling. It's immediately soaked in blood. That's got to really hurt. I can't believe he's still conscious. One of the guards kneels before him and takes the ankle in his hands, closing his eyes, just as Dawn did to my wrist. Must be a Healer. How convenient to have one on staff.

A few moments later, the bleeding's stopped and Duske's able to walk. He saunters over to me, positioning himself so he's inches from my face. "You should have killed me when you had the chance," he says with a bitter laugh.

"Yes, yes," I reply, trying to sound nonchalant, while inside everything is trembling with fear. "But I didn't. So how about you keep up your end of the bargain? Tell me everything."

Duske grins. "Gladly. In fact, I'm looking forward to it. Ask away."

I swallow hard, getting up my nerve. Ignoring my pounding heart. "Is Earth just a game?" I manage to spit out.

Duske frowns. "It's not *just a* game. It's the most miraculous creation in the history of the world. It's a new form of reality. A virtual escape, if you will, for all that plagues the Terran people. An amazing recreation of Terra the century before the war."

"Some escape," I mutter, glancing over at the drawers of bodies.

"Well, yes, we're still working out the kinks. Right now it's too expensive to run on a long-term basis. Do you think we want to be stuck intravenously feeding players for their entire Terran life spans? Or worrying about disposing of their bodily fluids? Also, we've found that after a few weeks, the Terran mind starts to decay from the fully immersive experience. So it's far better to pull the 'Gazers from their misery before their organs rot and their bodies are rendered unusable."

"But you've promised these people a new life on Earth! Instead, you kill them."

"But don't you see? They *do* get a new life. We speed up the game. Twenty Earth years can pass within a day of Terran time if we want. When someone commits to a full emigration we put their life on fast forward. By the time their mind starts to decay, they've already experienced an entirely full life. They're old. They're *ready* to die." He smiles, obviously proud. "And in return, here on Terra, we solve the overpopulation problem and help fund government programs. Besides, all of our subjects are perfectly willing to go."

"But if they knew how they'd end up …"

Duske shrugs. "What's the difference, because they never will. They'll die peacefully, thinking they've lived out an entire life in paradise. What could be better than that?"

"What about Mariah?" Dawn interrupts.

"Ah, Mariah," Duske says. "Beautiful, sweet Mariah." He wanders over to the back of the room and looks adoringly down at the naked body lying on the slab. "We started noticing her poking around Earth about six months ago. She tried to give a false identity, but there's not much our daemons—the program's security subroutines—don't pick up on. Not to mention it's nearly impossible for a celebrated rebel like her to keep a low profile. We were amused by her interest, and so we let her take a peek around, knowing she would never find anything wrong. Not on the surface."

"And then she got addicted?" Dawn asks.

"Sure." Duske shrugs. "If you want to call it that. The more she jumped back and forth, the more taxing it became on her brain. With all the 'Gaze she was inhaling, her life on Earth started seeming more real to her than her life on Terra." He smirks. "So that's when we decided to make our move—make it look like the infamous Mariah Quinn, would-be savior of the Dark Siders, turned traitor."

"Make it look like?" Dawn repeats. "You mean she didn't actually …?"

Duske stares at him, then starts to laugh. "Didn't actually betray you?" he asks. "You really think she did?" He shakes his head in mirth. "You two may have been together, but you obviously didn't know the girl very well at all. She was as loyal as they come. I mean, sure, she became a brainless, desperate drug addict, but still she refused to betray the Eclipsers up until the very end. And believe me, we tried a great deal to make her spill."

"So then, how did you know about our plans to sabotage the seminar?" Dawn demands. "You knew things that only she could have told you."

Duske smiles. "Once we realized that no amount of convincing was going to get her to talk, we simply allowed her to go 'Gazing in a specially doctored booth. While she was inside, we ran a brain scan and stripped her mind of all short-term memories. After running a quick analysis through a supercomputer, we got all the details we needed to thwart your pathetic plan. And Mariah never had any idea."

Dawn is silent for a moment, probably trying to digest this startling revelation. The girl he's been thinking a villain all this time is actually an innocent victim. He must feel so guilty for judging her. But how could he have known that in this instance two plus two did not equal four?

"But she still left us," he says at last, grasping at straws. "She still abandoned her people for a better life on Earth."

"Please." Duske snorts. "She didn't go anywhere. She was too sick. Her brain wouldn't have survived another trip. We didn't waste the resources. Once we had the information we needed, we killed her and sent in Skye here to start 'Gazing in her place."

"So then who am I?" I interject. My head is spinning. "Where do I come from and why do I look exactly like Mariah?" Even as I ask, I'm not sure I want to hear the truth.

"You're the spare."

"The spare?" I think I'm going to be sick again.

"Sure. A clone. Similar to the nTs. We took a sample of Mariah's genetic code and grew a new version. Then we implanted false memories of Earth, mostly stolen from our nonuser character designs. The idea was to send the new Mariah to Earth in place of the real one so people would see her there. We could relay back clips of your new life if we wanted, prove that Mariah had really migrated there. And if we needed you for something, we could bring you back. Hell, you never do know when a spare revolutionary leader turned traitor might come in handy." He laughs.

I stare at him, unable to even breathe. "You mean?"

He smiles. "Yes, Skye. You are that clone. You have the same genetic makeup as Mariah. Same fingerprints, same DNA. But your brain is filled with a false life on Earth that we created especially for you. You are not now, nor were you ever, Mariah. In fact, you are not, nor were you ever, a real person at all."

My face crumbles, tears robbing me of my vision. So, I'm not Mariah. I'm not the girl Dawn is in love with. I'm just a clone. A nonuser character. A fantasy. My whole life, every memory, is a lie.

"In reality, Skye, you've only been alive for about three months," Duske says.

"But how come ..." I'm grasping at the falling straws. "How come I remember sometimes? I mean, fleeting images, feelings. In Terra I feel like I have déjà vu all the time."

Duske nods grimly. "Our experiment wasn't a hundred percent successful. For some reason you seem to retain a few memories of Mariah. We're still not quite sure why. You even tried to escape us once. Do you remember? Before we implanted those memories in you? Back then you were a shell of a person, with no past, present, or future, and yet you took off, almost escaped into the underground. It could have been a disaster had my men not captured you in time."

The dream of my running through the underground flashes through my mind. I remember being frightened, absolutely terrified, not knowing where I was—or even who I was.

I had no idea that was because, in truth, I wasn't anyone at all.

TWENTY-ONE

We're thrown into a bare cell on the other side of the building, similar in style to the one that caged Glenda, though *style* may be the wrong word. The cell is filthy, the walls stained fecal brown, the floors damp and reeking of piss. A rickety cot in the corner is the only furnishing, clothed with thin gray sheets and a ratty yellow blanket.

"Sorry about the room," Duske says as the guards lock us in, not really sounding all that broken up about it. "It's the best we can do on such short notice. Next time, do warn us when you'll be dropping by." He pauses. "Oh, wait," he adds, as if something just occurred to him. "There won't be a next time. So sorry." He peers between the bars. "Better say your good-byes now, dearies. In a couple of hours, Skye here will be going under another little memory transplant."

"Memory transplant?" I repeat, my mind still reeling.

"Oh yes," Duske says. "It's a two-part procedure, actually. Part one will get rid of all the memories you currently have in your head. It's like one big magnet, erasing your brain like a disk. And then, after that happens, my doctors will perform the second part. They'll inject you with a little memory cocktail we've whipped up, give you a brand-new identity. We're going to turn you into a Mariah who has spent time on Earth as herself. She remembers all of her past revolutionary activities but has now found peace and happiness in her new world. She has returned for one night only, to speak at my Moongazing seminar and let all the Indys know just how wonderful Earth really is."

"That's crazy!" I cry. "I'd never—"

"You'd never what?" Duske asks, his face darkening. "Lie for me? As far as you know you'll be telling the truth, my dear. When the doctors are through with you, you won't have any recollection of this conversation. Or *any* conversations, really, besides the made-up ones we'll inject into your head. Sorry to break it to you, sweetie, but remember you're just a clone to do with what we like. With just a small dose of serum injected into your cerebral cortex, we can transform you into anyone at all." He pats the bars of the cell. "So, it was nice knowing you, *Skye*," he says. "I look forward to meeting the new you very shortly. Maybe I'll even throw in a crush on me this time. So we can finish what you started."

He turns and exits the room, flanked by his guards. The metal doors clank shut, leaving Dawn and me alone in filth and darkness. I consider screaming and yelling, and even begging for freedom, but I know there's no use, so instead I resignedly wander over to the cot and slump down on the grimy mattress. It creaks under my weight, but I'm so wrapped up in my terrified thoughts I scarcely notice.

Dawn joins me, his face ashen. He kneels in front of me, taking my hands in his. He brings them to his lips, pressing my knuckles against his soft mouth, capturing my eyes with his. We sit there for a long while, thoughts whirling madly inside our heads, but nothing seemingly worth saying out loud.

"I can't bear this," Dawn finally says in a choked voice, breaking the silence. He drops my hands and rises to his feet, pacing the cell like a wild tiger, caged. "To lose you again. It's just …"

I sigh, feeling very old, even though I now know I'm a mere babe of three months. "Didn't you hear a word Duske said? You're not losing me again. I'm not Mariah. Your precious Mariah is lying in a drawer."

"I meant lose you again like when you went back to Earth. As Skye," Dawn corrects.

I screw up my face in frustration. "But don't you get it? I'm not Skye either! I'm no one! I'm just some freaking clone that, at the end of the day, doesn't really even exist. You were right when you said being with me is like being with a shell. That's all I am."

Dawn turns to me, eyes wild, face haunted. "Skye, don't say

that," he says. "Don't buy into their game. You're a person. Just like me or anyone else. You're real. Special."

"Special? Please. I'm nothing more than a puppet designed to promote government propaganda. Everything about me, everything in my head is all made up." I squeeze my hands into fists, angry tears blurring my vision and pity wracking my insides. "Admit it, Dawn. You never loved me. You only wanted me because you thought deep down I was really your ex-girlfriend. But I'm not. And I never was."

"You're wrong," Dawn exclaims, dropping back to his knees in front of me. "You're so, so wrong. Sure, my early affections for you may have been sparked because I thought you were Mariah. But I've known for a while now that you aren't."

"Yeah, right."

"I'm serious," he says. "Mariah was a wonderful person, and at one time I loved her more than life itself. In a way, I probably always will hold a special spot for her in my heart." He rakes a hand through his hair. "You can't imagine what it means to me to find out that she didn't really betray us. That, even weakened by addiction, she stayed strong and never sold us out. Never took the easy road. What a girl she was!"

"Yes, yes, the great and wonderful Mariah," I mutter, trying to keep the bitterness at bay. His lauding is not exactly making me feel any better.

"It's funny," he says, stroking his chin thoughtfully. "I figured that finding out the truth would finally allow me to put my anger aside. But the weird thing is, it's already long gone." He smiles. "And that's got a lot to do with you."

I cock my head. "What did I do?"

"You were just you. Passionate. Self-sacrificing. Patient. Kind. You helped even pigheaded, stuck-in-the-past me realize that it really is possible to learn to love again. To fall head over heels for someone who is totally different than Mariah but equally as special."

"But how can you love me?" I ask, choking on my words. "I'm not even a person. I'm not real."

"Are you kidding me?" Dawn asks, incredulous. "In the short time you've been here, you've done so much. And not for your own gain. When given the chance to go home, you decided to stay. You risked your life by seducing Duske to get his thumbprint.

Then you risked it again by coming here with me. You did this all to save a people you didn't even know. To redeem a world that isn't even yours. And you weren't after fame and glory from your heroics. You helped because you couldn't bear to see people suffer. You've done more in the few months you've been alive than most people do in their entire lives. I'm in awe of you. And I'm in love with you."

Tears fall from my eyes as I listen to his words. Could it be true? Could at some point his feelings have really shifted from mourning Mariah to loving me?

"Before you came I'd given up hope. I'd quit the Eclipsers and resigned myself to living an empty life," Dawn continues. "You changed all that. Now, when I look at you, I get this crazy feeling inside. A feeling that we could take over the world or something." He searches my face with an earnest, open expression. "Mariah means nothing to me anymore. I love you, Skye."

It's all I can bear. I throw myself into his arms, burying my head into his shoulder, sobbing. "I love you, too," I cry. "So much more than anything, ever. You say I'm noble, but the truth is, one of the main reasons I came back was for you."

Dawn pulls out of our embrace, then leans forward to press his lips against mine. I kiss him, knowing that this may be the last time I recognize his lips. He lays me down on the cot, crawling on top of me, and kissing me over and over again. Every caress—every touch—is a knife through my heart as I realize it may be the last. I desperately try to burn memories of each touch into my brain. Memories that can't be erased, no matter how strong the magnet. The trail of kisses against the hollow of my throat. The tender fingers tracing my waist. How is it possible I could forget all of this? Forget him? I'd easier forget my very self.

Oh god, this isn't fair.

We fall asleep in each other's arms, but it's not a restful slumber. I keep waking up, panicked and worried about falling back into dreamland and losing my last moments of reality. I want to remember this night forever: the warmth of Dawn's arms wrapped securely around me, his body spooning mine. His heartbeat, his musky scent, his sweet breath exhaling in my ear— priceless sensations that should embed in my brain as everlasting memories, not be robbed from my consciousness to further a government plot.

But there's nothing we can do. And soon, way too soon, the prison door clangs open. Jarred awake, we leap from bed, realizing the time is here. The point of no return is upon us too soon. Two guards enter the cell. Dawn steps in front of me, fists raised. He's not letting me go without a fight.

But the guards aren't interested. They club him several times until he stumbles, then collapses to the floor. "No!" he cries, pain and fear choking his voice. "Don't take her! Don't you bastards take her from me!"

The guards laugh. One of them kicks Dawn in the stomach. He bellows in rage, helpless and emasculated on the filthy floor. The guard with the club approaches me, waving it in my face with a smirk. "You going to come along quietly, Sister?" he asks. "Or would you like to be 'managed' as well?"

"Screw you," I growl, kicking him in the groin. If I'm going to go down, it's going to be fighting. After all, in a few minutes, I won't remember the pain anyway. But these guys will.

The guard doubles over, stumbling backward. The club goes skidding across the floor. I make a dive for it, my one hope, my one chance, but the second guard reaches it before I do. He picks it up and strikes me hard enough to make me see stars. I collapse. He laughs and motions to the first guard to help him pick me up. One takes my shoulders and the other my feet, and they carry me outside the cell and onto a gurney. They must have expected they'd have to beat me. Or maybe they would have even if I hadn't resisted.

I look back at Dawn, who's still lying on the floor. There's blood on his face. Tears flood my eyes. This will be the last time I ever see him. Or at least the last time I recognize him.

"Skye," Dawn calls out in a hoarse voice. "I love you. No matter what happens, never forget that I love you!"

"I love you, too, Dawn," I tell him, forcing the words from my throat. They seem so useless. Though, at least for him, he'll be able to remember.

Is it better to have loved and forgotten than to have never loved at all?

"What a sweet good-bye," sneers the guard. "Too bad in a few minutes you won't know this guy from Duske."

Furious, I spit on him. The guard just laughs, not even bothering to wipe the loogie off his cheek. If only I had my sword, I'd chop him into a thousand pieces. A thousand and ten pieces, so even his mother wouldn't recognize him. And I'd do it slowly, too. So he'd feel every cut. So he'd know what it's like to lose something he cares about.

But I'm weaponless, powerless, and so I lie helpless on the gurney as the guards wheel me down the hall and into a sterile, all-white room—a sharp contrast to the disgustingly filthy cell. From the stethoscopes and hammers and blood-pressure cuffs hanging on the wall, I gather this is some kind of doctor's office. But I know I'm not just here for a checkup. The guards drag me up onto the bed and bind my arms and legs in four-point restraints, then exit the room.

A few moments later, a man in a white coat enters the room. He's about fifty, slender of build, with graying blond hair and a stethoscope around his neck. He pulls a chart from the wall and peers down at it before speaking.

"So, you're here for a memory transplant," he says, hanging the clipboard back on the wall.

"You'll never get away with this," I tell him, though I'm not sure what the hell will stop him. "You can erase my memory a thousand times. But I'll find you, someday, somehow. I'll track you to the ends of the earth—er, Terra—and make you pay for what you've done."

"Do whatever you feel is necessary," he says mildly. I squeeze my hands into fists, furious that I can't get any reaction from him.

He places the cap over my head and flips a switch on a large metal machine next to my bedside. A whirring noise starts. "Here we go," he says. "Don't worry. This won't hurt a bit."

But he's lying. A moment later, icy cold shards stab through my scalp. The machine's whirring grows louder and louder, its only competition: my screams of agony. I can feel tiny fingers invading my brain, robbing my thoughts, sucking out my memories. Oh God, it's really happening.

I desperately try to cling to one simple image: Dawn's face. I etch it firmly in my consciousness. If everything else goes, at least maybe I can somehow hold on to that. Somehow, some way. Grab the memory of his love and not let go, no matter what the pressure.

But it's like trying to hold on to grains of sand. Eventually, like everything else, even Dawn slips from my grasp.

TWENTY-TWO

I open my eyes. I'm in a small white room, strapped to some kind of bed in four-point restraints. There are instruments everywhere, as if this is some kind of doctor's office or something.

But how did I get here? And where is here? And while we're asking the questions, who am I, anyway?

I have no idea.

TWENTY-THREE

I lie, tied to a bed, trying to think, trying to process, to remember, for what seems like hours. It's no use. I can't recall my name, never mind who I am or why I'd possibly be lying here, strapped to a bed. All I know is that I'm terrified and my empty brain races a mile a minute, trying to make sense of it all.

A middle-aged man in a white lab coat enters the room, flanked by two uniformed guards. He lifts a plastic cap from my head and pulls out a lighted instrument from his pocket to peer into my eyes.

"Who are you?" he asks in a conversational tone.

"I was hoping you'd be able to tell me that," I reply.

I notice the guards tossing each other self-satisfied glances. Evidently my answer pleases them, though I don't have the faintest idea why it would. The doctor says nothing, continuing with his examination, listening to my heartbeat with his stethoscope and then following up with a check on my blood pressure. I know all the tests he's doing. I get what each of them is designed to do. I understand words, can interpret body language. So, how come I can't remember who the hell I am or what I'm doing here?

"She's good to go back," the doctor announces to the guards. "She'll have to rest a couple of hours before we perform stage two of the operation. Go ahead and inform your boss that the procedure was successful."

I cock my head in confusion over his words. Stage two of the operation? I'm supposed to undergo some kind of surgery? More surgery? I glance down at my body, searching for marks of some previous procedure. But there's no evidence I was ever touched.

"What's going on here?" I demand, my voice quaking.

The doctor waves a dismissive hand. "Don't worry," he says, walking over to the sink to clean some instruments. "You'll understand everything after phase two." He turns to the guards. "Well, what are you waiting for?" he demands. "Take her back to her cell."

"They haven't removed the other prisoner yet," one of the guards says.

"What does it matter?" the doctor says. "She won't know him."

Appearing satisfied, the guards step up to my sides and unlatch my restraints. They help me to my feet. I'm weak, but I can walk. I wonder for a moment if I should fight them, try to get away. But where would I go? Best maybe to bide my time and figure out what's going on before I make any rash moves.

I regret this decision a moment later when they drag me into a small holding cell, near empty save a small cot in one corner. I wrinkle my nose. The place is filthy. Disgusting. The stench is nearly overwhelming. I shudder. Am I a prisoner here? And if so, who are my captors and what do they want from me?

The guards shove me into the cell and lock the door behind me. It's then that I realize I'm not alone. There's a teenage guy in here, probably the one they were referring to, squatting in a corner of the cage, his head buried in his hands. When the cell door slams shut, he leaps to his feet, his face white and questioning. His eyes fall on me and I gasp at their beauty. They're so blue they almost glow. And the way he's staring at me ... as if he knows me. As if he's had a lifetime with me. I search my empty brain for recognition, but none comes. I have no idea who this guy is. If he's a stranger or soulmate.

"Skye!" the guy cries as he rushes over, throwing his arms around me. Alarmed by his sudden embrace, I jump back, but he grabs on, clamping down on my shoulders with strong hands. Reflexively, I knee him in the groin. He stumbles backward, hunching over, hands over his privates. His squints up at me, his expression a mix of physical agony and mental anguish. Suddenly I feel bad that I hurt him. Though, in my defense, he shouldn't have just jumped me like that.

"Nice to see you again, too, Skye," he says, retreating to the cot. He slumps down and it groans under his weight. "Déjà vu all over again, I guess."

"What is that supposed to mean?" I demand, keeping my back to the cell door. "And who are you? And who—" I start to ask about my own identity, but think twice before the words escape my lips. I might not want to let on how vulnerable I am right now. He may try to take advantage. Make up some story to get me on his side before he rapes and murders me.

The guy stares at me for a minute, with a level of horror I've never seen before on a face. (At least that I can remember.) Then he buries his face in his hands and wails. "God!" he says. "I can't do this again. I just can't."

I shift from left hip to right, not sure what to do, what to say. The poor guy looks completely devastated and I have no idea why.

"Look, guy," I try. "I'm sorry I kneed you and all. But I'm a bit lost, you see. Not sure where I am or what I'm doing here. First I wake up in four-point restraints. Then I'm dragged into this disgusting cell. Then you jump all over me and ..." I shrug. "I assumed the worst, I guess."

The man draws in a deep breath. "Right. I'm sorry, too. I didn't mean to scare you. I was just happy to see you alive. I forgot for a moment that you wouldn't remember me." He scrubs his face with his hands, then rises from the couch, hand outstretched. "Hello, I'm Dawn Grey, your fellow prisoner here in the Terran government jail."

I stick out my hand hesitantly. He takes it and pumps it twice. His grip is strong, firm, but there's a bit of a tremble just beneath the surface.

I decide to go for it. Who knows, maybe he can help me. We *are* both stuck in the same cell. "Do you know who I am, by chance?" I ask, crossing my fingers he'll be able to at least answer that.

"Yes. Of course," he says. "You're Skye Brown."

Okay, we have a name. I run it through my brain to check for resonance. Nothing. But at least I have something to call myself now. "And why are we here, locked up?" I question. "Did we commit some sort of crime?" Could I be a bad guy? That seems so unlikely, yet why else would I be behind bars in a government prison?

"If you call fighting for freedom a crime," Dawn says cryptically.

"God, I wish I could remember," I groan, plopping down on

the cot and rubbing my temples.

"It's probably not worth trying too hard," Dawn says, sitting down beside me. "They're only going to fill your brain with new memories in a few hours. I doubt you'll remember any of this conversation."

I look up. "New memories? What about my old ones?"

"They erased them."

"Erased my memories? You mean, like, on purpose?" I stare at him, even more baffled than before. "Why would anyone want to do that?"

Dawn shrugs. "Because they need you to convince a bunch of innocent people to spend a great deal of money on something that will kill them."

I don't understand half of what he's talking about. But I do know one thing. "Look, I may not know who I am, but I do know there's no way I'd do something that would end up with people being killed."

"Not now. But you will tomorrow. Because when they implant new memories in you, you'll suddenly believe that Moongazing's the ticket to happiness. And you won't remember anything about the dangers."

I slump my shoulders, defeated and scared. I have no idea what he's talking about, but none of it sounds good. If only I could remember something!

I feel a warm breath on my cheek and turn to face Dawn. He slowly reaches out and cups my chin in his hand, finding my eyes. It's as if he's searching somehow, desperately attempting to locate my lost self deep inside. I stare back at him, trying as hard as I can to remember his face. His earnest, soulful eyes. How could I forget someone as beautiful as him? How could I forget my own self?

"Don't worry, Skye," he whispers, gently brushing away the lone tear that's dripped down my cheek. "I won't let them hurt you. I can't stop them from implanting new memories in you, but I do promise that somehow, some way, I'll save you in the end." He pauses, his eyes cloudy. "You won't remember me when I do. In fact, you'll probably think I'm some crazy person set on kidnapping you. But it doesn't matter."

He drops my gaze and stares down at his lap. "And then I'll just start over," he says, more to himself than me. "I'll make you love me again. Somehow. Some way. If it takes the rest of my life, I'll never give up. They can erase your memory a hundred times. I won't stop making you love me all over again." He rises from his seat and begins to pace the cell. "I once gave up on Mariah. I let her go. Let her pursue her own death. I won't make that mistake again." He stands above me, then drops to his knees, grabbing my hands in his and squeezing them tightly. "I'll protect you, Skye, no matter what. I'll never let go."

I can feel tears cascading down my cheeks like so much rain. The passion and meaning in his words are overwhelming, almost too much to bear. He loves me. Truly. Madly. Deeply. Have I been deserving of such an epic love? Did I once feel the same about him? And if so, how could I have forgotten? How could such powerful, life-changing love have slipped through the cracks of my consciousness and flowed uselessly down a drain?

I throw myself into Dawn's arms, unable to resist the offered comfort. I start to sob into his shoulder, out of frustration, out of fear, out of anger at all that has been stolen from my mind without my permission. Through it all, Dawn holds me tight, stroking my back with both hands, kissing me softly on the side of my neck.

"I love you, Skye Brown," he murmurs. "And somehow, someday, you will love me again, too. I promise."

And the scary thing is, I realize as I cuddle closer, I think I already do.

TWENTY-FOUR

I cry for a long time, but eventually, the tears dry up and the sobs start to trail off. Dawn pulls me onto the cot and we cuddle. He feels so good, arms wrapped around me protectively, and I snuggle in closer. I may not remember him, but I believe with everything left inside me that he's someone I can trust. After a while, my eyelids grow heavy and sleep overtakes me.

When I awake, I find Dawn leaning over me, watching me with intense eyes.

"What?" I ask self-consciously, sitting up, wondering what he could be staring at.

His face reddens. "Sorry," he says. "I just didn't want to miss a single memory of you lying here next to me."

I smile. "You're sweet."

"Maybe sometimes," he says, grinning shyly. "But only to you."

I cuddle back into his outstretched arms again, seeking that loving warmth he's only too ready to offer. He smoothes my hair and kisses me softly on top of my head. And even though we're in a disgusting prison cell, a small part of me wants this moment to last forever.

It doesn't, however. Only minutes later the door bursts open and the two guards step into the prison. We jump to our feet and Dawn grips me tightly.

"Time for phase two," one of the guards announces. "Let's go."

"No. We want to see Duske first," Dawn says, keeping a firm grip on me.

The guards laugh. "Yeah? Well, Brother Bill and I would like to see Sleazy Sheena down at the strip club. But right now, it looks like none of us are gonna get our wishes." He holds up his club. "Want another taste of this? Come on, big boy. Have at me."

Dawn swallows hard, then turns to me. "I'm sorry," he whispers. "There's nothing I can do now. But I promise I will come for you. Try to hold on to that thought. That, and the fact that I love you. More than I can ever explain."

I can feel the tears spring to my eyes again, and I throw myself into his arms for a final hug. I feel like I've only known him a few hours and yet the bond between us is unbearable to break. But the guards aren't in the mood to wait for our hug to come to its natural conclusion. They yank me backward by the collar, wrenching me from Dawn's grasp. Our fingers lock for one moment and our eyes meet, a thousand truths passing between us in just one glance. Then I'm pulled out of the cell, kicking and screaming. Try as I might, I can't fight them. They're too strong.

They drag me down the hallway and back into the operating room where I first woke up. The man in the white coat is still here. He nods to the guards after they strap me to the bed. "Thank you," he says. "You may leave now. I'd like to begin the procedure."

The guards hesitate by the door. "We were ordered to stay," one informs the doc. "In case she causes trouble."

The doctor snorts. "This little lamb?" he asks, giving me a disdainful look. "I think I can handle one little girl. Besides, when she wakes up, she's going to think we're best friends."

"Like hell," I growl, but no one pays attention.

The guards grunt, then head toward the exit. Maybe they figure they can go catch that strip show after all. The doctor closes the door behind them. Then he heads back to my bedside, his casual expression fading into one that's much more serious.

"Don't worry," he says in a low voice that I have to strain to hear. "I'm an Eclipser. I'm on your side here."

"You have a funny way of showing it," I hiss back. "Erasing my memories and all."

He frowns. "Listen to me. I had to make it appear genuine. That you really had lost all your memories so they would believe the procedure was a success. But I didn't erase them. Not really. They've simply been flash-frozen in your brain. Everything you knew before the operation is still intact—it's just inaccessible to you at the moment. But now I'm going to flash-bake you, reactive your cerebral cortex. You'll be yourself in just a few more minutes."

I stare at him, eyes wide, hoping, praying, begging that what he says is actually true. "So, I'll get all my memories back?" I ask, crossing my fingers for an affirmative.

"It'll be as if you never lost them," the doctor says with a nod as he places a gel cap, threaded with wires, over my head. "But you can't let anyone know you've got them back. You have to promise to act as if I injected the new memories just as they ordered me to. Once the procedure is complete, you have to start playing the part of Mariah. A Mariah who's been living on Earth and loves it there." He plugs a cord leading from the cap into a tall, thin red metallic machine by my bedside. "You'll understand this better once you get your memories back."

"I hope so," I say. "Because at the moment I really don't have any clue as to what you're talking about."

"Don't worry. You will," the doctor says, patting me on the shoulder. "Very soon."

He flips a switch on the metallic machine and the cap begins to heat. It feels as if lightning bolts are piercing my skull and bugs are burrowing into my brain. I open my mouth to scream—

And suddenly I remember everything.

"Dawn!" I cry out before I can stop myself.

The doctor rushes to my bedside and clamps a hand over my mouth. "Do you want to get us both killed?" he hisses. "Remember what I told you! You have to pretend you're Mariah."

"Sorry," I mutter. But Mariah loved Dawn, too. "Listen," the doctor says in a hurried voice. "The Eclipsers are mobilizing. They're planning to sabotage the Moongazing seminar, just like they tried to do before. But this time, there's no one to stop them. When you get there, just follow their lead, okay? Pay attention and you'll realize what you need to do." He removes his hand from my mouth. "So, Mariah," he calls out in a loud cheerful voice. "Are you excited about speaking at the Moongazing seminar?"

"Oh yes," I say, matching his tone. "I can't wait to tell everyone about how wonderful Earth is. And how wrong I was to lead a revolution against the government who's found us such a paradise."

"Uh, let's not overkill," the doctor whispers.

"Mariah, darling!" Duske calls out, choosing that moment to swagger through the door. "It's so good to have you back."

"It's good to be back, Brother Duske," I say, watching as he removes my restraints. "Though, of course, I miss my home. When do you think I'll be able to return to Earth?"

"All in good time, my dear, all in good time," he says. Out of the corner of my eye I catch him giving the doctor a thumbs-up. "But first, remember, I need you to speak at my seminar tonight. To tell the Indys all about the amazing new world you have discovered on Earth."

"Right," I say, sitting up and shaking out my wrists and ankles. "I'd love to. After all, who wouldn't want to go to Earth? In fact, I don't know why more Indys haven't migrated there already. It's a true Garden of Eden."

"Indeed, my dear," Duske says. He gives a smirk that I'd like nothing more than to smack off his face. "Indeed."

We leave the surgery center and Duske escorts me back to his mansion, setting me up in my old bedroom. I notice that someone has scrubbed away all the bloodstains. Once I'm alone, I lie back on the bed, staring up at its canopy, wondering how Dawn is faring back in the prison. I only wish there was some way to get word to him. To let him know I have my memories back. I can't bear the idea of the poor guy languishing in his dirty cell, thinking he's lost me all over again. If only I could tell him that I'm okay. That I remember his love for me. And mine for him.

I look over at the clock. Three hours till the seminar. I wonder what kind of sabotage the Eclipsers have planned. What will they say? And will they really be able to prove to the Indys what a death trap their government has created?

They have to. The entire future of the world rides on what happens tonight.

TWENTY-FIVE

The Moongazing convention is being held in a large auditorium in the center of Luna Park. From what I can see from my quick peek behind the curtain, the place is packed beyond capacity. I guess the infamous Mariah Quinn as keynote speaker really draws them in. Fine by me. The more people who hear the truth, the better.

In my hands I shuffle through the pages of the speech Duske prepared for me. The one I'm not planning to read. I wonder how quickly the government will catch on and realize that I'm condemning them rather than reciting their propaganda. Perhaps it'll be once they hear the word *paradise* replaced with *deadly virtual reality that will burn out your eyes and rot your brain*. Or maybe it will be when I replace the words *new life* with *genocide, designed to rob you of your cash and vital organs*. How much will I be able to tell them before I'm dragged offstage? And will I be sentenced to death for my crimes against the government, or will they attempt another erase?

A lump forms in my throat. I know I have to do this. So many lives depend on it. But at the same time, I don't want to die. Especially not before I see Dawn again. Not that I'm positive he's still alive himself. Would they have killed him? Did he die thinking I'd forgotten who he was? If only I could have one more minute with him. One brief moment to throw my arms around him and squeeze him tight and let him know that I remember everything. Every whisper, every caress, every evocation of love.

At least if he's still alive he'll hear of my last act, when word of my speech trickles down through the underground. At least he'll know that I sacrificed my life for the people. I hope he realizes that every word will be dedicated to him.

"It's almost time, my dear," Duske says, coming up behind me and yanking me from my troubled thoughts. "Are you ready for your glorious debut?"

I turn around and toss him a guileless smile. "I'm ready," I say brightly. "So very ready."

"Good," he says. "I will go out and introduce you. Warm up the crowd a bit. When I call your name, you step out onto the stage and then read the speech that I gave you." He pats me on the shoulder. "We'll have the slides you took of Earth projected onto a large screen behind you. Feel free to reference those as you speak."

"Great. I can do that."

Duske smiles, then leans forward and kisses me lightly on the cheek. It takes all my willpower not to swipe away the moisture he leaves behind on my skin. Instead, I force myself to return the gesture. "I'm glad we're working together now, Brother Duske," I say softly, looking up through my lashes.

He grins like the fool he is and ruffles my hair. God, didn't he learn his lesson the first time around? And who gets off hooking up with clones, anyway?

"My dear," he says, "I do believe this could be the start of a beautiful friendship."

Oh, so do I, Duske. So do I.

He steps out to center stage and gestures for the stagehand to get the show on the road. A moment later, the curtains slide apart and the senator is illuminated by a single spotlight. From backstage left, I can now see out into the crowd. It's standing room only and everyone's going wild, cheering, screaming. It makes me sick. I hope they have brains enough to listen to what I have to say.

"Thank you, thank you!" Duske says, leaning into a microphone. A whiny feedback hisses for a moment, then dies away. "But I'm not the one you should be applauding. For tonight, as you know, we have a very special guest. She just arrived from Earth, where she has spent the last few months living a brand-new life. A life aboveground, out in the sunshine. A life full of new friends and new relationships. Untold riches and the companionship of animals. In short, our guest is much like the legendary Eve of the Bible—and she has been to Earth and found a real-life Garden of Eden."

The crowd erupts into more cheers. They're loving this. If only they had any idea of the truth, where their friends and family really ended up after visiting this so-called Garden of Eden.

"People of Terra," Duske shouts, then pauses dramatically. "I give you ... Mariah Quinn!"

And here I thought they were loud before. Now the crowd goes truly crazy. Their applause and screams are deafening. Unnerved, my heart beating a mile a minute, I step out onto the stage. My knees are wobbling, my hands are shaking. But I swallow down my fear and join Duske by the podium. He makes a grand show of bowing low to me when presenting the microphone. Then he steps to the side of the stage, leaving me in the spotlight.

I glance behind me and, sure enough, just as Duske said, my photos of Earth are projected onto the wall. Currently there's a shot of Central Park on a sunny afternoon. People are lounging on blankets, sampling picnic goodies. Two softball teams compete on the field. A man stands frozen in motion, tossing a Frisbee to his girlfriend. I have to admit, it does look a lot like paradise. And then I remember that none of it is real.

So, now what? I glance around, looking for some sign, some hint that the Eclipsers are in the house and ready for action. The doctor told me there was a plan in place; I just wish I were clued in on what exactly it entailed.

The spotlight shines down on me. The crowd stirs, restless. Duske frowns from his position at the side of the stage. I realize I'd better get this show on the road or people will start getting suspicious.

"This is a picture of what they call Central Park," I explain, pointing to the photo behind me. "As you can see, it's an aboveground park right in the middle of the city. New Yorkers like to come here on their days off, to read and eat and play ball or just hang out. They have a zoo and exhibits and lakes, and in the summers they perform Shakespeare in an outdoor theater."

The crowd oohs and aahs, clapping politely. I click to the next slide, feeling more confident. At least I know what I'm talking about. And when the Eclipsers decide to make their presence known, I'll be ready for them.

Suddenly, the applause dies midclap, a dead silence falling over the room. I glance behind me at the slide presentation, wondering what on earth has shut them up. It's then that I realize it's something not on Earth at all.

Projected on the wall behind me, in startling living color, is one of the photos we took in the morgue: a naked, bloated Indy lying on a slab. So, this is what the Eclipsers have planned. They must have hacked into the slideshow somehow.

"No!"

I whirl around to see Duske charging at the slide projector, face enraged. But before he can reach me, he's tackled by two of the onstage guards—evidently Eclipser plants—and sent flying to the floor. They club him, then clamp handcuffs over his wrists and drag him offstage. I watch, shocked, stunned, not sure what to do next. I glance around the room wildly, wondering if any other guards will suddenly burst through to interrupt the presentation. It's then that I catch sight of Hiro, standing at one of the exit doors in the crowd. At the next is Kayce. At the next, Tayrn. All three nod to me, prompting me to go on. I realize the Eclipsers are not only in the house, they've got complete ownership of it.

Time to get this show on the road.

"But I'm here to tell you not to be fooled by such luxurious lies," I say into the microphone to my horrified audience. Their panicked murmurs die away and they listen with rapt faces. "Moongazing is not a journey to a new world. It's not a one-way ticket to paradise. In fact, Earth doesn't really even exist. Well, not anymore." I click the remote and the slide switches to a view of the computer control center. "This is where they create Earth. It's a virtual reality simulation. A *game*, if you will, based on what Terra looked like before the war tore it apart." I click the slide again, to another computer room shot. "That's why you need the drugs. They trick your brain into believing this video game—*this illusion*—is reality."

My audience is silent, their faces pale and shocked. I've got their complete attention now, that's for sure. Time to move in for the kill. "Problem is, your bodies aren't able to handle this simulation," I explain, clicking the slide again. We're now back at the morgue. "A few weeks or months after you go on your so-called pilgrimage, your mind begins to decay. Your eyes burn out of your head. You'll die. And the government will dump your body into this morgue and likely harvest your vital organs."

"But why would they do this?" cries a teenager in the front row. "Why would the Circle sponsor a program that kills its citizens?"

"Easy," I reply, clicking the slideshow to reveal yet another burned-out body in a drawer. "We have an overpopulation problem, and the Circle of Eight's figured out a method of genocide that no one will object to. Not to mention it's a great moneymaker for them."

"What about you?" demands an older woman a few rows back. "You went. And you didn't die."

I swallow hard, but as I flip the slide, I find my answer: Mariah's corpse flashes on the screen. The crowd gasps. I stare at them, still too unnerved to look at my own dead body.

"This is what happened to the real Mariah," I say. "She became addicted to Moongazing and it led to her own death. You think I'm Mariah, but you're wrong. I'm simply an nT, produced by the government to trick people into thinking your precious princess is still walking around and enjoying life on Earth." I glance at the Eclipsers, still guarding the doors. "But thanks to a few brave rebels who refused to give up, I know what side I'm really on."

The crowd erupts in murmurs, the Indys anxiously discussing all that has just been revealed. Satisfied that I've done my part, I walk offstage and locate the Eclipsers, who are holding Duske captive.

"By the way, I have my memories back," I inform him as I approach. I resist the urge to make "nyah-nyah" noises.

"So I see," he says, not looking very happy. "Not that they were ever *your* memories to begin with. But how lovely that you're able to take ownership of them all the same."

Furious, I slap his face as hard as I can, my hand making a loud noise as it connects with his cheek. "That's for trying to turn me into someone I'm not," I spit at him.

He narrows his eyes. "Please. You were never anyone to begin with."

"That may be true," I agree. "But I *am* someone *now*. Someone important. And you know what? I like that person. I wouldn't trade who I've become for any alternate reality in the world."

"Neither would I," says a voice behind me.

I whirl around, my eyes widening and my mouth dropping open in shocked joy. "Dawn!" I cry, running to him—Duske forgotten—and throwing myself into his arms. He twirls me around, squeezing me tight. "You're here! You're okay!" I bury my face in his shoulder, wanting to cry and laugh, sing and scream, all at the same time. "I thought maybe you were …" I trail off, unable to finish.

"I told you I'd find you again," Dawn reminds me, setting me back on the floor. "Though, maybe you don't remember."

"Oh, I remember," I assure him, a huge grin on my face. "I remember everything. And I'll remember it all forever. I promise."

"I know you will, Skye Brown," Dawn says, leaning down to kiss me. "Because I plan to remind you every day for the rest of your life."

EPILOGUE

Three mornings later I wake up in Dawn's arms back at my house. Our house. We've decided there's no reason to keep separate residences anymore. After all, we don't want to spend any more time apart from one another then we have to.

Dawn sits up in bed, glancing at his watch. "We should get moving. We have a big meeting with the Eclipsers in an hour," he reminds me.

I yawn, stretching my hands above my head. "Let them wait a few more minutes. I'm too comfortable to move."

He kisses me softly on the forehead and lies back. "Me too."

"Besides, I know what they're going to say," I groan. "That we need a new plan. Something to follow our glorious victory."

"You're starting to learn. An Eclipser's work is never done."

"It seems a shame we can't just rest on our laurels for a bit," I joke. "After all, we did destroy the government's number-one moneymaking program and unite the Indys against them."

Dawn chuckles. "It was great," he agrees. "But it's only a start. While we did get the Indys to rebel against the Moongazing project, it's not like we took down the Circle of Eight. You saw the newsfeed last night. The Circle's spin doctors have already started working. Senator Estelle, Mariah's mother, vilified Duske and blamed the entire Moongazing fiasco on him, not to mention her daughter's death. She made it seem like the whole program was his brainchild alone and nothing to do with a government conspiracy." He gives a rueful smile. "Now all the Senate has to do is stage a trial and execution, dismantle the 'Gazing booths and suddenly they're big heroes to the land. The Indys will be grateful as their grand and glorious government saves them once again."

I make a face, knowing he's right. "Then I guess we just have to keep fighting."

"And we will," Dawn says resolutely "And so will the Eclipsers. And the Dark Siders. And I think this time we've managed to sway quite a few Indys to our side as well. And more will come every day. Slowly but surely, we'll win this war. Someday we'll be a free people again."

"And you and I will be together. No matter what," I say. Right now, that's what matters most.

He smiles. "Truly a force to be reckoned with."

There's a small woof of agreement as Noah leaps onto the bed. The dog wags his tail, his mouth open in a lazy pant. Pushing his furry body between us, he curls up on top of the blankets. Laughing, we reach out to pet him, running our fingers through his impossibly soft fur.

"I think Noah is pretty happy we moved him from the animal shelter here to your house," Dawn notes.

"Lots more begging opportunities up here with us suckers."

"And lots more doggie cuddles for us."

"You know," I say. "That should be our next mission. Find old Noah here a mate. Maybe we can start a whole new breed of companion animals. I think the Dark Siders would like that."

"What do you think, Noah, old boy?" Dawn asks, scratching the pup behind his ear. "You want a girlfriend?"

Woof! Noah barks in affirmation, wagging his tail eagerly. He jumps on me and laps one cheek. Dawn leans over, presenting me with a far less sloppy kiss on the other. I giggle and return kisses to both of my boys, more content and happy than I've ever been.

After all, with this kind of light in my life, who needs the moon?

ABOUT THE AUTHOR

Mari Mancusi used to wish she could become a vampire back in high school. But she ended up in another blood sucking profession—journalism—instead. Today she works as a freelance TV producer and author of books for teens and adults. When not writing, Mari enjoys traveling, cooking, goth clubbing, watching cheesy horror movies, and her favorite guilty pleasure—videogames. A graduate of Boston University and a two time Emmy Award winner, she lives in Austin, Texas with her husband Jacob, daughter Avalon, and their dog Mesquite.

To Contact Mari:
Website: http://www.marimancusi.com
Facebook: http://www.facebook.com/bloodcovenvampires
Twitter: marimancusi
Email: mari@marimancusi.com

For More Information on **First Kiss Club** books:
http://www.firstkissclub.com

For More information on **Mari's Blood Coven Vampires** series:
http://www.bloodcovenvampires.com